STRAY CATS
FROM A WAYWARD
WORLD

Pat McGrath

W. H. ALLEN · LONDON
A Howard & Wyndham Company
1981

481023773

Typeset by Computacomp (UK) Ltd,
Fort William, Scotland.
Printed and bound in Great Britain by
Biddles Ltd, Guildford
for the Publishers, W. H. Allen & Co. Ltd,
44 Hill Street, London W1X 8LB

ISBN 0 491 02498 3

Many special thanks to Francis Bennett
and W. H. Allen for their sponsorship and
support, to Amanda and Christine for
their patience and help, and to Victoria for
her part in all this.

Part One

STRANGERS

Chapter One

A few years ago, if asked about myself, I could only speak in terms of the future and things I planned to do with it. I rarely included anything from my past because at the time I was on a single-minded course—forward. I had no illusions about the work involved though. In fact the challenge of the work kept the adrenalin pumping from head to heart and I was lucky enough to get a fix on what I wanted to do pretty early in life. The only thing that was complete about me was the promise and vision of myself in ten years' time. With that vision I moved on from school, college and university, doing everything for a reason so that the details of the future me that I saw became all the more defined.

There's nothing remarkable about that and nothing strange about a young person changing direction either. But there may be something remarkable about the circumstances that turn you around, or edge you, like a juggernaut pushing your own modest vehicle into a different lane. Fate often displays diversion signs, especially to people who nurture long-term plans, big ideas and high intentions. So it is up to me soon to pinpoint where the changes came in my case, whether they would have occurred on their own or whether they came about as a result of an experience that feels unique to me. It's a theoretical question but it swims back into my mind from time to time.

To say that one moment I was travelling in one direction and the next I was travelling in another sounds dramatic. Ultimately it was, though it began quietly enough with a telephone call that aroused no more than mild curiosity, until it was followed by several more. A young man who had important business with me but would not leave his name either with my mother or father. I was out each time he called, taking time off from the dead-headed textbooks that had been dictating to me for the past four years.

7

Racking my brain didn't help identify the guy and I certainly had no idea what this 'important business' could be, though he added that it was 'personal' when he failed to get through to me the third time.

It began to intrigue me before it began to irritate me but by the time I was sitting on a 747 with Diane squeezing my hand, and the No Smoking light had come on at precisely the time I felt like lighting up half a dozen, I'd forgotten all about it. I thought no more of it until we were on the return flight from Athens and I wondered: suppose the bloody plane crashes and I never find out what those damned telephone calls were about?

Needless to say, and much to my surprise, it didn't crash. From the brown tree-dotted mountains, tavernas and indigo waves of Greece I found myself back in London—as though I'd never left it but had just had a long dream—with one evening to go before stepping into the offices of Marlon Markbyss & Co. I'll never forget that wet Monday morning, especially as Diane and I had been sitting in the sunshine of the Saronic Gulf trying to get rid of our last Greek change at the hotel beach bar the morning before. I felt a little lost, which was more than I had done in Athens, as I watched veteran office girls, clerks and businessmen rush along Gracechurch Street in the drizzle that seemed to make tall buildings, old and new, lean over one with calculated gloom. But I shrugged that off as I entered the dim Gracechurch Passage. The anonymous telephone caller was again far at the back of my mind as I pushed the reception door open, thinking the future starts here—at last.

There were four solicitors in this practice, plus the managing clerk. Marlon Markbyss, the principal, was a tall, thin, middle-aged man with black hair just beginning to turn grey, who wore black-rimmed glasses. He had built his firm up from a one-man practice to the small but busy company that it now was. He prided himself on the relaxed atmosphere, the team spirit that prevailed and a high turnover of clients. He dealt with the staff and clients with the same gentle authority, a fatherly finesse that was helped along by sympathetic lines in his face, indicating at times the weight of responsibility that he carried. 'Premature decomposition is an occupational hazard in this profession, young man,' he jocularly told me during my first half-hour in his office.

I was introduced to the other three solicitors and made to feel welcome. They were smooth, polite and friendly, urging me to consult them as soon as any problems arose. We were in the business of first of all putting people at their ease and they certainly managed that for me.

My first problem, however, couldn't be found on the premises. The managing clerk, one Mr Goldberg, we were told by his secretary Greta, had gone 'to the Bailey', so I didn't meet him until he walked into the office at about 5.00 pm. Immediately I sensed that I was not going to find him so easy to communicate with as the others. Everything about him, from his tone of voice to the expression on his face, denoted condescension. On first meeting there didn't seem to be much smoothness about him, or diplomacy. His first question was a blunt 'Who are you?' although my guess was that he actually knew. 'I want to see you in my office in five minutes and ask Sue to make me some coffee,' he demanded in an arrogant tone; Markbyss would have put the request or instruction in a much more congenial way.

Surrounded by depositions and files he questioned me in his office from behind a mist of cigarette smoke that seemed to add to his sense of superiority. He wanted to know about my degree, my interest in the law, what I expected and what I intended. 'You appreciate,' he observed, 'that the days of just walking into the law are over and that even in this profession people are qualifying to find that there are not enough jobs for them.'

I was very much aware of that. I wasn't afraid of the work and wanted the stimulus of challenge the law could offer. Somebody has to pull through, I pointed out, without bothering to add that I intended to be one. Perhaps I was wearing a pinstripe strait-jacket of naiveté but you can't beat the convictions of the naive, although I had a strange feeling that Goldberg was going to be my first challenge.

'That sounds all right,' he finally shrugged dismissively. 'You'll learn more by working for me anyway ... Post these letters for me, please, Mr Heyward ... try not to post the tray, will you?'

His built-in tone of sarcasm annoyed me and I became extra alert when he was around. He didn't seem to fit in with the others but I felt as if he was trying to make me feel as though I didn't fit in.

Whatever, he was the thorn in the side of my first day although I guessed I would be able to square up to his arrogance if I had to.

All the same, I was glad to get home to moan about him that evening—only to find my mysterious telephone caller had rung that afternoon, still without explaining himself.

That week Goldberg was engaged at the Old Bailey most of the time and I wasn't sorry that he was out of the way. He headed the litigation department, his office was inundated with boxes of deps relating to pending trials. I discovered that all the girls in the office quite liked him. They assured me he was great once you got to know him, though you could never argue with him. 'Dig a hole and Jake will fill it,' as Greta told me. 'That's why he's so good at his job. He never defends a client unless he understands and appreciates every single aspect of the prosecution's case first. He would have made a good barrister as well—he's got the gift of the clack and he thinks quickly and intelligently.'

He would have made a good footballer, I thought, because when he walked back in from the Bailey on Friday afternoon with another victory notched up he was so pleased with himself, that he reminded me of a player who had just scored a goal and won the bloody cup.

Personally, I wasn't all that concerned with criminal litigation anyway. I was more interested in company law and chancery work, which meant following in the footsteps of Markbyss, who specialised in these areas. But for the first few weeks it was Goldberg who commandeered me to do his running around and sit in behind barristers at Crown Court trials that he couldn't get to because of his star cases at the Bailey.

Having spent four years reading law it was a strange and slightly overwhelming experience having to walk into the various institutions armed with forms. It was an exercise and a half learning one's way around the corridors, looking for one department or another which would be tucked away in the dingy corners of the labyrinthine High Court. As I worked out the procedures and the mechanical errand-boy stuff, I learnt how to deal with the pedantic and occasionally belligerent clerks in the central offices. You had to assume confidence when facing them, even if you had none, to get whatever you needed done. Thus one learnt the art of bluff quickly; it was a matter of walking into the place as though you owned it. During a summons before Master Boldinger I got my documents a little mixed up. The Master kicked me out and told me not to return until I'd got it right. I felt stupid enough, especially in front of the female clerk who was opposing my summons for the other side, but I had to sort the papers out quickly and walk back into his chambers apologising and carrying on as though I was the Kiddie. In a way I could see what Goldberg might have been getting at. Degree or not, you could learn a lot of unforgettable lessons by landing on your arse.

The first time that I ever walked down these dull red-floored, yellow-walled corridors was when I was fourteen, with a small school party led by a dolly teacher that I had a crush on. It was part of a British Constitution outing, and it was a sunny day, though not much of the sun manages to get through these neo-Gothic windows. It was that day that sparked off my interest in the legal profession. My class-friends were all middling to extremely bored but I was fascinated by the anachronistic atmosphere of the place, admired the cut and style of the passing lawyers going about their mysterious business.

A clerk in the Chancery Division must have fancied Miss Alexander as much as I did. It was vacation time and everything was closing up early, not much was going on, and the clerk allowed the six of us to peep up into the giant attic to glimpse the dusty cobwebbed files that dated back over the centuries—fights, arguments, actions, Jarndyce *v.* Jarndyce, stern judgements, people and problems forgotten and buried in the mysterious dust.

Walking along the corridors eight years later brought that occasion back to me now that I was one of the pinstripe suits walking along, though there was no longer any mystery involved. But during that first week I still found the names on the doors intriguing: Master Jager, Master Dazzle, Master Abraham.

Delivering a brief to a set of barristers' chambers in Middle Temple Lane played back to me the schoolboy vision of blonde Miss Alexander guiding us through the lazy peaceful sunshine and shadows of the Temple. I was sucked in by the absorbing dignified silence, esoteric and soothing. Today the buildings were the same but the rain drilled down, washing away the fantasy that had brought me here with ambition and confidence. I was free of college now and was adapting to the down-to-earth machinery, the practical problems of real people in real situations. For me it was the slow start, the boring forms and procedures and delivering briefs to counsel, the shit jobs, plodding about in all weathers, the sense of starting from the bottom. But I was

11

paddling in future prospects that had become more real to me, a self-absorbed and only child, than the fact that my mother and father were not my natural parents.

They had never tried to influence my choice of career though they highly approved of the one I did go for. They were very supportive, even though they underestimated my desire to get out there and to get away from the insulation of Wichfield. The view of the rest of the world from that community is rather limited. College made me all the more restless and dissatisfied with what I saw as my colourless past and background. Although I was outwardly cynical towards the public-school friends I made at university, I secretly admired their self-assurance. Perhaps I had some sort of insane illusion that they could not be as screwed up as everybody else.

My parents took Diane and me to a candle-flickering restaurant to celebrate my degree. They had been waiting for a moment like this ever since I came into their hands. 'We're very proud of him,' Alison leaned towards Diane. I cringed, but the evening seemed to belong to them rather than to me.

'In a few years' time we shall be celebrating again—celebrating Nicholas becoming a fully fledged lawyer,' Gareth beamed, candles flickering in the lenses of his glasses.

It seemed difficult to believe that such a day could be so close when I was only just beginning to be active in that world. We were all oblivious of the fact that I would qualify in a different way from most other law students.

On my return to the general office one evening after the girls had gone home I saw a monumental pile of boxes hogging the office floor, containing depositions in the Hepburn fraud case. I knew at a glance that it was one of Goldberg's. Four thousand pages for him to read, digest and correlate into a defensive brief for a trial that would keep a QC and junior in refresher fees for six months. My head swam at the thought of the task involved. But the managing clerk was tailor-made for this sort of challenge. He immersed himself in the complex allegations, invoices, statements, exhibits, the defence of a man with his liberty on the rocks.

The fact that some of the lights were still on indicated that somebody was still there. Markbyss's room was empty when I looked in to return some files, so I left them on his desk and walked off to Goldberg's room to return some work to him. From the corridor I could hear emphatic voices that stopped me from entering. Mr Markbyss, I could see through the frosted glass panel of the door, was leaning with one elbow against a filing cabinet.

'You are inundated with this type of thing,' Markbyss was saying. 'You know exactly how much you're going to have your bloody work cut out on this Hepburn extravaganza, I've seen the depositions. We'll have to hire a fleet of taxis to get them from here to the Temple and on to court. That's five or more major trials looming up on the horizon. I'd like to know what you think you're going to do if most of them come up in the lists at the same time!'

'They won't,' Goldberg responded confidently. 'But if by some unhappy coincidence we seem to have a monopoly over the Warned List I shall get one of my contacts in the Clerk of the Lists office to do some juggling. Don't worry, I've got everything under control. There's no problem.'

'Yes. But you know well my feelings on all these epic Old Bailey dramas of yours,' Markbyss carried on. 'They gobble up time and energy which in my view could be profitably spent elsewhere.'

'I can't agree.' Goldberg spoke casually, drawing on his cigarette, I imagined. 'A few years back the property market was going wild. There was so much dough about people were gazumping each other hand over fist—it was a joke! Even then the litigation department here was making as much money as the conveyancing. When the climate changed some solicitors concentrated more on company law and litigation. We already had a strong litigation department on the basis of these big cases. I don't see how you can argue with the hard cash it's put into the office account. It speaks for itself, surely.'

'*My* argument, as you well know by now'—I could visualise Markbyss leaning against the filing cabinet with that serious smile on his face—'is that more up-market clients, as it were, and more smaller cases would require a good deal less of your time, fewer headaches and as much, if not more, remuneration. You are going to be working endless hours on this Hepburn saga alone. Then you've got Mathison and the bank job. In which time you

13

could be concentrating and employing your talents on smaller matters that would accumulate the same sort of rewards at the end of the day. You have enough monkeys on your back without adding a gorilla.'

'Our reputation is such,' said Goldberg, 'that if our number wasn't in the book and the brass plate wasn't on the door people would still come looking for us and find us. We have a reputation second to none.'

'We also have a growing company law department as well as conveyancing and chancery work, with some very influential clients coming in,' Markbyss insisted. 'The two worlds don't mix in the waiting room. And as things are at present we don't have enough staff to cover all the appointments that crop up. We can't afford to plant Nicholas behind counsel at the Bailey for weeks on end. This afternoon I had to interrupt my work three times in order to take urgent calls for you. You see, that's just one of the problems. Everyone's at panic stations but you can't be contacted because you're always out of the office somewhere, dealing with one of these bloody great Cecil B. Demille epics at the Bailey!'

'That's a problem all but solved,' Mr Goldberg assured him. 'I am considering the hire of the kind of bleep device used in hospitals to page doctors.'

'Good Lord, are you serious, Jacob?'

'Certainly I'm serious. These bleeps are available for hire at the rate of eight pounds per month. In the event of an emergency cropping up—and they very often turn out to be Mickey Mouse situations—but in such a case Greta will phone a given number which in turn will bleep me. I shall slip out of court and phone Greta back and deal with the situation.'

Markbyss laughed. 'Ingenious, Jacob. I can just visualise Mr Justice Beaumont's face when his courtroom starts bleeping.'

'I doubt if the sound of the bleep will carry as far as the bench,' Goldberg replied with a slight hint of disgust.

With the amusing prospect of Jake's bleep in mind I returned to the general office to wait for their little debate to finish. This one was tame; they sometimes turned into shouting matches. Apparently they'd had this running disagreement for the past fifteen years and everybody expected it to go on for the next. It flared up three or four times a year. I could understand that Markbyss didn't want bailed suspects flicking through *Country*

Life alongside his influential clients. He didn't need Jake's type of case.

In the reception I flicked through a pile of while-u-were-out memos and found three for me. The first from a client in a small county court action Markbyss had given me to practise on. The second was from Diane, asking me to ring her back 'when u feel up to it'. The third was another from the mystery man, who had gone quiet for a few weeks but was now back on the lines again. Having got the office number from my father, he was trying here as well and still having a frustrating time of it. I scrawled on a memo: 'Sue, if the phantom phonecaller strikes again ask him to phone this office between 9.30 and 10.00.'

Then I turned to sorting the files out for Goldberg. I perched on the edge of the copying machine and was in the process of scribbling reports on various matters I'd dealt with when the door swung open and Goldberg walked into the room.

'Don't sit on the Xerox machine, Mr Heyward, you'll make a copy of yourself,' he said facetiously as he walked across to Sue's desk. He flicked open the telephone ledger to take account of all the calls that hadn't got through to him that afternoon. 'Did you pick up those appeal forms I asked for?'

'Affirmative.'

'And the Coleman brief? You delivered that to Purnell's chambers, I hope?' He spoke without looking up from the book. I always got the feeling that he was waiting to catch me out on something.

'I wouldn't forget the Coleman brief,' I assured him. 'I know how much Coleman needs a barrister and how much Purnell needs the fee.'

'Indeed,' sniffed Goldberg, slinging the book aside. 'Now then, Mr Heyward. I saw you the other day reading the Wilson papers. Allow me to ask you a question. The policeman has identified our client as being the suspect he pursued down a no-through road. As you read, the suspect allegedly sprang up onto the wall and vanished over the other side. Wilson was arrested at his home the following day and identified by PC Fox. Bearing these circumstances in mind, if this were your case what defence tactics would you apply?' Goldberg perched on the edge of the desk and folded his arms. I lit a cigarette and thought about it.

'It was 2.00 am, therefore it was dark,' I recalled from the

15

police statements. 'I would find out how many street lights there were in the vicinity, and how many obstructions—such as parked vehicles. I would of course want to know where these street lamps were located. The wall at the end of the road is twelve foot high—impossible for anybody short of an Olympic athlete to jump up on. If the police officer was not close enough behind the suspect to grab his legs as he scrambled up and over the wall, then how was it possible to clearly identify a man in the dark who had his back to him and was running away—bearing in mind the distance that there must have been between them?'

'The police officer says that the suspect glanced over his shoulder at one point,' said Goldberg. 'What do you say to that?'

'A positive ID is still suspect. There is plenty of room for a mistake. If the officer was close enough to make a positive ID in the dark he would surely have caught the man as a tall wall slowed him down. If I were the defending counsel it's an aspect of cross-examination that I would pick up. Other than that there are a few things I couldn't comment on until hearing what the client has to say.'

'But if you were the police officer in the witness box what do you think your answers to those suggestions might be?' demanded Goldberg.

'I'd say, "I'm not a normal person, I'm a policeman and have been for thirty years. I'm especially trained to see people in the dark, together with which, I eat a hell of a lot of carrots. Sir!".'

Mr Goldberg yawned and rubbed his eyes, looking worn and tired. 'All right ... leave all this other rubbish until tomorrow. Put those files on Greta's desk.' I did as he suggested and he glanced at his watch. 'Mr Heyward. How are you fixed for a cup of coffee somewhere?'

That took me by surprise. As I'd been on the defensive with him from the first I was wary now as well, though I was in the mood for some refreshment after a day of running around. I also wondered what he would have to say to me beyond the realms of the office.

'While I phone my wife,' he took a 10p piece from his pocket and handed it to me, 'I'd be obliged if you would deposit that in my parking meter. Make sure there are no traffic wardens about while you are committing the offence.'

After feeding his meter I stood on the street corner and waited for a few minutes until he emerged from the antiquated dimness of Gracechurch Passage. We walked into the narrow streets and alleyways of Leadenhall Market, a Victorian backyard in a London skyline of mirror-window office blocks and ancient steeples, its old walls of the last century staring up at the multi-eyed blocks of this one.

'This is an interesting part of the City,' I observed, to create conversation more than anything. 'It has atmosphere. At least until you stick your head out into Gracechurch Street and get your brains blown out by the traffic.'

'Atmosphere?' scoffed Goldberg. 'The City is changing. I've worked in the City for twenty-five years now. I remember it when I was a junior clerk. The atmosphere is hiding behind all these bloody great glass-and-steel erections. The City is all frothy coffee and parking meters these days!'

In one of the dim alleyways we found a sandwich bar with a few City stragglers flicking through the *Standard*, a girl sitting on a stool reading a fat paperback, waiting for her accountant boyfriend no doubt. A cat sat under one of the tables, scratching itself to death, waiting to have this territory to itself for the night.

Jake ordered two cups of coffee. An expression of slight contempt appeared on his face when the insipid concoctions were placed in front of him. He asked me if I wanted to eat as well, but I said no and offered to pay for the coffees. 'What are you getting busy for?' he wanted to know. We sat across the table from each other by the window.

'Well,' he clinked the spoon in his cup and stirred. 'Tell me how you feel about the work now that you've been with us for a few months. Do you feel that you're getting on all right. Or do you feel that you're not getting on all right? Which of the two, do you think?'

'I feel that I'm getting the experience that I need. That's important enough,' I answered guardedly.

'I think it is, I would be inclined to agree with that,' he nodded, tipping the sugar from its sachet into the foam of his coffee. 'If you stick close to me you'll learn a lot,' he went on modestly. 'Now that you have shown over the past couple of months that you have some potential and initiative I can give you more interesting work than issuing writs and delivering briefs. Next Tuesday I want you to attend Old Street Police Station to

17

supervise an identity parade in which a client of ours by the name of Brelsford will be taking part. You know the procedure for that of course!'

'Of course.'

'Good! That's what I want to hear. It pleases me that you can be entrusted with work without constant supervision. Your predecessor was something of a Mickey Mouse who could hardly add up a bill of costs, it seems to me. I don't have the time to breathe down the necks of incompetent shmocks all day long. So, you will supervise the ID parade at Old Street for me. You will also phone Brixton Prison and make an appointment to interview one George Wilson, of the twelve-foot wall leaping fame, where you will take a statement recording his age, occupation, previous convictions, his version of what happened or what did not happen, his account of the arrest and subsequent police interviews, and his response and comments on the verbal statements of the police. You can fit this in with your other work at your own discretion, bearing in mind that we must brief counsel in the next few weeks. Any problem with that?'

'None at all,' I said, beginning to feel some more progress taking place in the slow-moving world of getting anywhere in this life.

'Incidentally,'—he sipped his coffee—'how much are we paying you?' When I told him the figure he agreed that there wasn't much to it. 'I'll have a word with Mr Markbyss about it in a day or so. You work harder than most of them … Leave it to me.' We both looked up to find the book-reading girl hovering around our table asking if there was an ashtray. 'We're using ours but you can share it. Where are you sitting—over there?' Goldberg asked. 'Have you got a long hand?'

She laughed, stubbed her cigarette out and returned to her stool.

'By the way, Nicholas. Did you get the message about the young man that paid you a visit this evening?'

'No, I didn't. What young man was this?'

'He came into the office at about 5.30 looking for you on a private matter. He said that his name might not mean anything to you and he would prefer not to leave it with anybody for the moment.'

'That saves me from racking my brain any further trying to

18

figure out who the hell he is,' I nodded. Then with curiosity: 'What did he look like?'

'About your age. Medium height, slim, scruffy, with jeans of an ancient age and a lavatory brush growing out of his chin. I would say he was a Scouse, judging by his accent.'

'I missed him by twenty minutes this time,' I reflected. 'I've had about half a dozen calls from the guy and missed each one. Now he's making the effort to materialise in person. I hope he catches me soon. Mysteries are all very fine and fascinating to start with, but they tend to become irritating after a while.'

'You've chosen the wrong practice to work for if that's how you feel,' he spoke sardonically. 'We have represented on several occasions a man called Harwood, a haulage contractor in the East End. We got him out of a fix at the Bailey years ago, since when he has not been in any trouble. Then last night—or should I say today—I was awoken by the telephone ringing itself silly at two o'clock in the morning. It was Mrs Harwood, who was in a near-hysterical state and quite incoherent. When I had calmed the woman down I managed to find out that her husband had been taken away from his office by a group of policemen to God knows where for God knows what reason. So with a client having disappeared from the face of London, I was compelled to get up, get dressed and drive all the way down to his office. There I met Harwood's manager. He told me about the police swoop but knew nothing of what it was about or where the police came from.

'At 4.00 am I arrived at the local police station, expecting to find my client in custody there. But they knew nothing about the incident either. We started checking all the police stations in the area and still nobody could enlighten us. So there we were with a wife whose husband had disappeared, a solicitor whose client had vanished, and the police baffled—a man arrested on their manor, without their knowledge, by a squad of phantom detectives. How do you fancy that for a display of mystery and melodrama?'

'It sounds positively sinister. What happened next?'

'In the hours that have ticked by since, the plot has only thickened. Still none of us knows where Derek Harwood is, who took him or for what reason. I've been on the phone throughout the day to high-ranking police officials and an investigation is being made. I'm expecting a call from the DI at Doughty Road tonight. It's hilarious, isn' it!'

19

'What kind of record has Harwood got?'

'He has a bit of form for receiving and dishonestly handling that goes back about twelve years.' He shook his head and looked out at the dusky passageway. 'Nevertheless, he's entitled to the same rights and protection as anybody else in the country. The law doesn't simply exist to use against people, it exists to protect them as well.'

I started to relax with him for the first time. He talked on about various cases that he had handled over the years—'You must have read about that one in the newspapers, Nicholas'—and some of them had been headliners, it was true.

It was dark outside by the time we left. The girl with the book had gone—I hadn't noticed whether a boyfriend had showed up or not. Jake offered me a lift to the station but it wasn't far so I decided to walk. 'Be in early tomorrow, I've got a lot of work for you to do,' were his parting words.

The City tower blocks were lit up like electric chessboards standing up behind the shoulders of smaller buildings. I walked past the banks, the amber lights and the mouth of Threadneedle Street, where the traffic was thinning out now that business was finished for the day. A police car came blue-lighting it down the wrong side of the road, the object of their mission heading for a place in Jake's filing cabinet if they didn't move themselves, I thought.

There was a flash of lightning, signalling the end of another short summer. In the next few minutes a sudden cloudburst followed it. I moved faster, cursing myself for not accepting a dry and comfortable lift in Jake's shiny Rover after all, and banged into a bone-shaking pram that was being wheeled along. It was full of rubbish and the force behind it was a little grubby-faced woman wearing a filthy headscarf, two dilapidated overcoats and a pair of miner's pit boots. She was pushing this pram along briskly, as though she hadn't noticed how treacherous the weather had turned and couldn't hear the gut-rumbling in the sky. I apologised for banging into her, then thought how curious she looked wheeling past the modern glass facade of the Bank of Abu Dhabi, then merging once again with the darker, older walls of the City. Some soup wagon near the river probably kept her going, and I shuddered at the thought of the cold naked life she led, before I made a mad dash to Liverpool Street and shelter.

20

Chapter Two

A gust of wind flicks through garden trees, shaking leaves in their autumn death-rattle. I walk up Forest Rise back to the comforts that I would exchange for a slag-heap flat in Camden Town or somewhere that would airlift me from this apprenticeship existence. 'There's more than enough time for that,' say my parents, the king and queen of common sense. They've given me nothing if not a sense of the practical, which is an asset in my particular design for life.

Wichfield is a conservative little cul-de-sac in Essex, flanked by fields and woods. A row of skeleton trees haunts the horizon of subdued fields. They stand stock-still against the overcast sky, so defined that they seem to have minds of their own.

'*What nonsense,*' echoes the voice of my mother.

'*Why nonsense?*' my father's voice returns in memory. '*An imaginative enough thought for such a young child, surely.*'

'*Trees with minds of their own,*' laughs my mother.

My father melts into the background. Master of his own classroom, he is not quite the master of his own home. They hold each other at arm's length. Therefore I have grown up to hold them both at arm's length, especially since I found out they were not my real parents. Sometimes in the past I felt like James Deaning it across the room and shaking some action and life into Gareth, but grew up to accept them as they are, with their perennial niggling, their never quite knitting together.

For years I've had an overwhelming desire to get out and the closer I pull the future towards me the more it becomes a gut feeling. Alison was all over me sometimes, yet still I felt out of reach—not because I didn't care for them, but there was a block somewhere. My desire to escape was always positive rather than self-destructive rebellion. I had priorities though.

21

Diane, in a pub one night, read my tarot for fun. I humoured her as she interpreted the cards I had selected. One of them was what she called the searcher—or hermit—looking out into the distance, scanning the horizon for something extremely important to him. There was a dog tugging at his cloak, trying to attract his attention to the fact that he was standing on the jewels already and need look no further.

I laughed heartily. She raised her eyebrows at me as if to tell me that it confirmed her theory, that I'm orientated too much to the external world, and missing out on something important. 'I'll be missing out on a job if I don't remain serious and practical at least until I qualify.'

She shuffled the cards, disdainfully shrugging her shoulders. 'You're still missing the point,' she said resignedly.

'Where did you get those Mickey Mouse cards from anyway?' I needled. 'The Mind and Body Exhibition, that marketplace of Nirvana and VAT?'

'What a sad and cynical young man you are,' she responded haughtily, which made me laugh all the more and grab for her hand—but it retreated for cover underneath the table.

'Anyway,' I said, 'whoever heard of a mystical solicitor?'

Every once in a while she questioned my attitude to life, as though she was unsure of it. She didn't mind my being a lawyer but she seemed to wonder whether I was just striving for a role to play, and looking for a stepping stone to a juicy income and interesting social spheres. We'd known each other for two years and she was still suspicious of me.

But so what? I chose a career that was challenging, that I would enjoy and that would take me somewhere. That seemed to be what life was about. If you knew what you wanted and had the methodical drive to get it, what was wrong with being lucky enough to have something worthwhile in a world of vanishing jobs? I don't want to stand still and just accept things as they are—who does? I don't want to go down either, so that leaves but one direction.

'What sort of a day have you had today, Nick?' Gareth asked after we had sat down for supper.

'Hectic. What is better than sitting in the office all day indexing

22

title deeds or something. You know, old Jake took me for coffee after work. Extraordinary!'

'That's this rather rude managing clerk of yours, isn't it?' asked my mother.

'Yes. He even insisted on paying for the coffee. Then after asking my opinion on one case, he proceeded to discuss another with me as though we were colleagues of equal footing. I'm to be recommended for a rise in pay also.'

'He can't be as bad as all that then,' Alison said optimistically. 'Still, they must think a lot of your capabilities to offer you an increase so soon.'

'Why shouldn't they though?' asked Gareth, pouring gravy onto his meal. 'He puts in a fair amount of overtime for them. Nobody can say he lacks enthusiasm.'

'Well, it's the only way to get anywhere,' Alison said once again. It was one of her lifelong stock phrases.

I told them of the work Goldberg proposed to delegate to me and of my imminent first visit to Brixton to interview an incarcerated client. 'It will be an experience, albeit a depressing one. But I'm quite looking forward to it.'

'It won't be at all depressing if the newspaper reports are anything to go by,' scoffed my mother. 'What with their colour television sets and what not. Prisons used to be places of punishment. Now it seems that any hooligan or villain who wants a holiday paid for by the rest of us just has to get himself put inside.'

'They come to us to get them out, not get them in,' I said, irritated by the absurd remarks she was capable of making. Alison stored more proverbial chestnuts than the average squirrel stored actual ones. Though at least squirrels sometimes have the decency to forget where they've stored them.

'I'm surprised at you, allowing newspaper nonsense to impress you with their sensationalised distortions,' my father spoke up. 'You know that the best way to sell a newspaper is to turn a molehill into a volcanic eruption if there's nothing else of news value.'

'They didn't have life so easy in prison in the past,' Alison insisted. 'There were no televisions, none of the recreational privileges of today. You went to prison for doing wrong and were treated accordingly. That was in the days before pampering and

23

do-gooding was all the rage. You can bet there are many people outside prison finding life more difficult that some of these gentlemen on the inside.'

'You've never been near a prison, mother. On what do you base your thesis, pray?'

'The facts speak for themselves, dear. There are too many clever lawyers like your Mr Goldberg getting violent criminals off on legal technicalities.'

It would be bad news for somebody if Alison was ever called up for jury service. Her hackneyed no-smoke-without-fire attitude made me realise that people like Goldberg were all the more necessary, for she could get that call-up at any time.

'You don't have to be a lawyer to imagine the wheeling and dealing that goes on in conference,' my mother complained.

'Oh you mean plea bargaining do you, mother?' I laughed. Sometimes the only course with Alison is to turn a discussion into a music hall routine. Tease her a little. 'But plea bargaining is such fun, mother.'

'Don't be facetious,' she said, much to my delight.

'The ideal is to keep those scales balanced and the lawyers as impartial as possible,' I repeated. 'Don't you think it is a sound concept—to give every man the right to respond to accusations made against him? Without that, what happens in other parts of the planet can happen here. Anybody can be convicted without even opening their mouth.'

'There is no one thing responsible for such things as a rising crime rate,' Gareth spoke up. From his point of view as a teacher he started going on about cutbacks in public spending badly affecting educational standards, accentuating unemployment.

But even with two of us against her, Alison never lost an argument. She stuck to her guns with pedantic determination, seemingly appalled that the rest of the deteriorating world couldn't see the logic of her own common sense. The nearest she ever got to conceding defeat was usually by changing the subject. It was her character, as Gareth always put it.

'Well, at least by the time Nicholas has completed his articles he'll be specialising in clean company work rather than all this sordid criminal work they've got him rinsing his hands in at the moment,' Alison said.

'I'm sure the prison visit will be an education,' Gareth nodded.

24

A few minutes of silent eating went on.

'Heard any more from your anonymous caller? Did he catch you at the office?'

'Not only that, but he actually turned up there. I was still on my way back from court - so that put the boot into that once again. But now he has something more than a Merseyside accent. He has a face and I have a description of it. He told Goldberg that I wouldn't know his name in any event.' I repeated Jake's impressions of the man.

'That makes him sound more ominous than he did in the first place,' said Alison.

After supper a pecking match broke out between my parents. He wanted to listen to a concert on the BBC while Alison moaned because she wanted his help in clearing up the supper things. Domestic matters couldn't wait.

As usual I blank out their little squabble, switching them off as I wander into the lounge and switch on the TV. As a young kid this switching them off used to make me feel guilty, particularly as I knew they had adopted me, and perhaps loved me all the more for it—'We didn't just have you,' Alison had explained. 'We *chose* you especially.'

The television presents me with the richer-than-life colours of an American courtroom drama. A handsome young attorney appeals to the jury as he defends his weekly innocent client. If only court trials were really as emotive as his, I grinned, switching it back to where it belonged.

I turned to the telephone and dialled for Diane. She was a little restless and irritable, wanting to know where I'd been skiving off to all day. 'You never seem to be in your office when I phone,' she said accusingly.

'I don't just sit there, moving crap from one end of the desk to the other, you know. I've been rushed off my fucking boots all day.'

'Well, now it's time for you to relax with an attractive young lady over a drink in a pub somewhere.'

'You must be joking. You know I haven't touched one of those bloody textbooks since just after we got back from Greece. I can't ponce around much longer, let's face it.'

'Don't be such a drag. You've got plenty of time. Think of all those stiff sentences—then think of *me*, burning with desire for you.'

Diane is fond of shooting the shit to get what she wants, though it didn't take much to talk me into pushing the studies aside for the evening.

I borrowed Gareth's car, and was soon spinning down black, country lanes beyond the village, with a friendly draught slapping my face at the open window, sudden bends jumping out of the darkness. The dark road made me think of the night I met Diane, two years ago. I was on a cheap holiday, dossing down in a dormitory situation in the Plaka district of Athens. On my last weekend I went off island-hopping but missed the last ferry that evening from Aegina to Piraeus. I resigned myself to a night under the stars and went looking for the subdued nightlife. At about midnight I wound up outside a taverna in the fishing village of Perdika. I collared a table by the sea wall, and embarked on a plateful of *moussaka* and a bottle of retsina. I soon realised that the two girls at the next table were English, and one of them noticed the English packet of cigarettes on my table. We got talking and ended up pushing our tables together and passing the wine bottles around. Avril was the talkative one, though my eyes kept straying to Diane, who I suddenly wanted to draw into the conversation. When we discovered that our English homes were only about fifteen miles apart she started to open up a bit; her detachment evaporated thanks to retsina, on the one hand, and common ground, on the other. We sat there yakking about ourselves and each other till gone two.

During the course of conversation it emerged that I was actually stranded on the island for the night. They were staying in a hotel chalet a couple of miles down the coast, Diane offered me some space on the 'hard' floor, 'unless you really are a fresh-air freak'. I was glad of the offer, especially as I didn't want to lose sight of Diane so quickly. When we walked up to the coastal road at about 2.30 I felt light, relaxed and glad of their unexpected company after three weeks of wandering around virtually shtum.

The road was pitch-black most of the way. One could only see the dark shadows of nearby trees, goat paddocks, olive groves and mountains. You had to watch your step on the left unless you wanted a bumpy roll down a steep embankment, culminating in a moonlight dip in the sea. Diane shivered at the dark silence and

26

the pine trees, the stillness of everything that made her complain it was eerie.

It seemed a long walk, during which we couldn't see each other most of the time. Then we suddenly heard a distant engine coming from behind. A tin-can truck was rattling along this narrow road at about ninety. We clawed our way to the side of the road to let him pass without turning the three of us into *moussaka*. But there was a screech of brakes as the truck rolled to a halt just past us. The driver called back to us and in chopped-up English asked us where we were going. Avril told him the name of the hotel and he invited us to jump into the back of the open truck, which we did. Again it took off at high speed and we laughed at the thrill of it, hurtling through the darkness, leaving blackness and blackness behind, headlights beaming ahead at the narrow coastal road coming towards us, the branches of trees whizzing past our ears. I wanted the driver to keep bashing the gas forever—the ride ended too soon. He left us outside the hotel, weak-kneed and laughing.

They smuggled me past the night-watchman and I spent the night in a sleeping bag beside their double bed. The next day Diane and I walked up the goat tracks of a mountain, underneath an azure sky and spell-binding sun. Avril was on the beach writing postcards, and it was good to steer Diane away from anywhere else, though it was too late for anything to happen—I would be getting lost at Victoria before very long.

Avril pigeon-holed herself a 'socialist feminist'. She was formerly at the LSE, Diane told me. 'She's very involved in all sorts of groups and movements and political meetings.'

'I thought she was from heavy Highgate or somewhere. Though she keeps going on about the working classes I rather get the impression she's never so much as sniffed the arse of a factory. I know a lot of people like that back in London. Upper Street thinkers.'

'That's too cynical and harsh,' Diane had said, as we climbed over a crumbled wall to a part of the mountain which gave us a view of the bay and its islets. 'She's got a lot to give.'

'And you?'

'Me?' she laughed. 'I've got nothing to give. To anyone.'

'That's disappointing if it's true. But I doubt that it is.'

When we met again in London six weeks later, we started a

27

friendship that surprised us, saved as we were from the holiday fling that might have snuffed it, as holiday relationships tend to when they can't take the strain of going home.

As our friendship grew I learnt that she had left home while she was still at school, to go and live with a rock musician in a grot spot in South London. She had become infatuated with him and his lifestyle. He was totally opposite to her. She had come from a middle-class background with influential contacts with the champagne and caviar brigade, whereas Steve Donland hailed from downtown Dagenham. He sounded like a bitter and boring ache, who thought Dagenham was the universal centre of pain, poverty and police harassment. The more I heard about him the more my contempt for him increased, as I wondered how a prat like that went about attracting a good-looking girl like Diane. He wasn't content with her either. He put himself about whenever the opportunity presented its treacherous self. She went through the motions of leaving him three times, and on each occasion he took an overdose of drugs. He would become maudlin and suicidal, a helpless child who needed her. When he OD'd for the fourth time she phoned for an ambulance, but by the time it arrived she was hitchhiking back home to Abridge. A man gave her a lift, tried to touch her up—until she burst into tears. He suddenly switched from one role to another, becoming paternal and protective. He went out of his way to drop her at the door.

'Christ! Having a teenage daughter must be a hell of a worry,' I observed.

'It must be,' she laughed.

She had become hardened to men. Men didn't seem to notice things, and what were men anyway? She didn't want to get involved.

For the next six months we spent most of our time not getting involved. She went around with other men but the moment they showed any insistence or eagerness, or signs of infatuation, she dropped them. They irritated her. She never minded the fact that I went out with girls from university, though occasionally she seemed annoyed by my single-minded aspirations and studiousness. In some ways she seemed resentful that I had found my vocation and she had not found hers. She was stronger than she looked and I had an idea that when she did grasp her own steering wheel she'd be going somewhere.

Now here we are, two years later, I'm thinking, as I pull into the car park of the Forest Fountain. Things are different because I was the first self-possessed man to come up to her, enjoy her without being dependent upon her. Because I am slightly cold and determined, as she puts it.

I bought two drinks in the pink lighting of the pub where Dr Hook's 'Sexy Eyes' played innocuously from the turntable. Diane was sitting in an alcove with her elbows on the table, looking down at a newspaper. 'Hello, brute,' I spoke.

She looked up suddenly. 'Ah! The elusive Mr Justice Heyward! And you've bought me a drink. I am much obliged to you, your honour.'

I sat down next to her. 'I suppose you're reading your stars.'

'No, I'm reading the flats-to-let section. As you're always busy it's up to me to see if I can find something. It's always left to the woman in the end.'

'Have you seen anything?'

'You're joking. There's a single bed-sit supposedly suitable for a student—at twenty-odd pounds a week. They must be mad. The flats are all fifty plus. Here's a flat in Belsize Park: suitable for refined ladies. Oh! That's no good, you're not even refined.'

'Watch it, kid.'

'Sorry, babe, only joking,' she bumped her head gently against mine. 'Anyway, where have you been all day?'

'I was at court, learning how to argue for a living.'

'You'll have to take me to court with you one day. I've never been to one. You can pick out a nice juicy case for me.'

'You'd be bored stiff. They're interminable, repetitive and the seats start chiselling your buttocks away after a few hours. After a full day, rigor-mortis attacks the arse.'

'I wish you were going to be a barrister. Then I could come along to the gallery and watch you eloquently pleading for your client in all the silly regalia.'

'Not enough money in that for me.'

'I had a chat with your receptionist over the phone. She seems quite nice. What's she like to look at? Pretty?'

'Sue? Yes, she's not bad. I heard Goldberg commenting on the fact that she has some desirable property in the Bristol area and that he wouldn't be adverse to doing a sort of land search of the property.'

29

'Sexist pig. So you fancy her, do you?'

'No. I only have eyes for you.'

'You liar. I wonder why it is that men are such bastards.'

'Because women are so virtuous and goody that there has to be an opposite. But I wouldn't lie to you, Diane.'

'Women pull men with their eyes, men pull women with their lies.' She turned a page of her newspaper.

After this profound comment on human behaviour, I fancied changing the subject, although as I did so she gave me a that's-typical-of-men glance. 'I bumped into your father in Bishopsgate this evening.'

'He mentioned it as he was coming in and I was on my way out. He suggested I invite you over for supper on Friday. He's thinking of using your talents for something or other.'

'What do you mean?'

'He didn't elucidate. Something to do with business, I should imagine. He'll explain on Friday.'

'I wonder what he thinks I can do for him.'

'My parents have also given us some tickets for the theatre, for Thursday. It's called *The Intruders* and it's written by a young female writer. The intruders, apparently, are a gang of men who force themselves on a woman's commune. It's about the different ways that different types of women respond to the pressures of sexism et cetera.'

'I could do with a good comedy,' I needled.

'Bugger off.'

I wondered what it was that John Sinclair wanted to speak to me about. It was true that we got on well enough. I had enjoyed several parties at their Georgian house, where I had discovered that people like Lord Bamforth and his elegant wife were only people, where I had been fascinated by the anecdotes and stories, plus parliamentary gossip and drawing-room debate from such people as Jason Gregory the Tory MP. It had all illuminated the death-watch beetle of Wichfield and life at home.

We left the pub at eleven o'clock. I watched her drive off along the dark road, more in the mood for following her than anything else. Then I got into Gareth's Datsun and drove off in the other direction.

Chapter Three

The adrenalin that pushed me up Brixton Hill against fierce and strong gusts of wind started to dwindle as the greyness of the place tried to push my heart into my intestines. It dwindled all the more as I walked along Jebb Avenue, past the perimeter walls crowned with barb wire. At the sight of the prison chimneys belching smoke, I began to wonder what the hell I was doing here.

A ring of the bell at the great wooden gates brought a hefty warder to open the inset door, so that I could step into the echo chamber of tuneless whistles, jangling keys, iron bars, leaving my spirits outside as the door was closed and locked.

Having been escorted through one iron gate after another, I was eventually signed into a glass booth containing a table and three chairs. The client was brought in to me after a while. I put on my smile and offered him my hand.

'I'm from Marlon Markbyss & Co.'

'Where's Mr Goldberg then?' he demanded.

'He's tied up with another client at the moment. It has to be me, I'm afraid.'

'You one of his clerks or summink?' he eyed me suspiciously. 'Mr Goldberg is in charge of my case, I hope? No disrespect or nuffing, but you can appreciate I don't want any screw-ups, like.'

I assured him that Mr Goldberg had the situation under control and that he should sit down at the table so that I could take his statement.

'Mr Goldberg's a good lawyer,' he said. 'I swear by the guy, mesself. A down-to-earth sort of bloke. Not like the usual stuffed shirts yer get in soliciters' offices.'

'I'm sure he'll appreciate your faith in him.' I headed the first page of my notebook 'Statement of George Arthur Wilson who will say as follows'. We went for a wander down Memory Lane as Wilson tried to recall with understandable difficulty his previous convictions, which turned out to be a list as long as Miss World's legs.

The oppressive feeling of being surrounded by prison walls started to fade away as I became more absorbed in his story, his categoric denials and his challenging of every word of the police statements.

Several items had gone missing from the Bermondsey premises of his employer. Among them was an expensive tool box, which Wilson admitted to taking without his employer's permission. 'But', Wilson poked a thick stubbly finger in the air, 'I meant ter put 'em back the next mornin'. I wanted ter do a job for me ole mum and I needed a mason's drill to get through the brickwork. I knew, or thought, my guvner would have given me permission to take 'em, only he wasn't there at the time. So I took 'em in the belief that all was kosher and that there would be no hassle, that he wouldn't mind. I was amazed when it turned out that he did mind. But as you no doubt know, under the provisions of the Theft Act of 1968 a person shall not be convicted of theft if he can show the court that he took the article in the belief that he would have had the owner's permission if asked and took the article without intending to deprive the owner permanently. What bollocked things up for me was the fact that by sheer coincidence somebody turned the place over the same night. So in the death, the tools that I had were listed among the nicked gear. Now old Bill may well have toed it after one o' the burglars, but it wasn't me, mate. But they found out that I had form and the slippery slags try to have me over for it because I'm a handy nick. They don't have to do any overtime. If you've got form they'll fit you up with anything. Half that previous that you listed out there were as a result of fit-ups and grass-ups. When you've got previous you have to have your eyes up your arse where the law's concerned.'

'When you were arrested and interviewed,' I consulted the police officer's statement, 'the police allege that you said "All right, squire, I'll stick me hands up for this one. You clocked me right enough, it's a fair nick." What do you say to that?'

'I say they should change their scriptwriters.' He sat back, casually dragging on a cigarette. 'They'll be telling me bulls don't

32

shit next. What happened was that they were riding me—geeing me up, trying to get me at it. They wouldn't take no for an answer. So I sez have it your own fucking way. If you say I did it—so be it.'

'Try not to be so subtle if anything like this happens again,' I advised.

The statement was difficult to take because much of it was contradictory. I was often referring him back to a few earlier pages to remind him of an earlier observation that didn't fit in with a subsequent one. The curious thing about him was that he was continually paraphrasing this, that, and the other Act of Parliament, and criticising the police for their neglect of the Judges Rules, which in his learned opinion should be law rather than a guideline. He seemed particularly fond of the Theft Act and its subtleties.

Occasionally as I was scrawling his tale across the page I had a mind-flash of Diane's face, which seemed a comforting vision in the middle of this place. In some ways I wanted to get the interview wound up quickly in order to get out, though I then wondered why I felt so bothered by it. After all, I would be out soon enough, which was more than some had to look forward to.

The door opened and a warder stuck his head around it. 'Will it be much longer, sir? Only if we don't get him down soon he'll miss his tea.'

'Just a few moments.'

The warder disappeared. 'Cretinous vacuum,' muttered Wilson.

He read back his statement, signed it, and asked, 'What's the score then, in your opinion?'

'I think Mr Goldberg would tell you that there is a case to answer. You can see for yourself, in the event of a conviction a custodial sentence is possible, bearing in mind your record. But we shall do our best.'

'What about a brief though? I don't want that Geraint Everard wally. He's no bloody good. What are the chances of someone like John Faconti?'

'Minus zero. Mr Faconti took silk last year. But there are several competent barristers available to us. Don't worry, we shall separate the orators from the wallies.'

A few minutes later I was being escorted out into the fresh air

33

of a courtyard. Two uniformed prisoners carried a dustbin between them and my tall dark warder eyed them suspiciously. I looked up at the factory-style chimneys again. 'I don't know how you can do this job,' I said abstractedly, as we reached the metal gates of the main arch.

The prison warder looked a little put out and defensive. 'There's more to the job than just locking them up, sir,' he said, pulling out a large ring of jangling keys.

As I stepped out into Jebb Avenue and the prison door slammed and locked behind me, a sudden feeling of exhilaration soared through me as though I had just been released from a two-year visit. The fresh air and space, and the feeling that I could go anywhere, literally made me feel high. In the next few years I would be back and would no doubt grow indifferent to the place, but for the moment I felt a spring in my step as I walked away.

I arrived back in the reassuring streets, walls and crowds of the City. It was dark by now and my heart was light with a night at the theatre ahead, plus bed with Diane, for the plan was to stay at her home. From Brixton Prison to Featherstone Place—the luxury of relaxing in that big rich house, with whatever Diane chose to offer, being the best kind of goodnight to an eventful day.

Cutting through Leadenhall Market I turned into a blind alley and into the noble building that houses insurance brokers, shipping agents, accountants and Marlon Markbyss & Co.

Jake was standing at his desk, flicking through his messages, still in his black Crombie coat, having just returned from yesterday's trip to Southampton.

'How did you get on?' I asked.

'It's a big case,' he said, taking his coat off and hanging it up. 'A big case, Nicky, I can tell you that.'

'I imagined it would be, given the manner in which they nicked him. I heard it was the Regional Crime Squad.'

'That was a liberty,' Goldberg sat behind his desk and lit a cigarette. 'We shall be making a formal complaint, just for the record mostly. These regional crime squads are a law unto themselves. But usually, before steaming in for an arrest, as a matter of courtesy they call at the local police station and say, "Look, we're going to pick up so-and-so, would one of your boys like to come down with us?" This crowd didn't bother. Anyway.

It's the Hampshire gold bullion job. You may remember reading in the press last year that an armed gang hijacked a security van and got away with a million in bullion. Harwood has been charged with robbery, conspiracy and the attempted murder of one of the guards.'

'And we're going to do it, obviously.'

'Of course. Is there anyone better? So! We have a busy time ahead of us, Nicholas. There won't be any time for skiving off in coffee bars.'

'I'm not given to that sort of thing, actually.'

'Don't lie to me, shmock! Now then. When you're not wrapped up with all this company and conveyancing rubbish I want you to go up to the National Newspaper Library in Colindale and peruse all the national newspapers of the week commencing August 5th last year. Bring back to me copies of any relevant reports or references to the hijacking. Okay? And there's a pile of outdoor work for you over there. Sorrenson is urgent—it must be done first thing in the morning.'

I took from my attaché case the Wilson file and handed it to him. He opened it and read the statement, dragging on his cigarette and squinting through the clouds of smoke. 'Guilty bastard!' he muttered after a moment. 'All right. See if you can draft a brief to counsel and bring it back to me for checking. Then Greta can type it up. And ask Sue to make me some coffee before she goes. I'll have some chocolate biscuits as well if the greedy pigs haven't scoffed them all.'

The internal phone buzzed. Jake picked the receiver up. 'Hullo? Yes? Speak! ... Yes he is, what do you want him for? I'll tell him.' He replaced the receiver and opened a file in front of him. 'There's somebody in the reception asking for you. Close the door on your way out.'

I expected to find Diane in the waiting room. Instead there stood a young man of roughly my own age, dressed in a coloured lumber jacket and shabby jeans. The rough beginnings of a beard made him look all the scruffier, together with his long wavy but tangled brown hair. The vacant look on his face gave way to a sudden alertness in expressive brown eyes that looked up at the sound of my footsteps.

'Can I help you?' I asked.

'Are you Nicholas Heyward?'

'Yes.'

The visitor twiddled his cigarette with thumb and fingers as though he was unsure how to start. 'I've bin lookin' for you for some time,' he said. 'And now that I've found you I'm not sure how to put it without sounding a bit daft, like.'

'Why don't you start by telling me why you've been looking for me,' I suggested. 'I take it that you're the man that's been phoning me for the past few weeks.'

'That's right, yeh. You get about quite a bit. I could never catch you in, here or at home. Me name's Tom Delaney.'

'Well, what can I do for you, Mr Delaney? I gather it's a personal matter you wish to speak to me about.'

'Yeh. It is. Look—the atmosphere in places like this doesn't do much for me to be honest. You wouldn't have time for a drink by any chance, would you? There's a pub down the way. I'd find it easier to yap in there.'

'I'm afraid not. I have to meet somebody in the West End in about ten minutes.'

'Shit!' the man muttered under his breath. 'P'raps I could walk some of the way down the road with yer, then?'

'Well, okay—if you like. I was just on my way out as a matter of fact.'

I led him out of the waiting room and along the corridor of leather-bound law reports, out into the cold atmosphere of Gracechurch Passage and distant traffic.

'Now perhaps you can tell me what this important business is exactly?' I asked as we walked along.

'It sounds a bit ... daft ...' he shrugged, 'just comin' out with it like thatt, but I s'pose there's no point in messing around with verbals, so here goes. You see, I've recently found out something that will probably come as a surprise ter you, as it did to me. I've discovered that we're related to each other.'

'Related to each other? By birth, you mean?'

'Definitely. This is gonna come as a birrof a shock to yer, but the fact is you and me are brothers. We're actually brothers, as wild as thatt sounds, burrit's true.'

I stopped walking, causing him to pull up in front of me. He looked back at me for a moment, watching for the reaction.

'Yeah,' he went on. 'I imagined it would have thatt effect on

36

yer. You coulda blown me sideways with a whistle when I found out thatt I had a brother somewhere out there that I knew sweet bugger all aboutt.'

This time it must have been me looking into his face, searching for God knew what. A mirror image of myself, or some trace of something to confirm the ludicrous thing that I had just heard—something to put my brain back into drive again. But there was nothing except the face of a total stranger.

'Brothers?' I was too incredulous to laugh, though there was a ticklish feeling in my stomach trying to find the trigger.

'There's no mistake,' he said, taking a pull at his cigarette. 'I've double-checked it out. I've been to a spot of bother finding out about you, then tracing you. You see, I leernt aboutt t'ree years ago that I was an adopted kid. Thatt me parents aren't me real parents. I think you can understand—it came as a shock. I'll say it did. But I imagine thatt it's a story thatt's familiar enough to you, ain't it?'

There was nothing dramatic or urgent about the way he spoke. He was as casual as his clothes, with the thumb of one hand tucked in his leather belt while the other hand flicked cigarette ash away. With a nose that had been broken in the past, he didn't exactly look like a handsome brute, speaking to me with the unconcern of a stranger in the street asking the way.

I stared at him with a stillness inside me not dead enough to be total shock. My mind was flashing with lights from an unknown past that I had put aside for later. I didn't have time for family-tree climbing. Yet impatient fate might now be dragging my past out of its spiritual fog to tap me on the shoulder in the here and now. But I still couldn't believe it—it was some absurd joke.

'It wasn't all thatt easy gettin' anything out of my mother and father—my adopted parents, that is,' he continued. 'They didn't know a hell of a lot but apparently it was a third-party arrangement. The kind of which must be illegal now but was well within the law at the time. Me mam an' dad 'ad to tell me sooner or later, especially when the legal position changed, an' all tha'. But when thee did cough up with it—and when I got over the thing thatt I was goin' through aboutt it—I wanted to know more. I started gerrin off on the idea of finding me real parents. I said to mesself: I don't know what kind of people they are or what kind of person I might have been, or what would have

37

happened if I hadn't been farmed out. And the more I thought aboutt it the more obsessive type of thing it became ...'

We walked on past courts and passages, through the covered market where more office workers were short-cutting through to their connections for home. A dustcart rumbled along, picking up the market rammel left behind by traders. Shadowy figures of businessmen moved on the other side of the frosted windows of the Lamb Tavern.

I wanted to drag this scruffy-looking sod beside me into the public bar and find out where he was coming from after all, and was on the verge of doing that when I thought of Diane hanging around in the cold at Leicester Square, waiting for me, and perhaps getting hassled by some freak. We emerged from under the arches of the market, back out into the amber light of the narrow main road, its bumper-to-bumper traffic, and people stomping back and forth, determined to disappear from this square mile as fast as possible, even if it meant killing somebody in the process.

'When I found you, though, I got a real lift, y'know? Here's a flesh 'n blood brother oo I've never so much as bloody well heard of. What kind of a guy is he? Where does he live and what does he do? Maybe he knows something about me—our—real parents, our natural background. Maybe he's looked for 'em himself and found 'em. I've got another family somewhere. If I passed 'em in the street I wouldn't know 'em from Adam and Eve. They're complete strangers to me—no more than phantoms. I wanted to know, more than anyt'ing else, who these strangers were.'

'I'm sorry to disappoint you,' I said, catching my breath, though keeping the situation at arm's length so that I surprised myself with the coolness of my voice. 'I know less about all this than you do, apparently. What evidence do you have to actually connect us?' I wanted to know, a hot feeling of blood and uncertainty being pumped from heart to brain.

'Now that the laws have changed about adopted children no one could stop me from looking for my past, though there were plenty of obstacles. My adoption from the home was fixed up by a Catholic priest, right? He was the middle man. I started on him, though at first he evaded the questions. But I guess I ruffled his cassock so much that in the end he sent me off to look for this

38

home in Manchester. I discovered there thatt their records had been'wiped out in a fire in 1962, so thatt knackered thatt. The County Record Office had me certificate of adoption registered but notten else. The adoption certificate gives the name of the child and the adoptive parents only. So I went back to Father McGuire and pestered the shite out of him some more until he came up to the house wid me one night, which gave the ole feller a bit of a shock when he saw dis priest comin' in. We had a long chatt and me parents relaxed and it was quite a social evenin'. Me mother is a bit highly strung, and all along I t'ink she wanted me to grow old and snuff it not knowin' thatt I wasn't actually her biological son—as though she'd been playin' this weird game for the past twenty years—my son, my son. Like the priest said, it was her I had ter convince that I wasn't tryina pull away from my adopted family. And I wasn't. I just wanted to know.

'Thatt evenen I learnt that I came from a family called Mackin. The priest didn't know much about the circumstances but the children of the Mackin family had been taken into care, like. I was only a year old then, but there was another lad a year older than me—adopted before I was, via Father McGuire again. He was adopted by a teacher and his wife, who a few years later moved south and Father McGuire lost contact with 'em ...'

Apart from the sensations he had been describing concerning the mystery of his blind history, which I had been able to identify with, this was the first statement he had made by way of giving credence to his claim. It gave my heart an unexpected jolt, I remember that much.

'When I came to London I went up to St Catherine's House and rummaged around the bloody great index books, where I found my entry, Mackin. Thomas Gerard Mackin, and me real dad's name right opposite. I looked through all four index books for the year before thatt and found another entry. Mackin. Nicholas David Mackin. I forked out and paid for two copies, although I was low on cash and all this gear can come to a bit, y'know! Anyway, when thee arrived I saw the names of my real parents. Neil Mackin and Eileen Waterford. And your parents, on your beerth certificate, are the same. Thatt makes us brothers.'

We walked along by the tall banking walls of Lombard Street, in the midst of a throng of people heading for Bank Station. Blood is thicker than water, but this guy looked as out of place as the female vagrant wheeling her pram through the rain the other night.

'Do you have these certificates on you now?' I asked.

He took from the back pocket of his jeans a bunch of folded-up papers and handed them to me as we arrived in front of the Corn Exchange.

'Keep 'em for now,' he offered with a shrug. 'Give 'em back to me when we meet again. You'll be interested in meeting up for a proper talk sometime, won't yer?'

'Of course. If we really are brothers there's a lot we need to know about each other,' I nodded.

'Yeh. That's warr I thought. They split us up for a few years, whatever the reason. So there's a lot of catching up to do. That's a fact and a half. We're brothers but we don't know a thing about each other. Nor ourselves for all I know.'

'Is there a phone number I can reach you at?'

'No, I'm not on the phone. Perhaps it's best to fix somethin' up now, I'm ready any time you are.'

'Okay. How about Saturday evening? Earlyish. And here in London.'

'There's a pub in Bethnal Green Road. It's called The Spooky Lady and it's not far from the tube station. I could meet you there about seven.'

We agreed on this and he lifted his hand in a wave and said 'Ciao', before turning away and walking off into the crowd, hands in jacket pocket, shoulders hunched and his feet in no hurry, towards the Stock Exchange and bus routes to the East End.

I glanced down at the folded documents in my hand. A combination of anticipation and a bud of paralysis took over, leaving me suspended in the crush of the City rush homeward. I slid the papers into the inside pocket of my jacket and descended the steps into the grim guts of the tube station.

Chapter Four

Words swam around the roof of the Swiss Centre in dotted lights.
The brightness of neon signs blazed through the branches of trees
as a busker played to a cinema queue, competing with a chorus of
unseen pigeons. People drifted along, the usual mixture of West
Enders and night-outers, some going somewhere, others going
nowhere, standing around as if waiting for something to turn up.
Pubs, coffee houses, record and bookshops, dazzling bright sex-
aid shops, all crowded, and the warm smells of different kinds of
food past different kinds of doorways ...

I took it all in without realising it this time, my mind blanked
by the face and name of Tom Delaney. I walked through
Leicester Square as though it wasn't there, until suddenly I felt
somebody tugging my arm, pulling me out of my thoughts and
back to the lights of surrounding reality.

'Nicky, are you sleep-walking or something? You just walked
right past me. You haven't forgotten what I look like, I hope.'

'Diane. I'm sorry,' I laughed, feeling my head go zing at the
sudden switchback to the immediate present.

I kissed her as a record blared out of a shop doorway behind
her—the raging voice of a manic youth adding chaos to thoughts
already swimming around my head like the meaningless words of
the Swiss Centre. It was getting cold, Diane was the only warmth
around and the scent of her hair made me feel like sitting in a
quiet pub and talking with her rather than going to a theatre.

'What's been happening to you?' She flicked a strand of hair
out of her eyes. 'You're late, that's not like you. And in a dream
... is there anything wrong?'

'No. No, there's nothing wrong ... Look, we have time for a
drink somewhere. Let's see if we can find a boozer, I could
murder a drink, I tell you.'

41

We turned into a side street festooned with neon signs, peopled with punters looking in and out of the strip clubs and fuck-book supermarkets. I pushed open the door of a warm-looking pub and jostled my way through the crowd in the saloon bar, eventually returning to Diane, handing her a martini and taking a sip of my own flat, expensive beer.

'Have you got any cigarettes? That bloke in the prison smoked half of mine and I've bloody well run out. I'll get some before we leave.'

'What's the mattter?' she asked, offering me the packet. 'You seem slightly ruffled. Did the proximity of prison walls psyche you out a bit?'

'I must admit I didn't feel particularly relaxed, but I suppose one gets used to it. I had actually expected that experience to be the highlight of the day. But that has turned out not to be the case. My mysterious caller has turned up ... in flesh and blood. Claiming to be my flesh and blood, as a matter of fact.'

'What do you mean?'

She looked sceptical at first, as though she thought I was teasing her. 'Christ, there isn't another one of you running about is there?' she asked.

I showed her the certificates and she realised it wasn't a joke. Her scepticism was replaced by an expression of wonder as she read up and down the columns of data. The beer flooding my senses helped me unwind. I felt a bit drained because, on the one hand, I was interested in what had come to me and, on the other, I wanted to run a mile from it.

'It ties in with my certificate of adoption. I was born in Dalethorpe, Manchester. Gareth was teaching there until the early sixties. That is the date of my birth all right. And bits and pieces of Delaney's story ring true. We were both redeemed from the world of care homes and foster parents. He found out that his elder brother was adopted by a teacher and his wife, and brought to the south. I kept quiet so that I wouldn't put any words into his mouth, and he came pretty close a couple of times without being prompted.'

'What's he like?' she demanded. 'I mean, does he look like you? What's he like?'

'God, no. He doesn't look like me,' I said, though I had to think about it again: his face, hair, expressive eyes, broken nose, unshaven jaws ... 'No, he doesn't look, sound or come across as having anything to do with me. He's got a Liverpool accent and he looks a bit yobbo, to put it bluntly. I just haven't had time to digest it. I'm going on first impressions—just telling you what I know so far.'

'Yobbo?' she laughed. 'My God, won't Alison be pleased to have a scouse yobbo in the family?'

'You're not kidding,' I thought, though I didn't find it all that funny.

'I can understand why you were floating along in a state of shock.' She gave me the documents back. 'But you seem quite subdued about it. Aren't you excited about suddenly being on the edge of discovery, and all that? Finding out something about this missing part of you.'

'That depends on what I'm going to find out,' I smiled. 'Even if he is—my biological brother—it just doesn't mean anything to me. Spiritually, as you would say, he's just a stranger that walked in off the street tonight.'

'The brother who came in from the cold,' she grinned.

'If you want to be theatrical about it,' I said impatiently. 'Come on, then, toss that back. Let's go and get into somebody else's drama.'

We sat in the middle of a perfumed audience that night, but the lights and the play only got through to me in spasms. Several times I put my hand in my inside pocket to feel if the birth certificates were real or not. Delaney hovered about in my mind's eye, coming and going throughout the laughter of the audience, the action and the applause. I wasn't sure whether I wanted Delaney or fate to drag me back into a time that I would never remember anyway—at least not until I was ready, not until I chose to find out for myself.

Chapter Five

Twenty-four hours after the initial surprise I was still trying to get over it. Throughout the day, in the office, in a taxi, during a court hearing as I sat behind a waffling barrister, I had read the birth certificates over and over again. Mackin. The man was my brother, I knew that much. We came from one womb, and that just seemed incredible, although, as Diane had said this morning, it was always possible that something like this could happen. Yet twenty-four hours after meeting him the memory of his face had become vague and indistinct.

At home that evening I picked up one of the photograph albums. It was old, filled with family history in sepia. It would fetch a couple of bob in an arcade down Portobello Road with its frozen memories of a family—they had intrigued me as a kid— the heroic deeds that Gareth's father and uncles were involved in during the Great War. They illustrated family memories and anecdotes that went back seventy years.

Alison and Gareth were my real parents. I had my family and that should have been that. But I was cut off from these sepia faces. Somewhere there were other photograph albums featuring faces from another family tree. What did they look like, I couldn't help wondering for the first time in years. It seemed hard to believe that I now had a rendezvous with the real thing.

A friend of mine in Kentish Town had just acquired a mortgage, therefore he and his wife would be getting shot of their one-bedroom flat. After dinner at Featherstone Place I phoned them and arranged for a stop-over in London for the following night. Our expectations were high. Their vacant flat could be the chance we needed. And my adrenalin was in full flow because Diane's father had suggested handing over to the practice that I was articled with some legal matters that his company's in-house lawyer claimed were too complicated for them to handle. This would be a hell of a boost to my standing with Markbyss himself, as well as with Mr Sinclair and his contacts.

Getting into Diane's family felt right. As we drove into the East End early on Saturday evening it certainly felt more real than going to meet my brother.

I told Diane I'd see her later and she drove off to our friends in Kentish Town. Because it was early The Spooky Lady had just a handful of customers, couples that were vague figures sitting in booths in the dim lighting. Somewhere around the corner you could hear the clicking of billiard balls. Not far from the bar a teenage couple sat gazing down into a Space Invaders table and in the DJ's throne at the end a girl sat at the decks playing her fly-by-drink favourites to the empty atmosphere of the pub.

There was no sign of Tom Delaney. I sat at the counter and ordered a pint, then waited, contemplating the mirrors and iridescent colours of upside-down bottles. My concentration fixed on them as if trying to stop the gut-twisting anticipation that I felt.

The clock hand crept past seven and I began to wonder whether or not he was going to show. Every time the door opened I looked around to discover that it wasn't him. I was busily trying to remember what he looked like when suddenly I could feel somebody standing close beside me.

'Hi It's great to see you,' he smiled. 'What are you drinking?'

'Let me.'

'No chance. I'll get these in. Hey, love, can I have a couple down here when you're ready?' he called to the barmaid.

As he ordered a double round of drinks I looked at him again. He was wearing a flat cap, last week's beard, a choker, a tweed jacket, faded jeans. When the drinks came he suggested we move across to a booth behind the Space Invaders.

'Look at the way she's poured dem out,' he complained as we sat opposite each other. 'Amateur! There's more froth on it than anyt'ing else. Them heads don't arf mount up at the end of the night, you know?'

'Is this your local or something?'

'I get in here from time to time. It's all right at the moment. Later on it'll be crowded an' dead loud, wid plenty of talent around knocken back shorts nineteen to the dozen, if you're into all thatt. Peersonally I never stick to the same pub all the time. Most of the ones over thiss side of the Smoke seem like animated mausoleums, though there's one or two with some spark.' He took out a tobacco pouch and started rolling a cigarette. I offered him one of my proper ones but he preferred the one that he had rolled in a matter of seconds.

He was more relaxed than he had been the other day. This time it was me that felt some tension. I'd had a list of questions ready to fire at him but the situation seemed so absurd that it was impossible to drive straight into them.

'You live locally though?'

'I live in New Road—thatt's Whitechapel. You know it?'

'I don't know the road.'

'New Road is aboutt the oldest looken road in London,' he chuckled. 'In Liverpool I once lived in a block of flats called Riverside Mansions and they looked more like bloody dungeons. The people thatt sling these places together and stick names on 'em afterwards have gorra wild sense of humour. Still, the New Road gaff'll have to do for now, until I get mesself fixed up with something better. If I ever do.'

'What is it, a flat?'

He lit his cigarette and shook his head in a haze of smoke. 'No way. It's a squat. Flats are bloody gold dust in London, y'know. But I came down here because jobs are bloody gold dust in Liverpool, I'm lookin' for that happy medium wer jobs and flats can be acquired together. Don't laugh. Finding weerk down here's not as easy as you might think either.'

'How long have you been in London?'

'Two year, near enough. Earl's Court feerst, then over here when I got to know some people. Plus a few spells of wine drinkin' an' beach dossin', in France and Spain. I nearly turned into a bloody field mouse in Spain, but I enjoyed it. If I get some gelt under me belt I'll be on the trot again, given the chance.'

I took from the inside pocket of my jacket the documents he had left with me. 'In the meantime, you seem to be making prodigious efforts to find the lost family. How did you know where to find me?'

'That was a fluke.' He unbuttoned his jacket. 'Ole Father McGuire—remember, the priest?—he knew your mam and dad, and he knew that you'd gone to this place in Essex—Wichfield.

46

And your dad was still teaching. Well, Wichfield's not a very big place. I could get at the electoral register and then the directory inquiry for the phone number, and check out the schools if necessary. As luck would have it, you and your family haven't shifted since you moved there from Dalethorpe. You've been in Wichfield for as far back as you can remember, haven't yer?'

'That's right.'

'As soon as I got all that together I dialled your number. If your family had moved sometime during the past twenty year I would have been knackered. We wouldn't be sitting here now. But the gods were on my side for a change.'

'I'm sorry I missed your calls. My job is a bit hectic at the moment. But I was intrigued to know what the calls were about. Why all the mystery? You didn't leave a name or a message.'

He sat back and sighed, idly tapping his fingers against his glass with a distinct clink, clink. 'I'm not sure really.' He dragged on his roll-up. 'I didn't know whether or not the name Delaney meant anything to you or your family. I wasn't sure what reaction I would get. I didn't want to barge in on your family or anything—maybe upset somebody, for all I knew. I wanted to save the punch line until we were face to face. Ceertainly not in a message left over the phone. I thought I'd play it down and lay it on you in person. As for the chick on the switchboard or the Jewish guy, it had nothing to do with them.'

'I see your point. That was a good bit of foresight on your part,' I had to admit.

'Have you told your family yet?' he asked.

'No. I wanted to talk to you first. I almost feel that this is something just between ourselves, as if it has nothing to do with my adopted family. I wanted to get to know you a little before setting up some sort of meeting. But I shall probably tell them when I see them tomorrow night.'

'How will they feel about it, d'you think?'

'They'll be curious to meet you, obviously. My father is a gentle character, easy-going and agreeable. My mother will probably suggest that you get a haircut or something, but she means well.'

'What is your family set-up like? I mean, d'y'have any brothers or sisters?'

'No. I was an only child. Or so I imagined for a long time. And you?'

47

'I've gorra young sister. Kathleen. She's sixteen. My parents tried for years to have kids and somehow never scored. Then they adopted me, and a few years later they hit the jackpot and had one of their own.'

'How did you feel about the fact that you were adopted?'

'Like I told you before,' he leaned his elbow back on the table, flicking fag ash into the ash tray. 'It was a bloody mind-bender. Not that I loved me mam and dad any the less for it. They went to a fair amount of hassle to get me. It saved me from homes and from being fostered around from arsehole to breakfast time. The fact that I wanted to know more about where I really came from was no rejection of my adopted family. It made us closer in the end. I think of them as me real family. I gave them a bit of trouble because I was a bit of a tearaway—high spirits an' all tha'. But me ole man in his grumpy way allus stood by me. Bailin' me out and dealing with the pleece whenever I got into the odd scrape. He'd make a bloody good lawyer himself, although it's not the kind of family that lawyers come from.'

'What kind of a family is it then? What does your father do?'

'Not much now. He used to weerk on the docks in Liverpool, humping shite from ship to shore. Gallopin' lumbago put paid to that gear. Then he got a job in this light-engineering factory, owned by a company in Mayfair or somewhere. But two years ago the men in Mayfair said, "We're losin' too much bread, the plant on Merseyside has got to go." Me dad, who had just been made foreman, was among the ones that got the heave-ho. Dead chuffed about thatt, he was. In the best of places, guys of his age don't get offered jobs. In Liverpool he's got no chance. Anyway, when theers weerk about you might call it a weerking-class background, if you're into labels of that sort. Although the old feller wasn't amused when I joined the WRP.'

'What's that?'

'The Weerkers Revolutionary Party. Me dad is a traditional Labour supporter. Which to my mind is a choice between one fatality and another. I got a lift off of thinking that what the country needed was total change, and that reforms and stuff just weren't enough anymore. I didn't get off on any revisionist bullshite. At the WRP meetings you could hear speakers get up and start yellin' about revolution being five minutes around the corner. The people of Iran have risen against their imperialist

48

oppressors and are free. Up the Ayatollah. They said sumpin' like that was gonna happen in England at any time. You could see it beginnin' ter crack, with the left-wingers gettin' their hold even within the Labour Party. I had to laugh at the comparison with England and Iran. Khomeini is not exactly a champion of the weerking man. But it's true what one guy said: you have to have your eyes up your arse with all the propaganda flyin' about, playin' games with people's brains.'

'And so you're stuck for work as well?'

'Yeh. I'm what you might call a dole queue floater, in between one arsehole of a job after another. Ah've been doin' some casual work for this agency. Kitchen porterin' in disgusting restaurants up your way. Fenchurch Street, Fleet Street, Holborn. Scraping the encrusted shite out of the great vats, pans and pots that they bake the bastarding gunge in. Piping hot steel in piping hot water in a Turkish bath of a kitchen. Some of you pinstripe freaks don't know what you're eating. I wouldn't have been surprised to find a bloody second-hand condom in one of the pots. We'd get a half-hour break so we could gobble a free meal. By then I'd usually lost me appetite and would settle for a coffee, fag, and rest. Anything but the bloody grub. The money just wasn't weerth it, so I bailed out. Bastard of a job. So I'm in the market for something else.'

'Are you looking for anything special?'

'Well, I'm lookin' for some night weerk in a bed-testing factory,' he grinned, and his eyes sparkled. 'But failing that, I'll take anything that comes along and pays. You have to keep yourself afloat and watch out. Dole queue life can make you feel really demoralised, especially if you're stuck with it. The less progress you make in finding a job, the more discouraged you get. You can't make plans for fuck all. You just live from day to day, and hope the Giro spins out until at least the last minute. I thought things might be brighter in London. Why not come down and have a look around, I thought, I'll risk it for a biscuit, so down I came. What a piggin' life, eh, our kid?

'When I feerst came to London I was fifteen. It was my feerst runaway dash to the bright lights. I wandered around the West End, the usual scene, mesmerised by the coloured lights dancing up and down above the people on the pavement. I dossed in night shelters and slept rough, and it only seemed possible to make

49

friends or contact wid the guys floating around Subway 4, lookin' for a deal or offering one—really fucken depressin'. I got into all these soup kitchens and late-night tea-stands in places like Victoria and Parliament Square, yappin' with the dossers hanging around and kippin' in doorways. I hated it. But was fascinated by it. Then I got into it. The piss-takers as well as the philosphers, all the scraggy little scroungers, the losers and boozers—it was easy for me to accept their idea of survival. They're not thatt much a race apart and I laughed to mesself that we all might end up like that if the silicone chip t'ing gets out of control. Even now, six years on, I still go down to places like thatt and chat 'em up when insomnia sets in.

'I went back to Liverpool though and stayed there weerkin' in factories till things got so bad and weerk really became a bastard to find. Then when I was eighteen I came back to the Smoke with me feerst real long-term girlfriend and we managed to get this tight-arsed bedsit in Earl's Court. Being with someone you're having a strong relationship with makes all the difference to taking a big new city on. Our families thought we were daft—that you're better off being hard-up among your own. But here I am in cold London, drinking with you. Among my own after all, eh?'

'So it would seem,' I said, thoughtfully stubbing the cigarette out. 'You found me okay. What about our real parents? Did you pick up on any clues concerning them?'

'No, notten. All I could do was ask questions at home and find out from the priest where they used to live back in the fifties. I went down to the street in Dalethorpe to see if I could just check out the house. The house was gone, there was just these blocks of flats givin' each other the evil eye. It was useless askin' around for the Mackin family after all these years. Have you ever made any attempts to find 'em yourself?'

'No,' I shook my head.

'Why not? Weren't you bothered?'

'I don't know. I had more immediate things to deal with, it seemed. My law studies for a start. They've used up most of my energy in recent years. There was no time for turning detective over the missing link.'

'What made you go into law? A bit anti-social, isn' it?' he asked with what I could only assume was North Country bluntness.

50

'What the hell makes you think it's anti-social?' I asked.

He shrugged his shoulders. 'Big fees out of the big troubles of little people, I guess. If somebody'd come to our house in Liverpool and told me I had a brother in London in a lawyer's office, I would have laughed. Although I didn't know who or what I'd find when I started lookin', I might as well tell yer the truth.'

'What is it that you find so attractive about down-and-outs? You seem to look down on people trying to make something out of life, but I can tell you there's nothing anti-social about my work. We're not all just grab-alling Uriah Heeps skulking around looking for a pregnant wallet. But we do have to earn a living. Drinking tea in Spitalfields with our bewhiskered friends of the road is all very romantic. But who the hell wants that for a life, for God's sake? Is that where you want to be in ten years from now?'

'I know what I don't want. I don't wanna sell mesself short. I don't want to compromise mesself by jumping into the combine and gettin' all tangled up with thatt. All I need is a job, a place ter stay and a notebook ter create images in—and I'm *happy*. But I don't have to go to the extremes of prostituting mesself for a house in Hampstead or an ulcer in the City. Shite, there's a weerld out here, why buy insulation? Wash your hands of it?'

'I enjoy my work. It will provide me with the means for a comfortable life. I feel that we help people and that we provide a damned useful service. Therefore it is challenging and rewarding, not just in monetary terms. You meanwhile, don't seem to know where you're going—or even where you want to go. Washing pots and pans in the kitchen—isn't it you that's selling yourself short?'

'I admit I haven't found my own direction yet,' he conceded. 'Maybe I'm irresponsible and immature as well. Thatt's my look-out, sure. But the idea of tying myself to your sort of weerld seems irksome to me, as mine probably would to you. I can't relate to the establishment you're seervin'. None o' my family or friends have prospered on it, no way.'

'But isn't all this drop-out-and-drink-with-the-tramps-treatment a little passé?' I asked.

'Dropout? I was kicked out with two and a half million other people signing up on the bloody dole. I spent months trying to get

51

in and join me dad. In the end we were both kicked out and set aside, waiting for the executive Messiahs to come along and invest in a British industry full of old machines, low peerks, low pay, and conditions that no weerker in France or Germany would weerk in.

'Me dad never missed a day's weerk in his life. But look at him now. Strong and fit, with a good few years left in him to serve society, contribute to the country. But there's nothing for him, and he's on forty quid a week social security. He's got no choices, no freedom, no prospects, no future except a co-op funeral. There must be something wrong with the distribution of wealth and capitalist policies for so many people to be wasted like this. I used ter roll me eyeballs when I heard the WRP goin' on about capitalism being in its dying agony and all that trite Trotskyist bullshite. But I'm thinking again. It's seerved its purpose and now it's all used up but the Tories won't admit it. They're great at hanging on to values that belong to another time. I get the feeling they'd like to teern the clock back, with their vicious cuts in social services; widen the gap between money and breadline; cut back in education and make higher education, but for the privileged few, harder to get again; keep women in the home, lookin' after the family—as if women are superfluous, dispensable machines—when a lot of families rely on two wage packets to keep up with inflation. It's not exactly in the spirit of the anti-discrimination act, which is a law, and the double-faced bastards are always telling us that we must respect the law. Then there's that racialist proposal to stop immigrant women bringing their husbands into the country, while immigrant men can bring in their wives; Tory councils buying 38-thousand-pound limousines for the Mayor, and proposing to scrap school dinners for kids to cut the "expense". One week they're yelling the odds about the immorality of abortion because it's taking a life, the next they're calling for the introduction of the death penalty. Literally one week after the other! Shite! I cringe at the idea of such poxy hypocrisy. I don't wanna be like that, I've got that much self-respect.'

'It's a nasty unjust world, full of bullshit as you've said,' I agreed. 'But you have to live in it. You might as well make the best of it. There never will be equality, so why sacrifice yourself dreaming about it?'

'You're the one that's sacrificing yourself,' he smiled wryly. 'People accept where it's at because it's playing safe. You don't like the unknown so you hang on to the lifelong values. You don't have to deeply examine your own motives.'

'Whoever the government is, it was the people that put them there, remember?'

'That's just an example of what little choice people have got. They play safe. They don't believe the promises that are made but they don't have many alternatives. The public are bored with it but would rather have things stay the same.'

We agreed to differ on our attitudes to life. His views seemed to me to be a naive mixture of dreams and bitterness. His political views were his gut reactions to experience of life rather than the result of intellectual analysis. Our backgrounds were entirely different, so it surprised neither of us that our views on a number of things conflicted.

The pub filled up with more and more people. Tom was an emphatic and manic talker, words raced out in all directions; he would be a writer who never showed his work to anybody else. He was full of energy and rhetoric and ideas about everything. We got through about eight pints of beer and his talking subsided after he asked me for my life story, wanting to know about life in Wichfield, my adopted family, the school that I went to, the girls I'd been involved with. It no doubt sounded tame and 'bourgeois' to him although he thankfully didn't inflict that one on me. The more we drank the more we ploughed into each other's personalities. The booze expedited our opening up to each other. For someone who had little money he was fast enough on his feet when the glasses were empty.

He asked me what sort of music I liked. Jazz, folk and rock was an answer that pleased him immensely because it was common ground between us and we had a long discussion about the pubs and clubs in London where the music could be found. Nightspots like the 100 Club we both knew well, and we may have bumped into each other by the bar before now, for all we knew.

He seemed to question everything he discovered in life, mauled it around in search of worthwhile answers—without the benefit of a formal education that might have brought him to a few answers a little sooner.

'I've fallen into the bad habit of self-analysis,' he said with a

53

self-mocking smile. 'It's a flaw in my character helped out by this geerl I was living with til a few weeks back. She analysed herself day in day out, so that we couldn't move forward. Hated herself so much that she lashed out at people who cared for her. Before giving me me beerthday present she'd start a row and throw it at me because it was the only way she could give. All that wasted time spent peering into her chaotic soul, not to mention the energy spent on it. It started rubbing off on me. I always pick out screwed-up women, somehow. I'm following some sort of pattern that I can't seem to break. Maybe there's something wrong with me that attracts that kind of peerson. Maybe I should wurk on mesself and find out what it is, type of thing.'

'And waste more time? What's the point of that? You'll only get stuck up your own psychic creek without the paddle of return. You can't waste half your life wondering why you do things. Such futile self-indulgence should be kept for the deathbed. Maybe you should just move in different circles and meet people with some direction. Find something more positive than this mellifluous life-style of yours.'

'We are different, aren't we!' he said, with an infectious smile.

'That is something I think we can agree on,' I grinned.

'D'you play pool, Nick?'

'I used to.'

'D'you fancy a game now?'

'I haven't played for a few years. I'm a bit rusty.'

'Thatt's all right. Being as we're brothers I'll let you have the feerst game,' he grinned. 'Come on.'

Cold night air wasn't enough to sober us up as we walked through the dark streets well past closing time. Kentish Town seemed like a thousand miles away. I hadn't intended to be out with Tom so long but had been absorbed by his energy and life more than by the content of his monologues.

'D'you wanna come back to our place?' he asked, turning his jacket collar up against the cold. 'We've got some coffee and some Lebanese Red, if you're into naughty cigarettes.'

At just after midnight we arrived in New Road. The house that he lived in was on a corner. Sprayed on the side of the house was much graffiti including the giant letters: WOGS OUT. The house may once have been a respectable Victorian abode but now

54

looked like a ramshackle hovel, the lower windows adorned with corrugated iron.

Inside the building was the smell of dampness and paraffin. The electricity was on and he led me along the hall and into a large room at the back of the house. It wasn't so dreary in here, with the gas fire switched on. The room was spotlessly tidy, with armchairs and settee, a table holding stacks of papers and notebooks, a bookshelf crammed with books, a record and tape rack next to a small stereo record player; a fluorescent light illuminated the room from the corner.

'Make yourself at home. I'll get some coffee. Stick some sounds on if you want,' he struggled out of his jacket. 'D'you take sugar and milk?'

Whilst he was in the kitchen I took a look at his bookshelf to see what his reading habits were like. I wasn't surprised to find a few works of Karl Marx there and laughed inwardly at Diane's suggestion that she invite Tom to have dinner with her father. But there were other books that I was surprised to see: books on Greek and Roman mythology, feminism, poetry, psychology, surrealism, witchcraft, drugs; names as varied as Huxley, Kerouac, Camus, Dickens, Hesse, Jung, Laing, Toynbee, Shakespeare, Plath jumped into my scanning eyes—not a James Bond in sight.

As I turned around I suddenly met the chubby face of a large tabby cat that was staring at me dreadfully from one of the armchairs.

'What d'you call him?' I asked, rubbing its chin as Tom walked in with two mugs of coffee.

'That's Oliver Twist,' he laughed, handing me one of the mugs. 'You feed the greedy bastard but he wants more all the fuckin' time. Don't yer, yer whore!'

He put some music on, an early Springsteen album, and while he rolled one of his home-grown cigarettes I stroked the cat and drank some coffee, totally devoid of the energy to get to Kentish Town. I watched him putting the joint together. Whether it was the alcohol or not I still couldn't relate to him as my brother.

There was something there that drew me, but that could have been simple friendship and nothing else. All we seemed to have in common though was the fact that we liked the same music.

'Don't you ever wonder why our parents disposed of us?' I asked.

'Yeh. Frequently. There must have been a bit of a story behind it, with the two of us in care.'

'If we had been kept together you and I would be the same kind of people. Same accents, same background, perhaps even the same kind of outlook on life. Who can tell?'

'I can't help but wonder what went on. One day I'll find out though. I'm sure of thatt, our kid.'

Two brothers, disconnected from their beginnings, getting drunk and stoned and reaching into each other's skulls; disapproving of each other's values and trying to cross over into each other's range of experience; we wanted to know each other well, although we didn't want to be like each other. Suddenly I wanted Gareth and Alison to meet him. I wanted us to be drawn together. I wanted to go to Liverpool and meet his family. Such blood-bond tying and the desire for it took me by surprise.

The marijuana gave my drunkenness a lift, as if turning my intoxication on its edge and clearing my vision a little. I hadn't smoked the stuff since I was at college and nearly coughed my stomach up on this.

'If the pleece came kicking that door down yed need a lawyer yourself,' he grinned.

'I was just wondering what my principal would think if he could see me now. He'd probably sever my articles if he thought that I was smoking pot in a squat.'

Tom laughed. I asked him how many people lived in the place. There were six of them. The house was owned by a property developer waiting for planning permission to do something with it. Forced entry had given birth to it as a squat, thanks to a man called Eddie, who occupied a room upstairs, having spent months getting nowhere in search of accommodation.

'Diane and I are hoping to get a flat ourselves,' I told him. 'But living in London is expensive. Especially on my present income.'

'Move in here,' he suggested.

'Here?' I laughed. 'You must be joking!'

'Why not? There's plenty of room, kidder. No rent to pay. Just a fiver a month towards the rates and a few quid in the kitty towards gas and electricity. You're a stone's throw from your office in the City. What more d'you want?'

'I don't think my lawyer employer would like it if one of his minions were squatting in somebody else's property. It would be bad for the firm's image. Especially if this property developer happens to be one of his clients.'

'He wouldn't know about it,' Tom spoke enthusiastically. 'It's a great idea. What better way would there be for two long-lost brothers ter get to know each other? Living in the same gaff. Why not?'

'A place like this is not what I had in mind anyway. Nor what Diane has in mind either, I should think. Somehow I don't see myself as a squatter.'

'Neither did I, but I'm doing it out of necessity,' he pointed out. 'You should open a few eyes by being a bit unconventional. Don't get into that pompous stereotype stuff. The legal profession is a bloody dinosaur, protecting affluence and middle-class values. That's why it won't change and why the people in it don't change.'

'What does your family think of the way you live?' I asked. 'It sounds as though it's a close-knit family, but aren't they disappointed to find you floating around the countryside?'

'I suppose they are,' he admitted. 'But not surprised, I'm sure. They would have been surprised if I'd gone to university myself. Me dad is one of the best. I respect him a lot, although there's something amiss at times. He doesn't talk much but you can tell his present worklessness gnaws at him.'

'Where did you develop the taste for all this heavy literature?'

'I got all them books from Sandie. She was a dead intelligent lady, but self-destruction wasn't in it! In spite of the dead-and-alive school I went to I liked readin' and she kind of took me away from the sci-fi and the crap.'

'What happened to her?' I asked, before taking a powerful draw on the joint. It made my throat roar with pain but turned my brain inside out in an elated sort of way. The smoke drifted around slowly and serenely, and my thoughts floated around with the same gentle buoyancy. It was too late to go to Diane now even if my legs could get it together to carry me out of here, which was doubtful. When I closed my eyes, instead of darkness, there were coloured patterns looping the loop.

'She had a drug problem,' he said. 'She was on sleepers for her nerves, being the highly-strung sort. They were prescribed—it

57

wasn't a Subway 4 situation. In the end she got hooked. When she got scared enough to try and do without 'em her system started bucking on her. We lived together for three years. It's insane to stand by and watch someone go through that.'

He walked to the table and came back with a dog-eared photograph of a dark-haired girl nursing a baby on her lap.

'The kid in thatt is mine, Uncle Nicholas. Your nephew Damien. But he lives with her mother now.'

'Yours?'

'Yeh,' he nodded with a grin that denoted he was proud of his son.

'Nice kid,' I said. He was a big-eyed baby, smiling, and the girl was quite attractive with long, straight, black hair and dark eyes that gave her a Mediterranean look.

'Where is she now?' I handed the snap back to him.

'It's a long story, brother,' he half-laughed. 'But aren't they all? This one began three years ago in Liverpool when I met Sandie in this club. In them days I didn't wanna settle down or anything like that. Me motto was fuck 'em and chuck 'em. So I never useda stay with the same geerl for more than a few weeks at a time. But when I teamed up with this one I felt really made-up, y'know. A rapport developed, which might not have been love, but we got a lift off it all the same. She was full of nervous energy, passionate and really moody, but we had a great time, takin' in music, poetry readin's, fringe theatre, drinkin' and writin' an' gettin' off on all that type of thing.

'We moved in together and after about six months we found out that she was pregnant. I didn't freak out when I heard there was a kid on its way, which surprised me. I'd always thought mesself to be too immature to be a father. But Sandie got shite-scared. We were in London by the time she had the baby. After he was born her high feelings and low feelings went from bad to weerse and the gear she was takin' for post-natal depression just seemed to make things rougher. She started escapin' from the realities by poppin' the pills: Tuinal, Sodium Amytol, Valium, or any shite she could get her hands on. She just cracked up and there was notten I could do ter stop it. It was suddenly like havin' two kids, a baby and a disturbed teenage daughter. I was at the end of my bleddy rope with it, and self-preservation was forever tempting me to do a runner, while a stronger force was keeping

58

me feet nailed to the floor. I couldn't leave, although watching her continually stoned or continually crying in pain had me in this bastard of an emotional half-nelson type of thing.

'She was doing things without knowing what she was doing, and it freaked her out when she was told later. She would attack me like a wild animal sometimes, then on other occasions she was just like a five-year-old kid. It was doing my head up, you know. A couple of times she overdosed and I got her to the hospital. They pumped her out and before I knew what was happening they'd pumped her back onto the street to get on with it. For twenty quid the GP she was with sold her twenty barbiturate capsules and she was off again.'

'Where was the child while all this was happening?' I asked.

'Sandie got scared of what was going down. We took him to her mother's place in Liverpool while we got things sorted out. She tried to reduce her dosage. We were in this pub in King's Cross one night. Suddenly she just collapsed on the floor in the middle of this boozer and started jerking and convulsing and making these choking noises. It was bloody frightening, I've got to tell yer. I stuck her comb in her mouth to stop her biting her tongue and tried to keep her where she was, as she was clawing at the carpet, at other people's ankles and stools, at my face.

'This scene went on for a couple of months. I started to wish that she would overdose once and for all and end her own agony as well as mine. That sounds really bad to say it, but she was destroying herself in any case.

'In the end we got her to agree to go to this rehabilitation place called Rendezvous House.'

'I've heard of it,' I nodded.

'They tear you to pieces there,' he said, taking a pull on the joint, turning the volume of the music right down. 'Strip your personality down like a stolen car, layer by neurotic layer. Constant encounter groups, rigorous work-schedules, 24-hour discipline. There's no stepping outside the grounds, no correspondence or communication with the rest of the fucked-up world—not until you've worked on yourself. I've heard people say that, given the choice, they'd settle for prison rather than go through the programme at this joint. But Sandie agreed to go in. At her induction they told her that she'd probably be in there for two years. It takes a long, long time to unravel twenty-three years' worth of hang-ups and neurosis.

'For both of us this place breathed a welcome blast of fresh air over us because it seemed like an answer. There was an end to all this bizarre hell after all. I felt punch-drunk with relief and maybe she didn't feel so condemned to death as she had done. A ton weight had lifted off us and for a week before she went in things were suddenly back to the way they were at the beginning. The rapport came back as we crammed as much into her last week at large as we could: cinema, concerts, theatre, art exhibitions, readings. She liked to dance, which I don't, but I took her to a disco. Every penny I'd put by was ploughed into making it a good week, a sendoff, and a way of keeping her mind off the drugs, on the one hand, and to prevent her from worrying about Rendezvous House, on the other.

'When Friday afternoon came around that outburst of life and loving had to come to a bloody sharp end. It hit us that it was finished and my guts suddenly churned at the thought of the ordeal she was about to go through. Not that I could understand why any of this was happening. But it was happening and there were no two ways about it. She was scared again and it was visible on her face. Looking at somebody else's face in pain can be a hundred times worse than having the pain yourself. In the back of the minicab I took her in to London Bridge, she said, "Tom, I'm frightened!"

'Jesus! Me guts turned and me eyes went fucken stiff. I put me arm round her and told her daft weerds, like it's for your own good and there are no short cuts to getting better. You've got to learn how to cope with life and the sooner you do the sooner you can live. Saying that it was the only way didn't seem to help, and yet we'd tried everything else.

'The train journey from London Bridge to Caulton Park was loaded, really charged. Things were flooding into my brain, all the love and the shit and the stress and the strain of the past three years. All the hassle and pressure had numbed and deadened me feelings. Suddenly they were back again, making me wonder how things could turn out like this, making me choke on the guilt that I felt for wishing that she'd kill herself, making me tired of myself for judging conditions in people that I didn't understand. I wondered what I could have done but didn't do. We'd had a close but stormy relationship and a baby during the past three years.

60

Suddenly I wasn't gonna see her again for another two years. I sensed that that was the end of everything. People change after a two-year separation and although I told her I'd be there when she came out, if she wanted to come back, I think we both knew things might not work out like that.

'I carried her case through the town and up this really steep, mile-high hill. My heart was goin' away like a two-bob watch as we climbed up it and I started to get flecks of rain in me eye. At the top of the hill was a potholed track, with shrubs and bushes on either side. We walked along it until we came to the entrance of a driveway that led up to the front door of this stony-looking manor house. This was it. Rendezvous House, the answer to all Sandie's problems, with the rain drilling down on it.

'We walked up to the front door and I put her case on the step and rang the bell. I gave her a quick kiss, told her to take care, and then headed back across the gravel towards the exit, thinking I'm fucked if I'll look back. All sorts of sensations were playing star wars in my body and brain.

'When I got to the end of the drive I did look back. She looked haunted—isolated—like a lost kid standing there with her case, waiting for the bastards to open the door. I bailed out and into the track. The potholes were already rippling with puddles. It was slashing it down so much by then that there was a stream of water gushing along the side of the track, looking for a drain to disappear into, which was just what I felt like doing. Then I looked through a crack in the bushes and saw that the doorstep was empty. They'd taken her in and that was that.

'The windows of the place were open and you could hear distant voices from inside but they were too far away to make 'em out. What are they doing to her? I wondered. I was on the verge of rushing in there and rescuing her from their fucking mad therapy and brainwashing bullshite. I know this might sound daft, but I walked up and down that track, gettin' soaked to the skin, for twenty minutes. I just couldn't leave. I was paralysed, wanting to tear into there and bring her out. Then I remembered it was them that was rescuin' her. I'd only be doin' more damage.

'When I finally pulled me weight out of there I couldn't wait to get lost again in London. I couldn't get drunk enough that night, our kidder. But when I got over that, I had to accept that it would have been worse if she hadn't gone in and there was no doubt about it. I thought, if you can gerra job and get some money together maybe there'll be something for her to come out to in two years. That made me feel better, although so far I haven't advanced much in that direction. But there you go. That's what happened to Sandie.'

'I'm sorry to hear that. When did all this happen?'

He leaned his head back to look up at the smoke flattening itself against the ceiling where the paint was cracking. 'She's been in the Rendezvous House for a couple of month now. I hope she sticks it. If she ever sorts herself out she'll be one hell of a person. Anyhow!' He hauled himself up into a sitting position. 'That's enough of that! I'll jump on these thoughts for the next two years and live my rolling-stone existence again.' He gave me a twisted smile.

'Enjoy your freedom while it lasts,' I laughed to jolly him up. 'It sounds as though you did what you could.'

'Hey!' He shook his head as if to wake himself up. 'I'm sorry to blitz yer with all tha'. It's the feerst time I've been able to get it off my chest since it happened. I must be suffering from a touch of alcoholic remorse tonight, but it was bound to come rushing back to the surface with someone.'

'That's all right,' I nodded for want of anything else to say. 'That's what brothers are for.'

'Yeh,' he laughed in a stoned, emotional sort of way. 'Hey, look. Why don't you make some more coffee and I'll roll another joint? I fancy getting wide-eyed and needless tonight, our Nicholas.'

The cloud of his despair had passed. Another joint was lit to permeate the air and shroud the demons of the mind for a while. I made coffee in a spartan kitchen with damp ancient walls and a battered old whistling kettle that took ages to boil. I was stoned myself, wondering what I was doing in this doss-hole when I could be lying in a warm bed with Diane. Then bits and pieces of our kid's last story, illustrated by the snap of Sandie, drifted into my smoke-cloaked head. Everybody has got their own lot to put up with, but if I were him I'd want to shelter myself from the netherworld rather than embrace it and invite it home. Then thinking of asking things home, I thought of Gareth and Alison meeting the man. I knew for sure my mother wouldn't understand him, God bless her. But that was tough. Having come to seek me out, he deserved to enter the realms of the family. He had said earlier that I was welcome to visit his family home in Liverpool and sample northern hospitality. We owed that much to each other after all.

Chapter Six

Sunlight forced my eyes open. For a startled second I could neither work out where I was nor what day it was. It had been such a deep sleep that it blocked out for a moment the memory of how I came to be in this alien room. Then the night before rose from the dregs of my sleep like a phoenix, with the face of brother Tom.

I was alone in the room. The gas fire hissed in the mist of my first cigarette of the day. By the time it burned down to the tip I would be wide awake, with a bit of luck. Don't bank on it, I thought, lifting my head from the camp bed. I had a hangover for a start and was much in the mood for a shower, having slept fully clothed all night. I'd be lucky to find a tin bath in this joint, judging by the state of it—although Tom kept this room scrupulously tidy.

A car hummed past the window, disturbing for a moment the dead silence of the house. I hauled myself up into a sitting position and put my jacket on. After a night on the booze my throat was desert-dry. I'd drain a bottle of milk if I could get to one.

Looking out of the window I could see it was a nice morning. Sunshine drenched brown and gloomy buildings across the road. An old woman stood on the opposite doorstep, arms folded across her thin chest, watching a couple of Asians walking up New Road.

It was eight o'clock and I imagined Tom would still be asleep somewhere. I went out into the kitchen to make some coffee and spark my braincells back into action. This time yesterday I was doing the same in the elaborate kitchen of Featherstone Place. The setting couldn't be more different, but I felt happy with the contrast. No doubt Diana would wake up in Kentish Town and

64

wonder where I'd got to. She sometimes made fun of my reliability, so it wouldn't hurt to be unpredictable for a change.

The front door went bang, sending a shooting pain through my hangover, and Tom came in carrying a tin of paint and a brush.

'Jesus,' I muttered, sitting down at the cluttered table. 'Go easy on the door-slamming this morning, Tom, for Christ's sake.'

'Sorry kiddo,' he laughed. 'Have you got a fog on this morning or something?'

'If you mean do I feel as though somebody let me have it with a house-brick last night, the answer is yes.'

'I don't get many hangovers mesself. The dope seems to even things out for me, so I'm all right. Did you sleep well though?'

'Like a corpse. You're up early. I was going to leave a note and shove off before you woke up.'

'I go through phases where I don't need much sleep.' He sat down at the table, taking his tobacco out. 'Too much neervous energy. I've just been touching the house up with a spot of paint.'

'What? At eight in the morning? You must be mad.'

'On impulse I wanted to make the place look more desirable. That cretinous graffiti was lowering the tone of the neighbourhood. I don't like the National Front using my home as a writing pad.'

'Lowering the tone of this neck of the woods can't be easy, I would have thought.'

'You're a snob, Nicky,' he grinned cheerfully 'It'll do you good to slum it for a bit. We should swap places for a week and both see how the other half lives. How would the community of Wichfield take to squatters in their midst?'

The suggestion amused me. 'I should think that ten percent of the population would put their houses up for sale. There would be petitions flying about right left and centre, and all the committees would be up in arms. What do your neighbours here think? Or don't they care?'

'They don't seem to. There's this couple living next door. The husband is not quite the ticket. He's convinced somebody is tryina do him in. He told me that somebody at work loosened the nuts on his pushbike so that it would fall apart while he was riding in the traffic and he'd get killed. He keeps taking his wife's rice puddings up to the police station to be analysed. He's more worried about his phantom murderer than he is about us.'

65

'He sounds like great fun.'

'Yeh. You can't beat good neighbours.'

'I'd better go. I hadn't intended making a night of it and I've got some things to sort out in Kentish Town. With a bit of luck I'll be living there soon, so we'll be closer to call on each other than we are now.'

'Great stuff. I was thinkin' we should organise a real night out together. We like the same music and that can't be bad. Let's arrange a night to take in some of the London nightspots.'

'Okay. You'll have to phone me during the week. Give me a ring tomorrow. By then I will have fixed it up for you to come over to Wichfield to meet the dreaded lower-middle classes.'

'Thanks,' he laughed. 'In return I'll take you to a WRP meeting. We might persuade you to swap your pinstripe for a guerrilla war outfit.'

'Don't bet your dole money on it.'

I was glad to be out in the fresh air once the front door was closed behind me. The sun emphasised the grimness of the buildings, but turning my head to the left I saw that one of the stern walls had been rescued from the gloom of neglect. It was a kaleidoscope of colour, thick rich paint depicting East End life: fat women shopping, bored unemployed youths huddled on street corners, children playing marbles, a dog barking at a fat cat safely out of reach up a tree, children playing on skateboards and a policeman talking to a black child—street propaganda but good to look at in the general eye-sore of houses. It reminded me to take note of what Tom had done to the walls of his own squat that morning. It didn't take me long to locate the piece of graffiti— WOGS OUT—which Tom had transformed into a cartoon strip. The W was transformed into a butterfly, the O into a face, the G into the profile of a man smoking a cigar, the S into a potato cat, the U into a cup of coffee and the T into the profile of a clown. An earnest young protester and revolutionary, objecting single-handedly to a world that doesn't give a damn. His wit fed my humour and so did his desire to change the world.

We walked past the ponds and other strolling couples on Parliament Hill and came up into Hampstead by genteel backstreets and cobbled walks. In a quiet leafy street just off Rosslyn Hill we called into a flat where friends of Diane lived.

They were two art students, Simon and Robert, short-haired, clean-cut and gay. Robert was gentle and quiet, and ultra-talented from what I'd seen of his canvases, whilst Simon found it difficult to talk without condescension to the foreigners amongst us who were not artists. He had an air of superiority which annoyed me although I had to credit him with the fact that he also had talent.

The afternoon crept by slowly with cider and cigarettes plus art-school tittle-tattle, so that I had the impression, after listening to who was sleeping with who, that they had gossip down to a fine art, if nothing else.

'We may be moving to Kentish Town soon,' Diane told them. 'Some friends of Nick's are giving up their flat and we're getting an introduction to the Victorian landlady who owns it. If it works out you'll have to come around and see us.'

'Let's hope you do get it,' Robert raised his cider glass. 'I should think you'll both be glad to get away from the family domain. It'll be good to have another couple to call on.'

'And when Nick is a big fat lawyer,' Simon spoke cynically, 'you'll be able to look back on those Kentish Town days and think how horrible and poor you were in grubby little Kentish Town.'

'Lady Margaret Road isn't particularly grubby.' Diane sipped her drink.

'I'm sure it will be after Nick has made his money and bought a house in The Bishops Avenue,' he joked without smiling much. 'You can tell that Nick is only just starting out in the legal profession, because he's slim. I'm willing to lay odds now that by the time he's in his thirties his chin will be hanging over his collar and his belly over his belt.'

'You don't have to worry, Simon.' I spoke politely. 'As you are a friend of Diane, and if I'm affluent enough, I shan't charge you any legal fees when it comes to handling your bankruptcy case.'

Diane and Robert both found this remark a little more amusing than Simon.

Simon was obviously contemptuous of my choice of profession although he never came out and said much in the way that Tom had done. Simon mistook snideness for subtlety and the only time that his condescension let up that afternoon was when Diane raised the subject of my meetings with my new-found brother. It caught his imagination, and his infantile gossip, his tedious

67

theories on art and his continual down-grading of other people's work gave way to questions about my unusual experience.

All in all Simon did nothing much more than annoy me. He was double-faced and pretentious and I felt a sudden affection for Tom, his squalid home and his aimlessness.

Walking along Forest Lane that night I looked at the dark lawns, crimson porch-lights and warm illuminated bay-windows. Everything immaculate. The paintwork of each house complemented the house next to it. They were individual but there was a united stand against anything vulgar. Passing some of the houses I could catch a glimpse of our neighbours moving about in their showpiece lounges.

I'd spent a carefree and colourless childhood here, and now that I would soon be leaving I felt the combined sensations of wistfulness and elation—premature nostalgia, if you like. Sad as it would be in the last minutes of leaving, it was also like a weight off my mind to be going. I felt buoyant, with cartwheels of thought spinning inside my skull—about Diane, the flat and Tom. But there were two things to discuss with my surrogate parents now: the arrival of my brother and the imminent departure of myself.

They were watching television in the lounge, an adaptation of a Graham Greene novel, and my mother was sewing a cuddly toy which would eventually be a Christmas present for one of my young cousins.

'Well, here he is.' She looked up as I came in. 'Hello, stranger. Did you have a nice weekend? We were beginning to wonder whether you and Diane had eloped or something, weren't we, Gareth?'

Gareth nodded without taking his eyes off the film.

'Not yet.' I sat down on the empty settee.

'Not yet indeed,' my mother half-laughed. 'It's a bit early for that. You'll have plenty of time in the future for all that sort of thing. But I shouldn't think you'll go far wrong with Diane. She is very good-looking and seems a sensible girl as well.'

'I don't know,' I scoffed. 'You pay 30-odd pounds a year for a colour television licence for the privilege of watching black-and-white films all the year round.'

'Well, Gareth likes these old films. And you know what a

Graham Greene addict he is, with his five pounds a copy for each new book that comes out. If it were up to me I wouldn't bother with the telly at all,' she said. 'Anyway, how was dinner on Friday? What did you have?'

'A spoonful of caviare and roast duck in a wine sauce.'

'Mmmm. That sounds nice. Hear that, Gareth?'

'Yes, yes. Very nice.'

'What was the proposition then? With Diane's father!'

'He wants Markbyss to undertake some work for his company. It's the kind of work that I might get a bit of commission on.'

'Oh good. I'm glad that you're getting on well with her family. They sound like nice people. You never know, it might do your career some good in the future—open a few doors for you.'

'As long as you don't go down on your knees to anybody,' Gareth spoke up. 'If you do go down on your knees to anybody, you never get up again.'

'I'm not saying he should go down on his knees to anybody,' Alison whined irritably. 'I'm saying that it can't do him any harm knowing people. They've got him running around prisons and courts after all sorts of rogues at the moment but that won't take him very far, will it?'

'It'll take him further than the dole queue and that's a fact,' observed Gareth.

'You needn't worry about me,' I told them. 'I'm not about to get on my knees for anybody. I won't have to.'

I allowed a few seconds to pass by without anybody saying anything. Then, 'Does the name Delaney mean anything to you?'

'Not particularly. You, Gareth?'

'Not offhand,' Gareth chomped on his pipe.

'Or Father McGuire perhaps?'

My mother stopped her sewing and looked up at me curiously.

'Father McGuire was the priest who helped us with the adoption, Nicholas. What about him?'

Gareth had taken his eyes off the TV set now.

'The strange young man with the mysterious telephone calls,' I said, 'I know who he is and why he was so persistent in getting in touch with me. In fact I spent Saturday night at his house in London. His name is Tom Delaney.'

'And who is Tom Delaney when he's out and about?' my mother spoke as though she could guess the answer herself.

69

'Last week he finally caught me at the office. He had with him some documents that he had bespoken from St Catherine's House. They were birth certificates—his and mine. Our names might be different but the parents' names on the certificates are the same.'

'I told you!' she said to Gareth. 'Didn't I tell you it had something to do with that! I had a feeling. Call it intuition if you like, but when you told me that the man had a northern accent I had a feeling it was a voice from the past.'

'Yes, you told me,' Gareth agreed resignedly. 'How did he find us, Nick?'.

I sat back and lit a cigarette, then related to him the conversation I'd had with Tom. They listened, Gareth with obvious interest, but my mother wore a blank mask so that I couldn't tell what she was feeling.

As I described him to them with only one half of my mind on it, the other half was whirling into me once again the kind of sensations Alison must have gone through in life. She was a natural fussy mother, always wanting children of her own, yet not allowing herself this in case she passed on to a son the disease that had slowly killed her father. After adopting me that void in her life was compensated for and it seemed as though she did not want to be reminded of where I came from in the beginning. I sensed that I'd had a lot to do with holding their marriage together over the years. In a sense I felt that they were both more married to me than they were to each other. Such suffocating affection was one reason for getting away, yet how could I do that without feeling guilty? But obviously I would have to make the break sooner or later. A new wave of hate for my biological parents soared through me because they had created this situation.

'I want him to meet you,' I said. 'I'd like to invite him here for dinner some time.'

'Oh you must!' Gareth said, turning the TV off.

'Of course!' said Alison.

I went to the kitchen to make some coffee. I felt happy that she was taking it calmly and wondered whether I had been more paranoid than she was. From the age of twelve onwards I had lived in an atmosphere where I felt others knew more about me than I did. Now I felt good at the idea of pulling my past towards me. Until last week the only thought I'd had on my mind was my work. Now something else was important; it was an unexpected twist of fate.

'Why didn't you tell us about this before?' Alison asked as I set the tray down in front of them.

'I wanted to get used to the idea myself first. It took a while to sink in. I was used to feeling as though I were an only child and when this dishevelled-looking character stepped into our plush waiting room calling himself my brother it took me by surprise, to put it mildly.'

'I'll bet it did,' Gareth nodded.

'And now,' I said, 'I have something else to tell you. It's about Diane and me. Diane may have this advertising job in the bag. And we also have the chance of a flat in London.'

'I opened my mouth about elopement too soon then,' my mother said stiffly. 'What the hell do you want to go off and live there for at this stage in your career, you fool? It's a damned expensive business these days, living in London, and you don't earn much money yet. It's noisy, it's dirty, it's a strain. At least while you're living at home you don't have the worry of rent and bills and so forth. And there's plenty of peace and quiet in which to study. It would be mad of you to go and live in town right now!'

'Diane is capable of earning a reasonable income,' I told her. Her father could probably see to that, if nobody else, I pointed out. Anyway, with our combined salaries we would manage until I qualified. The rent on the flat amounted to about fifteen pounds each and we were sure we could handle that. It would save me a lot of valuable studying time as well, without the daily drag to and from Wichfield. Alison wasn't convinced but she was a model of calmness. She wanted to know how Diane's parents would react to my 'shacking up' with their daughter. I laughed and teased her about the fact that it was she who was the old-fashioned one and that the Sinclairs had stopped clinging to their children years ago.

'Well!' Gareth said. 'You seem to have had an eventful weekend, Nicky. When do you and Diane intend to start keeping house then?'

'It isn't settled yet. But by the end of the month I expect.'

My mother shook her head thoughtfully, 'I'd like to see you

71

settle down comfortably with someone nice, certainly. But it's too soon.'

'He hasn't had enough life to settle down from yet,' Gareth chuckled.

Alison put down her cuddly toy. 'No doubt he will now.'

Chapter Seven

Tom phoned in the middle of Monday afternoon while I was sitting in my office drafting some forms.

'Howz it goin' then, Perry Mason?' he asked.

'Very quietly at the moment, comrade. And you?'

It wasn't necessary to ask, you could tell over the wires that he was enthusiastic about something. He was talking about a trendy coffee house in Earl's Court somewhere, that on Monday nights threw music and poetry gigs, and was I interested in coming down to watch him aim some of his words at the audience?

I swapped his invitation for the one from my parents for Sunday dinner and this seemed to fire his enthusiastic tone all the more. When I put the phone down I was frozen in thought at what was going on here. Snapping out of that, I phoned Diane to ask her if she wanted to join in tonight's arrangements.

She turned up at Dirty Dick's, where I was waiting for her over a drink, at about 6.30. She looked good, dressed up in a dark blouse and split skirt. It was tempting to take her back to the empty office for some poetry of the real kind.

She was looking forward to meeting my brother and thought how strange it was that she would know him just as well as I did. But there were other things on her mind as well: the farce that we would have to act out as a married couple to convince the landlady in Kentish Town that we were suitable tenants; and the interview she faced that week with a business contact of her father's—she wished to work in the art department of his advertising agency.

'Things can drag on for so long without anything happening, then suddenly everything starts moving at once,' she reflected.

Soon we were heading along the Embankment in her battered Spitfire, moving towards Tom's poetry session. I felt slightly tense again because it was only my third meeting with him and this time there was somebody else close to me getting involved, which for a moment seemed too soon. I hadn't got to know him myself yet, though it felt as though I'd been thinking about him for years.

Coming straight from the office, I felt conspicuous in my three-piece pinstripe as we walked into the general hubbub of the candle-flickering cafe, crowded with representatives of bedsitterland-in-jeans.

We followed the sound of the music down into the basement. A five-piece band was hammering out a rock song on the stage, with a young female vocalist in garish make-up and silver bum-swinging slit skirt, while one of the guys was Mick Jaggering around the platform.

We bought a couple of drinks and waited for Tom. I filled in time by describing the game that we had played at the identification parade that morning: warning the client to keep his hands behind his back because of his tattoes, then watching the door for the appearance of strangers dragged in from the street, a shake of my head dismissing half a dozen that didn't look right, before the line was made complete on my approval and the witness walked up and down, picking out our client anyway. He was a young tearaway whose back-street life was about to lead him into prison for a year or two.

'What a weird job you have,' she wrinkled her nose, then looked up at somebody behind me. I turned to find Tom standing there, dressed exactly as before, really glad that we could make it. He had a feeling that he might need friends among the audience tonight. I introduced him to Diane, whose smile was casual but her eyes were taking him in carefully as though she were trying to match both of us up, like me matching up the strangers with the suspect on the ID parade.

Tom seemed a little self-conscious at the unexpected presence of Diane, a little shy, which surprised me, but it was the kind of shyness that triggered off the nervous energy he had displayed when I met him.

Diane forked out for some more drinks. I asked Tom what we were all doing here. He liked words but the poetry circuit didn't seem to suit him. He could only explain that he had followed Sandie's footsteps into it with scepticism, scepticism that he still felt. He couldn't take it all that seriously but these gatherings served a purpose: you could meet new people; it took your mind off the dole office or the pub you couldn't really afford very often; it was one place where you could stand up and be listened to, even if people thought it was drivel. Until Sandie went into the rehabilitation centre he hadn't had much time for poetry readings, but afterwards time was something that he did have, more than he needed. This was one small way of dealing with his problems, be it futile or otherwise, though he warned me that he was 'no Shakespeare or notten', criticising himself before we had the chance.

He did his reading in between two bands at about eleven o'clock. The words were more inspired by the lyrics of rock songs than by poets; they were not poems for the sake of it. I missed half of the first one in anticipation of the audience giving him a cold reaction, though they didn't. Whether because of his nerve or because they could see that he wasn't from Hampstead and that he had something simple to say from wherever he did come from, they gave him a warm round of applause. I still couldn't help but wonder what was really going on in their minds.

I listened more closely to the second one, which he called 'Ode to Sandra Louise'. It was a story about a girl 'drowning in the river behind the trees' and his own reaction of shock and panic. 'The sound of your scream and that of rushing water broke the woody silence. I could only stand there—fascinated by your horrified face, and by the nature of the water's violence ...' When he tried to rescue her, as she had done him, there were always distractions or obstacles, especially the space 'between the whirlpool and the bank'. He went off to look for sticks, ropes or life belts, was distracted by clowns, teachers and social workers, and people asking him questions. When he finally returned the river was calm and the girl was gone.

His final poem was the most recent. He called it 'Double Exposure' and it described two brothers meeting for the first time after twenty years or more 'to discover each other on different sides of the law'. In its abstract way it conveyed to me Tom's frustration at knowing less about himself than most other people.

Diane's car was only a two-seater which meant that one person would have to sit on another's lap. Tom and I both agreed that this was one way of getting to know each other that we would give the go-by.

'Give me the keys, I'll drive,' I said. 'You'll have to sit on his lap. Tom, keep your maulers where I can see them.'

'Never mind his hands, babe. You keep your eyes on the road while you're driving my car,' she handed me the keys.

I drove along Victoria Embankment, the lights on the river fleeting past as fast as I could get away with. Diane had little room, huddled up on Tom's lap with her arms around his neck, his arms securely around her waist. There was something about it that was a bit of a turn-on, with the split in her skirt exposing her doubled-up legs.

She complained that she was hungry, so Tom directed me through the City to Bethnal Green, where he knew a place that was open all night.

We pulled up underneath the face of a cool, blonde, Martini girl enjoying a drink in sun-drenched paradise as she smiled down from a dismal East End wall. Across the road was the Majestic Café and although it was one o'clock in the morning it was doing a fair bit of trade. It was a dimly lit place, quite noisy and cluttered with grey and down-at-heel people at stained and messy tables making cups of tea spin out forever. A toothless and plump old woman sat resting her three chins in her hand, eyes following a passing car with less life than that of the Martini girl who stared at us from across the road. Next to her sat an old man with his arms folded tightly across his chest, cap on head, and trousers tucked into his long socks, nodding and smiling mindlessly at anybody who happened to pass by. Everybody looked down on their luck.

'Christ!' Diane exclaimed softly.

'What d'you fancy to eat?' Tom asked.

'In here? You must be joking. Look at those custard tarts.' She pointed to the glass display case. 'They're turning orange with age. And those rock cakes look as though they were actually quarried.'

Tom laughed. 'They do a nice line in caviare butties.'

'I'll take a chance with one of the chicken ones.'

While Tom queued up behind a couple of tramps, Diane and I found a table at the back. 'Jesus!' She pushed her hair over her shoulders. 'Look at the people here.'

'It's not exactly the Café Royal,' I agreed.

'They look like Capo di Monte figurines until they move,' she half-laughed.

'What do you think of Tom?'

'I like him. In fact, I think I'm in love all over again.'

'Really? How did that happen? Is he that much like me?'

'Not really. To look at, it's only the odd expression on his face that gives him away as your brother. And he's got the same doggy-eyes, which is one of the things that infuriates me about you sometimes. But personality-wise you're entirely different. On the surface you're logical, cool and reserved; he seems almost the opposite—demonstrative, gesticulating and open. He comes over strong one minute and weak another. I haven't worked out which is image and which is real. Perhaps they're both real.'

Tom returned with the sandwiches and coffee, at ease again because he was back on familiar territory.

'This place is a bloody freak-out,' Diane told him.

'Don't you like it?'

'It's different. I wouldn't come here on my own with all these hungry-looking old men about.'

'You would, with that daredevil streak of yours,' I pointed out.

'Well, not in a tight skirt like this,' she shrugged.

'I like it in here,' Tom said, lighting a cigarette and shaking the match dead. 'When I was a kid in Liverpool I was fascinated by steamy transport cafés and the coming and going of guys in lorries. The atmosphere of this place reminds me of all that.'

'I liked your poems, Tom,' Diane said. 'They seemed spontaneous. Full of energy and pictures. In one of them you spoke of the two brothers on different sides of the law. What did you mean by that?'

'I meant to put across that I found my brother actually weerking in the law, after spending my own life among people who feel alienated by such things. Solicitors and stuff were all part of the system thatt kept the likes of us in our place, along wid the police. It was all the same type of thing. Everybody I knew got into hassles wid the police when I was a kid. I was no exception. When I was fourteen I got caught climbing out of the back of a shop. Me dad had never had anytin to do with the police, though he didn't like them simply because he lived in an atmosphere where they weren't liked or trusted. But he came down to the nick thatt night, as polite as pie to the police. "I'm

77

sorry my lad has caused you all this trouble—Tom! Stand up straight when you're in front of these nice people!—but he's usually such a well-behaved lad, officer, I don't know what must have come over him—Tom, stand up straight in front of these nice people or you'll get summat! When I get him home, officer, I'll make sure notten like dis ever happens again." He bailed me out like thatt a couple of times—until I was seventeen when I actually got done for something really daft.

'I was lookin' for a job and a couple of mates of mine offered me a fiver if I'd drive this lump of lead to a bent dealer in this old VW. With the weight of the stuff, I couldn't get the car out of second gear and I was supposed to get this nicked lead from Liverland to Huyton. I was driving through Liverpool and I stalled the car right in front of this panda. The copper got out to find out why I couldn't get the car started. He tried turning over the engine and diagnosed thatt the battery was flat, so he offered to give us a push. Have you ever tried to bump-start a Volkswagon wid a ton-weight of lead in it? After a few minutes of huffing and puffing and grunting and pushing he started to wonder why the fuck such a little car was so fucken heavy. The result of his finding out landed me wid a heavy fine, I can tell yer.'

Tom's infectious laugh spread to us and opened up the door to more memories and anecdotes that made us laugh all the more. I noticed that Diane seemed to be captivated by him, his accent, his humour.

She asked him why he didn't stay on at school.

'Where I lived thatt didn't seem possible. Nobody expected me to be bright enough. We all knew where I was goin', including messell, and thatt was the docks or the factories. It was never discussed because it was taken for granted. We used to stand around outside the school gates. Jeans, leather jackets, all the gear, and we used to harrass all the grammar school and technical school kids on their way up the road in their immaculate uniforms. They were posh and by then we were well on the road to our walk in life, and they were to theirs. It was the feerst time I became aware of any tiered system in life—before thatt I'd never thought about it.

'At the school I was at, they tried to prepare you for the weerld that would be accessible to you and notten else. The first political teaching you had, for instance, was when you went to weerk and

78

got tangled up wid unions and confrontations with the management, who kept their weerkers at a distance—not like other countries, where they boost incentive and morale by involving everybody in all aspects. Then even thatt started thinning out.'

'What sort of work were you doing in the end then?' she wanted to know.

His list ranged from working in factories to labouring on building sites to doing seasonal work in holiday camps. It was a rolling-stone existence that he felt stuck with.

It was getting late when a fight broke out between a couple of the dossers on the other side of the café. Somebody had pinched somebody else's tobacco and suddenly there were curses plus skin and hair flying. The proprietor came out to cool them down and without turning anybody out brought the fracas to an end by handing the aggrieved tramp a fag from the loose-cigarette box.

'It's two o'clock,' I said. 'I have to be in the office early. We'd better go.'

Tom gave up his bedroom to us that night, and with Diane at my side it was like taking another step into my unknown—without feeling as wary as before. 'You mean he doesn't threaten your own self-image after all?' she mocked, as we tried to get warm in the cold bed. 'He's not the malevolent alter ego you imagined he would be?'

'I mean, now that I know something about the guy, I'm feeling more and more as though I want to know about the rest of it. He mentions catching up on lost time. I reckon the only way to do that is to catch up with all the lost details about us.'

I pulled her towards me, ready for her tonight: the warmth and touching, the whiteness of her under the quilt, her hands gently moving up and down my back, the expression on her face changing gradually from playful devilment to intense seriousness, the scent of her hair in my face, the change in breathing, the tensing and rocking into a flesh-tight grip, moving as if trying to find my past, my origins, in the flesh and blood of fucking all my energy into Diane, who, for reasons of her own, had to come back with energy to take something for herself.

Chapter Eight

On Sunday morning I drove into London and picked Tom up in Gareth's car.

'I've been lookin' forward to this,' he stuck his elbow out of the window as we drove along Commercial Road. 'Goin' back to your place makes me feel like we're gettin' somewhere—crossin' the barrier a bit, y'know?'

'They're pretty hyped up about meeting you,' I told him. 'My mother is nagging my father to do this and help her with that more than usual this morning.'

'Sounds like my old lady' he laughed. 'She always has a freak-out when a visitor is about to descend. A total personality change takes place and she drives the rest of us up the bloody wall.'

The cold sunshine poured through the trees of Epping Forest and Tom felt good getting out of London 'for some oxygen' again. Apart from hitchhiking to Liverpool in the rain a month ago, he hadn't been out of London since taking Sandra to Rendezvous House.

The day before this ride out to Wichfield Tom had met an acquaintance of his in a pub in the East End. This man was a sub-contractor doing demolition work. It was just him and a mate, a couple of mattocks and a coil of rope—they would be sent up onto the rooftops to start knocking the houses down from underneath them, bashing masonry to bits, hauling down blocks with the rope. The man was a fanatic about demolition and considered it a 'fine art'. He used to be a vandal but could now destroy buildings and get paid for the pleasure, doing society a favour rather than the other way around. 'That sounds like a success story of sorts,' I nodded.

'The thing is thatt the guy has offered me some weerk,' said Tom. 'Fifteen quid in me hand every day, to sort out the good bricks from the damaged ones. It's not a regular job or notten but it'll be good to be self-sufficient now and again. If I can stash away some cash for when Sandie gets back we'll have somewhere to go from. If it becomes a regular thing I'll be happy enough. Like I say, when Sandra does make it there's got to be a decent flat for her ter get home to—not thatt dive in New Road, or anywhere else around there.'

We pulled into Forest Rise and came to a halt outside the house. When I turned the ignition off and we got out of the car Tom stood there and gazed around. 'Jesus, listen to thatt,' he said. 'The silence.' He looked up the road to where it ended at a footpath that disappeared into the forest. 'My 'ead went fuckin' *zing* as soon as I gorrout the car and 'eard the *silence*.'

As we walked up the drive our next-door neighbour came out of his house. Mr Campbell, the chartered surveyor, exchanged pleasantries and asked me how I was getting on now that I was working in the lawyer's office. He looked at Tom curiously and I introduced him as my brother, much to the neighbour's surprise. Then I led Tom into the hall of the house and closed the door. Apart from the air freshener, the aroma of roast beef drifted down the hall. 'Dinner is nearly ready, I should think. Come and meet my parents.'

Alison greeted Tom with no sign of disapproval at his appearance. She shook hands with him and said she was pleased to meet him at last. Then he shook hands with Gareth, who offered him a drink. We all sat down in the lounge with a glass of something before dinner and Tom, who was nervous, talked cheerfully because any embarrassing silence would hurt.

'I'm really glad you invited me over,' he said, his smile shining openly as he tried a little too hard. 'It's good to get out of Whitechapel for five minutes. The streets of London, or anywhere, start shrinking around you if you allow yourself to get bogged down in a rut, or stuck somewhere too long. I like to walk around the city to clear my mind sometimes, but no matter where I walk in London these days I seem to have seen it all before. I definitely need a change of scenery.'

'Well, don't you worry. We wanted to take a look at you and find out all about you,' Alison assured him, sipping a glass of cream sherry. 'It's not every day a stranger turns up as one of the family, as it were.'

'You're dead right,' Tom nodded nervously, but still smiling.

'How long have you been in London, Tom?' asked Gareth.

For the first half-hour conversation was forged uneasily, although I knew there were questions in Alison's mind waiting for the opportunity to be asked. The situation seemed unnatural at first, but the drinks helped loosen the atmosphere.

'When you were making your initial phone calls,' Alison said, 'of course we had no idea who you were. But after a while I began to wonder. Did you come to London especially to see if you could find Nicholas?'

'No, I didn't,' he admitted. 'It was on my mind and I couldn't not have a try, although I didn't quite believe I actually would find anybody from the family I was really born out of. I couldn't quite get it together in me head when I actually found the name and number in the book. I phoned here, and you, Mr Heyward, answered the phone and told me Nicholas was out and did I want to leave a message, an' all that type of ting. I was using a pub phone at the time. I went back to me drink at the bar, hardly able to believe that I'd got the right people. I didn't say anythin' on the phone because I couldn't be sure. Me head was spinning and not just from the ale, and thatt's for sure. Then suddenly I knew. A feeling roared thru' me and I knew I was on the right track! I had this instinctive feelin' that this piece of paper I had was actually me brother's number. Then I started wonderin' what he looked like and even what this place looked like—what sort of job he did and whether he would get freaked out at my turnin' up or not, or whether he knew who my mam and dad were. He might have known more about me than I do.'

'And what did you feel when you actually met?' she asked.

'I don't know what I was expectin' in the end,' he said. 'I met him in his office and he was wearin' this really straight three-piece pinstripe and he looked and sounded a bit on the conservative side—a bit put out, naturally enough, at my sudden appearance. But I felt great, as though I'd found some sort of grail, daft as it sounds, as though fate was tryina rectify a mistake it had made twenty years ago. The fact that Nick and me look, sound and think entirely differently about life, and have totally different backgrounds, made me want to bridge the gap between us all the more.'

'Do your adopted parents know about your discovery yet?'

Gareth inquired.

'They do now, I wrote to 'em the other day,' Tom answered. 'They knew I was interested in finding me past. My mother, who's a bit neervous, an' on Valium and stuff because of me dad out of weerk and moody with it, she was a bit dubious about me lookin' for me mam and dad. She said, as far as she knew, I didn't have very stable parents and that I might get hurt if I did find 'em. They might not want to know—or they might get hurt by my sudden appearance if they've got their own lives together by now. But me dad understood my own need in trying to find out. Anyway, I haven't heard from them yet but I'm sure they'll be dead chuffed. I've told 'em Nick is a respectable young lawyer and I expect me mam'll be pleased to hear that, given the character of some of me past associates.'

Over dinner Alison asked Tom many questions about his family, his life and his plans for the future. Tom answered them in a friendly way. He had a knack of talking to people as though he'd known them for ten years. You had to look closely to see that this was the way he displayed his nervousness, as opposed to others who lapse into silence when nervous. This is the strange telephone caller, I reflected as we ate. Here he is a few weeks later having dinner with us. One big happy family.

When the meal was over he complimented my mother diplomatically and she was pleased to hear it. 'I don't suppose you do yourself many meals like that at home, do you?' she said.

'Notten like it,' he laughed. We were all more relaxed now.

'What would you really like to do, Tom?' my mother asked. 'I'm sure a bright young man like you won't be content with demolition work forever.'

'As long as it helps keep me goin', thatt and writin' poetry,' he said flippantly.

'Writing poetry?' my mother's pragmatic tone emerged. 'Well, I don't know—that's a bit airy-fairy, isn't it?'

'No,' Tom smiled. 'It's got notten ter do with fairies—hairy or otherwise.'

He was learning quickly how to keep Alison's 'reality' assaults at arm's distance without even having to be defensive. Even Alison was amused by him.

'You've got a little boy, so Nicholas was telling us. How old is he?'

Tom described his son to us and talked of the differences he saw in the boy each time he went back. He talked briefly of the boy's mother when asked about her by Alison. Both my parents felt that the rehabilitation centre was too tough. 'Not allowing the poor girl visits or letters. It sounds more like a prison than a prison.'

'It's all for a reason,' Tom said. 'A glimpse of the outside world too early could beckon her back into the streets lookin' for drugs and pushers and all sorts. The only treatment for someone hooked on drugs is extreme. It's hard to come off them in the outside weerld where they're close at hand. This is the best way in the long term. And even then Rendezvous House are only about fifty percent successful, if thatt.'

'It must be a hell of a worry to you,' sympathised Alison.

'She'll make it,' Tom sipped his cup of tea.

'The sooner she does the better,' Alison said. 'Then she can put some regular meals into you. You don't eat properly, do you? You're underweight, my lad. You could do with some more meat on you!'

'I can take care of mesself,' Tom laughed. 'Don't wurry about thatt.'

'Well,' Alison shook her head doubtfully. 'You know, you're welcome here any time, Tom. Isn't he, Gareth?'

'Most certainly,' Gareth concurred.

'I'll put some meat on him,' she threatened.

Tom laughed again.

After dinner we went for a walk in the forest. Tom marvelled at the idea of growing up out here with all these trees and the open countryside of Essex. It must have seemed quite different from a lifetime in Liverland.

'And now he wants to rush off and live in the midst of London concrete, dirt and petrol fumes,' tut-tutted my mother. 'Some people don't know when they're well off. Kentish Town indeed!'

We walked along the sunken paths, feet cracking bracken and dry brown fallen leaves. It was cold but bright. What leaves were left whispered news of imminent winter.

'They've started advertising Christmas things already,' said my mother. 'Still, I suppose it's not far off. What will you be doing for Christmas, Tom?'

'Ah don't know yet. I haven't thought. I'll probably go back up

84

and see the family and our Sandie's people.'

'They live in Liverpool as well?'

'Yeh. But it's not such a run-down area, which is one good reason for our Damien being there.'

'You'll have to come over for a drink with us before you go,' Gareth said.

Suddenly I wondered if it had occurred to my parents that they might just as easily have adopted Tom instead of me. He might have been brought up here by them and I by his family in Liverpool. A twist of fate had decreed otherwise but it seemed an interesting thought.

We took photographs by the lake, using up a reel of colour film. Alison photographed us separately and together, for the first time in our lives as far as we knew; our first pictures of Tom would fill some of the empty pages in the family albums.

At the age of twenty-two and in just a few hours Tom had almost become a second adopted son to my parents. This seems like a sweeping statement, I suppose, but that's the way it felt at the time. I was pleased, yet if some spiritual voice had warned me of it a few weeks before I might not have liked the idea.

After tea I drove him out to the Forest Fountain. I bought the first round of drinks and we sat at a table in front of the coal fire that was belly-dancing in the grate for the first time this autumn.

'Well, Nick,' he said cheerfully, 'your old lady doesn't seem so bad. I was wondering what sort of reception I'd get. I can see where you get your ideas and ambitions from,' he added, without the vague condescension that had emerged in flashes once or twice on our first night out.

'When I was a kid I ran away from home twice,' I told him. 'I ran away because I'd found out they weren't my real parents. They were shocked, because I was normally a well-behaved little boy and well brought up. I must have had some idea that if I ran far enough I would find my real parents. It was as though I expected them to be standing on some street corner by accident. I even had a vision of what they looked like. I fantasised about them and my imagination conjured up all sorts of romantic ideas about what had happened to create that situation. That was the beginning of my rebellious phase—you know, reacting against the family's values, and all that. My rebellion went in the opposite direction from yours. Maturity dragged me out of fantasy land. I realised that our natural parents were probably unsuccessful people in reality. My father is a tired teacher and my mother a frustrated lady who grew up wanting something out of life and had to settle for less, as most people have to, and no doubt I will. But I was determined to go up and not down, independently of what anybody else hoped for me. I was going to leave everything behind, get my teeth into a job that meant something—dealing with people and getting results. Success of some sort would mean that my beginnings didn't matter. My parents are happy with what they've got. They have more or less what they want. I don't. But I intend to.'

'It seems to be a kind of insulated weerld out here,' he said. 'I suppose Diane lives in an area like this.'

'Diane's place is bigger and more genuinely affluent. It has a totally different atmosphere. She grew up in a comparatively self-assured environment, whereas I come from a lower-middle class street where all the self-satisfieds are trying to outdo each other and get into the tennis club.'

'All these definitions! And by getting into Diane's family you're trying to join another club yourself?'

'I approve of social mobility,' I smiled.

'I wouldn't waste me time with all thatt status quo bollocks. But I could tell at a glance that this was a blue-belt area. Not many *Newsline* readers out here tonight, eh?' He looked around at the clean-cut, casual young executives scattered around the pub with their wives. 'They look nice and relaxed, having driven out to a quaint little country boozer in their bright insect cars, bought no doubt on a tax-fiddled income.'

When we got back home Alison had sandwiches prepared for supper. She had also fixed up a bed for Tom in the attic room. He would stay the night and then go back to London with me in the morning.

'Thanks for everything, Mrs Heyward,' he said. 'It's been a real nice day, I've enjoyed it and thatt's a fact. Peaceful, like. A home from home and all thatt type of thing.'

'Well, I trust it won't be another twenty years before you turn up again,' my mother said.

'No,' he laughed. 'You can be sure of thatt!'

'Feel free to come over any time you want a bit of peace and quiet,' said Alison. 'Not to mention clean air!'

'I will—cheers!'

I took him up to the attic. Last summer Alison had ordered Gareth to get it converted into an extra room and it had been done very well. It was warm and cosy with varnished wooden beams. You could hear the breeze and the trees rustling against the roof.

'Jesus, I like thiss,' he said, dropping onto the bed. 'I'd really feel made up if I could live in a mad attic-type of place like this. And I think this country air is knockin' me out a bit!'

'It's not so much the country air as the six or seven pints that you swallowed in the pub,' I suggested. Upon reflection he conceded that I might have a valid point. I wished him a good night.

'Yeh. Cheers, Nick.'

Back in the darkness of my own room I fell into bed, the beer adding to my force of gravity. I was eighteen months old the last time I had slept under the same roof as Tom, before we met up a few weeks ago. Neither of us had any memory of each other. I tried to visualise the two of us as we might have been all those years ago. It was a weird, weird feeling in my guts, leading on to thoughts of the recurring dream that I had experienced until I was fifteen. It would shake me awake with no memory of it, but I knew it was the same dream although I could not grasp it in waking daylight. Even in the midst of the dream it seemed as though I was so anxious to remember it that I would always lose it. And now—now I wondered whether all along it was just a dream about our missing past.

Chapter Nine

After several weeks the initial shock of Tom's appearance had died down in me. He helped Diane and me move into the flat, then we didn't see him for a few weeks. I got on with my studies as much as I could, and we began to enjoy a more hectic social life. We involuntarily became part of a clique. We were no longer separate people. When friends thought of me they also thought of her—we were Nick and Diane, a unit that had given up the status of individual existence.

But I knew that moving out of Wichfield was the best thing I could have done, and also knew that I could never live there again.

Although we didn't see much of Tom for a few weeks his presence was never that far away from me, whatever else was going on. He had set off the shadowy figures of my unknown family and they were on the move in my imagination again. Tom was a reality giving the shadows some sort of vitality they had lacked up until now.

Then after a month or so he started paying us visits, often dragging me out from under the textbooks to go off for a 'quick pint'. These quick pints often turned into about ten quick pints, followed by one long hangover. We would drag around various jazz clubs and other dives on big nights out that he was more able to afford now that he had some employment, albeit precarious.

One evening he brought a friend with him, a woman called Donna. She was vaguely reminiscent of the photograph of Sandra with long dark hair, dark complexion, slim build—but she was older, perhaps thirty. I thought she was attractive in a hard, been-around sort of way. She seemed quiet, if not aloof.

'You've got yourself another bird, then,' I nudged him as we left her and Diane sitting at a table in the pub while we got the drinks. 'She doesn't seem to be a great conversationalist though.'

'She's got notten to say about us,' he shrugged. 'We've known each other a while. We're just friends thatt's all. Pure fresh air, our kid.'

'That's a pity, you could do with a fling by now, I should think,' I laughed.

'You could be right. But I can't see it bein' with Donna even if I was into thatt idea. It's occurred to me though, I admit.'

'You're being very well behaved. I wish we middle classes had your morals,' I needled.

'You have,' he grinned. 'You just don't practise 'em.'

'You should go and live in Wichfield for a week.'

During the course of the evening Diane got talking to Tom. She seemed intrigued by him, and left me on the other side of the table to create conversation with his friend. I asked her how long she'd known him.

'About two years,' she shrugged. 'I dunno exactly, but it's summing like that. I met him and Sandie down Shoreditch, where I used to live. He's a nice guy, Tom is. I like him a lot. Genuine, you know what I mean?'

'Yes. I mean, I agree.'

'I didn't know he was lookin' for a stray bruvver though,' her deadpan face cracked into a smile for the first time. 'You seem bloody different from what he is, to look at anyway. And the sound of yer.'

'Well. We're not exactly identical twins, that's true. But we seem to be communicating in spite of our differences. How did you get on with Sandra? Was she genuine?'

'Yeh, she was great when she was straight. A bit moody. Sometimes on top of the world, the next minute she could be through the floor. She was about as genuine as a barbiturate-user can be. I don't know what sparked her problems off but if what Tom says is right it sounds like things hit the fan after she had the kid. I don't usually get on wiv girls but *she* was all right. She needed lookin' after when she was droppin' the downers, y'know? I used to live with this bloke who used to deal stuff, and she came round one night—really freaked out and pleadin' for some gear. Terry had the stuff all right, but he enjoyed a good wind-up. I think he liked to see women grovel a bit. He kept telling her he wanted to keep it all for hisself. Doing that to an addict is sadistic beyond belief, but he let her have it when he'd had a larf. Tom got to hear about the kind of people she was gettin' the gear from, so he come along next. He decided to do the dealing hisself, and bought a big amount of Tuinal from Terry. It was supposed to be a safety net for Sandie while she went to get help that never came from the doctors, *et cetera*. My old man ripped the cunt off. Every third capsule was full of make-up, so when Sandie was on the verge of a barb fit she'd take 'em and they'd do no good. Those fits can kill you if you have enough of 'em. She thought the barbs were doin' her no good and she upped the dosage, which made things worse. I saw it one night and I suddenly felt like turning a fucking knife on the bastard!'

'Your old man sounds like a laugh a minute,' I said. 'You should bring him around to our party. We like to meet fun people.'

'I left him,' she said, gazing beyond me at the thicket of people behind. 'Although he wasn't a complete animal. He'd had a hard life hisself,' she stared back at me. 'He was a good father in his way. He liked his kids. He just ain't capable of coping wiv his life. And I got tired of livin' in a hovel with the pigs kickin' the fuckin' door down every other night. I had a row with him. Then the next night I told Tom about the dud barbs and Tom ain't stopped lookin' for the bloke ever since. I hope he never finds him. Terry can be a vicious bastard and your bruvver just might not be hard enough.'

'Tom's life style sounds more unattractive than I had imagined.'

'He gets involved with all the strays and lame dogs,' she smiled. 'He doesn't fit in wiv the East End scene, but he'd do anyfing for yer, he's good like that. Him and Sandie helped me out. I had nowhere to go, wiv two kids. They found this empty house and opened up a squat for me. They stayed with me a bit til I got mesself sorted out.'

'You've got two kids and you're living in a squat?'

'Yeh. You should see the fuckin' gaff as well, mate. The place is arf caved in—it's damp, the electric wall-fittings come to life with the occasional flash of blue from time to time. Bits and pieces of the ceiling have a *strange* habit of *floating* down to the floor. There's a bloke and anuvver couple living downstairs now. They've done a bit of work on it, but there ain't much you can do to it.'

'The council are under a legal obligation to rehouse a homeless family.'

'Their first reaction was that being as I've got a *roof* over me head I'm not an emergency case. So Tom and one of his mates from the WRP went up to the council offices and had a go. Not that it did much good. They said I was the GLC's responsibility. The GLC said I was the council's responsibility. The Health people keep visitin', taking notes and goin' away again, but nothing gets done. It's a fuckin' joke.'

I took a sip of the golden whisky and its heat went straight to my stomach. 'It's hard to believe that people live in conditions like that these days.'

'It ain't ard to believe for me, mate,' she scoffed.

Chapter Ten

The casual demolition work that Tom had been doing was spasmodic and highly unreliable. Work came in dribs and drabs, though it was something to be hopeful about while he trekked around for a more secure job. Though as Tom said, security these days was a word to be used in inverted commas. He went up to a factory in Hackney for an interview. The girl gave him a biro to fill in the form, which was three foolscap pages long, crammed with questions about his past jobs, the schools that he went to, and his academic qualifications. He sat in the pot-planted foyer, behind him the ominous rumble of the production line, and his eyes swam at the extent of the form. He couldn't understand what difference it made to a Hackney factory which school he went to eight years before, or whether he had O and A levels or not. And why were they interested in his hobbies?

He had to resist the temptation to be flippant throughout the twenty minutes it took to fill it out, though he couldn't restrain himself when the form asked: Are you pregnant YES/NO? To this he replied, 'Chance would be a fine thing!' When he had finished he handed it across to the girl at the reception. 'May I present you with the unabridged first edition of my autobiography,' he smiled. She told him to take a seat and took the form into another room.

Ten minutes later he was summoned to this small room where a young lady, not much older than he, was waiting to interview him. She cheerfully invited him to take a seat, saying that she would just like to ask a few questions. Jesus, thought Tom, pulling a chair out—you must be skittin' me!

Question time ran on for about ten minutes, culminating with the enquiry: 'Why do you want to work for us, Mr Delaney?'

By now, Tom was beginning to wonder himself.

'Excuse me,' he said, 'but you have got this right, haven't yer? I've come about the job as an assembly worker—not the managing director vacancy.'

She laughed, but wanted an answer to her question nevertheless.

'Well, it's obvious,' said Tom. 'For the intellectual stimulus of the work.'

When she saw him to the door, saying 'We'll let you know,' he knew what that meant. His father in need of work would have played along with this game but Tom had thrown in the long-term towel in order to experience immediate gratification. She had probably written 'smart aleck' all over his application. He was used to not getting a job though, so it was only the waste of the bus fare that made him curse. Graffiti on an old wall that he walked by fed his humour: 50,000 lemmings can't ALL be wrong.

Over the months Tom and I would meet up in the City after office hours. We'd have a drink, then he would take me on a short cut through the sweet-smelling spice and squalor of Brick Lane. 'The richest part of England right next door to the poorest part,' he was fond of saying as we wandered down the dark streets that one had to admit were Dickensian slums and no less, a stone's throw from the Stock Exchange.

We found that we had a lot of small things in common. We liked the same books, possessed the same records, harboured the same interests—barring politics. I found that I was relaxed with him and enjoyed his company. Diane seemed to feel the same, and she had a strange habit of being a little curt about his friend Donna, who I quite liked. 'If you're into her that much why don't you bloody well sod off with her?' she would ask, toffee-nose style. 'I'll took after Tom.' It was said in jest, though I sometimes wondered. Their relationship registered somewhere low on the Richter scale between fraternity and desire. She often seemed to glow a little more when he walked in—her 'Hello, Tom' started to become suspiciously soft. Over the months I noticed that something unspoken was happening, something that was between them not me. It struck me particularly in a pub one night when I turned around and realised they were standing close together—closer than normal, brushing against each other lightly—their eyes getting caught in some invisible magnetism. I

93

was excluded from this and could say nothing about it. It would have been good to watch if it hadn't been a bit gut-wrenching with it.

I even wondered whether it was wise to leave them alone together but ultimately I couldn't believe that a scene would take place, given the nature of the three relationships. I was too close to be sure of what was happening anyway, and started to wonder how much of it was real and how much my own imagination.

One night we stayed at Tom's place in Whitechapel after an evening out. We were aroused from our sleep by the sound of glass crashing and something heavy hitting the deck in the room below us.

'Christ,' moaned Diane, sleepily. 'What was that?'

'*Mice.*'

'Go down and find out what it was.'

'No way. Go back to sleep.'

There was another crash which woke me right up. It sounded like a demolition gang had moved in underneath us. I dragged my jeans on and felt my way down the dusty staircase to the hall, banging my bare foot against an old bicycle parked in the darkness of the hall. Cursing, I hopped blindly for a moment until I reached the light of Tom's room. Limping in, I looked around at the devasation. Books were scattered about the room where they had landed. The bookcase was on its face, furniture was tipped up, glass was all over the floor. A bottle of wine had been smashed across the wall, staining the paper with thin liquid that ran down the walls like blood. Papers were everywhere, some turning black in curled-up balls of flame in the fireplace. Tom stood in the middle of it all, looking drained and wrung out, a broken lamp dangling from his hand. He'd been in a subdued mood all night, but this bloody lot took me back a bit. 'What the hell are you doing?' I asked.

He took a deep breath. 'Fuck knows, but who cares?'

'What's the matter with you, for Christ's sake?'

'I dunno,' he threw the lamp on the floor, stepped across the bookshelf and turned an armchair the right way up, then flopped down in it and lit a cigarette. 'Just letten off steam I s'pose, our kid.'

'That's an expensive way of doing it. It would be cheaper to go out and beat up the odd old lady or two.'

94

He smiled—for the first time that night. I picked up a chair and parked on it. 'So—what is it, Tom?'

'I'm just on a downer, thass all.'

'Why?'

'Why? Because I'm not gettin' anythin' done. I don't know why, there isn' a reason for everything. I'm just pissed off in the extreme.'

'Oh. I see. Well—you know—the next time you're feeling so pissed off why don't you come round to my place and smash it up? It's better to be among friends at a time like that. Don't stay on your own smashing things up.'

He laughed—his real Liverpool cackle. 'You'd make a dog laugh, Nicholas,' he said. 'I dunno, I guess it was alcoholic remorse again. It's been a bastard day. I went for a job this morning in Canning Town. I wanted to get some bread together. When Sandra comes back it would be handy to have some cash so that we can start on a different footing. A job would also keep me busy while we wait. I didn't get it. I went and had a drink and during the course of that I started to sink. Started gettin indulgent an' all thatt type of ting. There was people yapping all around me words just whistling around my earholes like bloody bullets, so I had to get out. Then the traffic was roaring through me brain and everywhere looked deerty and depressing. I wanted to get out of London and thatt was all I could tink of.

'Then suddenly, I wanted to talk to Sandra. I could see her face in me mind's eye, and I wanted ter touch it, like. It was a really powerful gut feeling. Call me the sweet old-fashioned sentimental type if you like. But I got on a train at London Bridge to Caulton Park. Walked all the way up thatt poxy hill agen ...' His words trailed off with the cigarette smoke.

'Why did you do that, Tom? I mean, it's a little soon, isn't it? You've accepted the rules. Did you think you'd be able to see her?'

'I knew I wouldn't. But theer was also a possibility that I might. Being within thirty yards of the place where she was made it seem possible thatt I might. Being outside Rendezvous House made her and our relationship seem real again ... In the end I just stood there in the bushes. It was dead peaceful. I wondered what she would think if she knew I was standing there outside like a spare part, a fart in a trance.'

95

'Then what happened?'

'I pulled back. I came back here.'

'You must be broke, aren't you?'

'Yeh. I am as a matter of fact. You couldn't lend us a coupla quid, could yeh?'

We laughed, but as I got back into bed, homing into the warmth of Diane, I was thinking of something else I had learnt about Tom. He had stressed that his relationship with Donna was platonic. He had surprised me by telling me that he hadn't been with anybody since Sandra. He thought about her more often than he let on, it seemed, glued to her absence like some sort of raggedy-arsed Gatsby. 'I guess I wouldn't step over anybody offering it on a plate,' he had shrugged. 'But I know if I took it I would just jerk off on 'em and not have much to say afterwards. I'd be screwing away like a two-stroke fantasising about someone else.'

A few weeks after this something did happen. To me it was unimportant—a fly-by-night incident casual enough not to be cared about. But it affected Tom in a curious way and during the next few years of his life would affect him even more. But at the time it seemed important for very personal reasons.

Tom and Donna stayed at our flat one night after a party. We made up two beds for them in the living room and left them to it. I wasn't particularly surprised when, the next morning, I came out and found them entangled together in one of the beds.

Diane followed me into the kitchen a few minutes later, in her dressing gown and hair messed up. 'So much for platonic pals. I thought those two were just good friends.'

'Well, if you're going to screw someone you might as well screw a good friend—that's what I always say.'

'Make me a cup of tea, will you, pig?' she demanded, sitting down at the table and lighting a cigarette. 'Christ. One moment he speaks fondly of his lost loves and the next he's laying darling Donna in our sitting room. Typical of men.'

'Bullshit. Two years is a long time in a relationship these days. You don't expect the guy to remain celibate, do you?'

'Men stick together as well, don't they?'

'Would you stay celibate if I wound up inside or languished in the head house for a couple of years?' I asked.

96

'I might,' she spoke with a coy glint in her eyes. 'If I loved you enough.'

'*Bollocks.*'

'Nicholas!' she pretended to be shocked. 'I don't wish to know what your favourite toy is!'

'Less of the moralising. Not to mention the piss-taking. Are they awake yet?'

'Yes, they were beginning to stir as I came through. Where's my cup of tea?'

Donna was the first to enter the kitchen. For a moment she looked slightly self-conscious, though she laughed and said, 'Sod it, I was gonna get up before you two.'

'You'd have to be up early for that,' I replied. 'Tea or coffee?'

'Whatever's easiest.'

'Did you sleep well?' Diane smiled faintly, with her chin on her hands and her eyebrows slightly raised.

'Quiet woman, or I'll blind you with this cup of tea,' I said with my best Groucho Marx impersonation. Donna laughed and confirmed that she had had a good kip though she'd had a really weird dream.

Then Tom came in, bleary-eyed, dressed in pullover and jeans, but with his shirt hanging out in the front and back looking like an all-round apron.

'Look at the state of that,' I said, as he rubbed his half-asleep eyes.

'S'truth,' scoffed Donna. 'All 'e'd need now is a cigarette 'older an' 'e'd look just like Noel Coward.'

It was as light and as casual as that, but Tom fell into a funny mood about it. He was surprisingly bothered that I might have thought something was happening with him and Donna. He wanted me to know that the mood and need of the moment had brought them together and would now push them apart. He was telling me because we were by now close, perhaps closer than we would have been had we grown up together. Only a little later did I realise he was explaining things as much to himself as to me, and I wondered at the object of the fixation he had that made him on drunken nights smash his belongings to smithereens, or travel as far as the path alongside Rendezvous House to look at it, thinking of her moving about inside oblivious of his nearby presence which could only do her harm. I wondered if he felt that

97

by screwing Donna he had lost another part of Sandra. Having operated in his teens on the 'hump 'm and dump 'm' principle, he was now for the first time unable to accept the transient commitment of a one-night stand.

Part Two

CATALYSTS

Chapter Eleven

'Perhaps he isn't coming,' Diane shrugged after a while.

'It's the first time he's broken arrangements with us if that's the case,' I said, puzzled.

'Well it's twenty-five to nine now. He was supposed to be here at eight. Maybe something came up.'

The door swept open and we both looked up, but it was a shuffling old man getting out of the corkscrew wind. The reflection of him in the night-time window seemed ghostly and transparent—more unreal than the giant face of the Martini girl.

'Let's go down to New Road and see whether or not he's forgotten,' I suggested.

Ten minutes later we pulled up outside the house. I knocked at the letterbox and a few minutes later a tall bearded man opened the door to us.

'Is Tom at home?' I asked.

The man shook his head and told me no.

'Any idea where he is?'

'Who are yer?' the man wanted to know, in an Irish brogue.

'I'm Tom's brother.'

'Oh! You better come in then.'

We stepped into the hall. The man closed the door and led us along to the door of Tom's living room. 'Look at dis,' he said, pushing the door open. We stepped into the room and looked around. It was wrecked. Books, records, papers, cushions, pillows, blankets—all thrown over the floor, and furniture dragged out of place.

'Jesus,' said Diane.

'What the hell's been going on?' I asked. 'Don't tell me Tom got into a bad mood again! Bloody maniac.'

'I expect Tom ain't in the best of moods,' said the man. 'But dis is as a result of the pleece bein' in a bad mood, not him.'

'The police? Why, what's happened?' I asked.

'They came round last night about six o'clock. Two plain-clothed fellahs. They wanted to talk to Tom, who was in the kitchen getting' hisself some dinner. Tom brought 'em in here and a while later he went away wid 'em. We haven't seen him since, but the police have been back twice today and turned the whole fucking lot over. They made a right pisshole of the place as you can see for yourselves, the filthy slags!'

'So Tom is still with the police then?'

'I couldn't tell yer to be trut'ful.'

'And you don't know which station these policemen came from?'

'I don't, friend. Could be any one o' the locals.'

I took another look around at the mess of Tom's room, then I wrote down the man's name, Eddie Regan, and Diane and I returned to the street. A gust of wind lifted at her hair as we stood in the depressing road for a moment.

'What are you going to do?' she asked. 'They could have taken him anywhere.'

'Like the man said, it must be local.' I looked up the street as if for a sign of Tom sauntering along towards us.

'What do you think it is—drugs?'

'I don't know. I can't see them going to a hell of a lot of trouble over a couple of drawers of pot, but you never know. Let's get back to Bethnal Green and work this little mystery out.'

At Bethnal Green tube station we went down to the telephone kiosks. I took out the telephone directory and turned to the Police page. My eyes scanned the page for the local numbers and as I picked them out Diane scribbled them down: Whitechapel, Limehouse, Shadwell, City of London, Bethnal Green. Then I set about dialling each number, saying the same thing to each duty officer: 'My name is Heyward, of Marlon Markbyss & Co. solicitors. I understand you may have a client of mine by the name of Thomas Gerard Delaney assisting you with some inquiries ...' Each time the duty officer would disappear for a while and then return with a negative response.

Then finally I made contact with Doughty Road Police Station in Old Ford. This time the duty officer returned to the phone with: 'Yes, sir, we've got your client here.'

102

I'd hardly said thank you before I slammed the phone down. 'That's the one,' I told her. 'Come on, let's go and see what the hell this is all about.' We walked back up into the street and back to the car which was parked underneath the bright face of the Martini girl enjoying her drink in paradise in the midst of these lights and dark buildings.

I took the A–Z from the glove compartment and gave Diane the directions to Doughty Road. The windscreen wipers swished back and forth against another downpour. My mind was racing, with adrenalin and apprehension burning through me like an electric current.

It seemed like ages before we arrived in front of the square red-brick building although Diane assured me later it was only twelve minutes. She followed me into the bright strip-lighting of the reception. There was nobody at the counter but I could hear the voices of policemen laughing and talking around the corner and also the muffled voices of people talking over a radio. We waited for several infuriating minutes before a uniformed, jacketless officer appeared. 'What can I do you for?' he asked with a condescending expression on his face.

I told him who I was and what I wanted to know. The officer disappeared for another five minutes, during which I paced the floor. Diane took out a packet of Dunhill, handed me one then lit one for herself as well. It might have been the first time she'd been in a police station but I was glad enough of her company.

The officer returned with a bunch of papers in his hand. 'Someone'll be out to see you in a moment, sir.' Then he wandered off out of sight again.

This 'moment' dragged on for about ten minutes. Diane looked at the map of the local area, then at the Wanted and Missing posters on the noticeboard. Finally a door to the side opened and a man in a suit and tie stepped into the room, bringing with him the aura of a hard young detective—which is often only marginally different from that of a hard young bank robber.

'Mr Heyward, is it?' he smiled superciliously.

'That's right.'

'Mr Delaney's a client of yours, is he?'

'That's also correct. Who am I talking to actually?'

'DC Villiers, sir.'

'So, er, what's this all about then, officer?'

'Well! We think your client can help us with certain inquiries we're making, and at the moment he's shaping up very nicely.'

'He's been here something like twenty-six hours apparently,' I pointed out. 'Is he going to be charged with an offence?'

'That remains to be seen, sir. As I say, at the moment he's in conference with one of my superiors.'

'How superior is this superior?'

'Chief Superintendent, sir.'

'What? What the hell is this inquiry in connection with for a Chief Superintendent to be involved?' I asked, surprised to hear that Tom was with such a high-ranking officer.

'It's a murder inquiry, sir,' the detective smiled.

'Murder?' Diane's startled voice came whizzing past me.

'That's right, miss,' he nodded.

'When can I see him?' I asked.

'Well, he'll be busy for some time yet,' said the officer. 'Why don't you pop back in the morning? There isn't much you can do at the moment. You'll be able to see him in good time, I should think, Mr Heyward.'

'Thanks for your help,' I said, finding sarcasm difficult to suppress.

'Well, I'd like to be able to put you more in the picture,' he said in a pally sort of way, 'but it's not down to me. Still, I've no doubt you'll be in the picture soon enough. Anyway. I'll see you later,' he waved his hand as he went back through the door, then closed it behind him.

'I don't believe it,' Diane said incredulously. 'Murder? Nicky, what's going to happen?'

I looked around at the counter where the duty officer was back flicking through more papers. I asked him if he could lend me a couple of telephone directories for G and M. He handed them over and I began flicking through G.

'What are you looking for?' Diane asked.

'Goldberg's home number. I've got to get through to Jake and I can't wait for him to turn up at the office at eleven o'clock. Now where did he say he lives? Barnet or somewhere.' I scanned the list of names until my eyes ached but there was no sign of his number. I then tried to find Marlon Markbyss's number. In bold letters and figures the office number in the City appeared, but no home number. Both were ex-directory. I cursed and walked out of the reception and on to the steps of the station. Silver specks of rain rattled through the night.

'Isn't this fucking ace? There's a guy in there, somewhere in this building, being interrogated by high-ranking police officials. A few yards away stands his brother—in law—who feels bloody impotent. Jesus.'

'There's nothing anybody can do tonight,' Diane said. 'Come on. Let's get home and you can talk to Mr Markbyss about it when you go into the office in the morning.'

I didn't want to go home. I felt entrenched in my mood and fixed permanently to the steps. Lights blazed from the windows of the police station in the rain. I could only imagine what Tom was going through at the moment. The rain seemed to separate Diane and me as I brooded on the experience, authority and skill of Jake Goldberg—if only I knew how to contact him. Then suddenly at the tail end of one thought another came to me.

'There's a book in the office,' I said. 'It's got the names and addresses of all the staff.'

'What's the good of that now? It's half-past twelve. Your office will be all locked up.'

'We'll wake the caretaker up,' I said. 'Come on.'

We got into the car and drove off. I saw everything and absorbed nothing as the rain came towards the windscreen and the car came towards the yellow lights of the City, its deserted glass towers and noble buildings. The streets of the City looked strange and empty at night, and in my overwrought state of mind things had a dream-like unreality, yet it was part of my training to deal with crises in peoples' lives every day.

We left the car in Lime Street and ran through some courts and alleyways until we came into Gracechurch Passage with its solitary lamp and shuddering rain puddles. Of course all the buildings were in darkness. Bert, the belligerent caretaker, lived on the top floor of number 9. He was an irascible old bugger, very strict about locking the building up at 7.00 pm every night. Anybody still in the building a minute late was usually reported to the landlords for contravening the terms of the lease.

I rang the bell several times. Ages seemed to pass and I wondered whether he was at home or not. 'Come on, you old bastard, get it together for Christ's sake,' I growled, ringing the bell again. Eventually we heard the sound of the ancient lift inside clank to the ground floor. Then the bolts on the other side of the door flew across and the door opened. Belligerent Bert stood there in his braces and vest, his moustache twitching with anger at being knocked up so late.

'What's your game then, at this bleedin' hour of the night?' he wanted to know, although he undoubtedly must have recognised me.

'Bert, I'm sorry—I wouldn't be here now if it were not a matter of urgency. I need access to the office.'

'No way,' Belligerent Bert shook his head emphatically. 'Arter sevener clock at night this place is out of bounds to all shipping merchants, accountants, insurance brakers and soliciters. That's in the lease, mate, an' it includes your guvners Markbyss 'n Goldberg. I'd be up and down on that bladdy lift all night uvverwise. So you might as well save it for termorrer, cos I'm on me own time now and I wanna get some bleedin' kip. This front door'll be open at seven in the mornin', so come back then.'

'You don't understand, Bert. My brother has just been arrested. The police are going to try and stick him up for a murder charge, I think. I need to get hold of Mr Goldberg fast. This is the only place where I might find his home number.'

'Werl!' said Bert. 'You shoulda said. If you'd cummout straight away an' said, you'd most likely be in 'ere by now!'

We stepped past him into the corridor and he bolted the door again. Diane and I were saturated, our hair heavy with rainwater. Bert waddled ahead of us, taking a large ring of keys from the pocket of his baggy trousers. He unlocked the reception of our office and we went in. Immediately I started searching through Sue's desk while Diane perched on the edge of the table and lifted her wet hair behind her shoulders.

'The bladdy ole bill are alwuz causin' trubble at ungodly hours,' Bert complained to Diane as I rummaged around. 'Right inconsiderate bastards they are! They've got nothing else to do. I 'ad me collar felt the uvver night. I wuz walkin' darn City Road with this duffle bag when this young copper pulls me. "Watchoo got in the bag?" he says. "Wossit got ter do wiv you?" I says back. "Got summink in there you shouldn't have, have yer?" he wants ter know. "Maybe I have," I sez, "and maybe I ain't." So he sez, "Maybe we'll find out darn City Road nick if you ain't careful." I said, "Don't you bladdy come it wiv *me*, mate." ' He rambled on but I was no longer listening, for I had found the book. The office seemed strange and haunted with just one light on as I flicked through the pages of the book. There it was: *Jake Goldberg, 5 Silesia Gardens, Totteridge*, followed by the phone number. I switched the switchboard back on and gave myself a line, then lifted the receiver and dialled. I glanced at my watch for the first time in hours; it was five past one.

The phone rang interminably and was finally answered by a woman.

'Can I speak to Mr Goldberg please?'

'Who's calling?' the woman asked.

'This is Nicholas Heyward—from Mr Goldberg's office. I'm calling on a matter of great urgency.'

'Hold the line then,' she sighed, and the phone was put down.

I sat back in Sue's swivel chair and waited. I felt tense and impatient. Then a few minutes later the phone was picked up again and I heard the reassuring and ruffled voice of Mr Goldberg himself: 'Hullo.'

'Mr Goldberg—it's Nicholas, from the office.'

'Nicky. What's the problem?'

'I've got a spot of trouble, Mr Goldberg. Yesterday evening my brother was taken from his home to Doughty Road Police Station where he has been ever since. They say he is helping them with their inquiries on a murder investigation, and they've turned his home over twice today and made a right bloody mess of it to boot. I don't know what they've been looking for there.'

'Have you been to Doughty Road?' he asked.

'I've just come from there.'

'Did you speak to any of the officers involved?'

'Yes, I spoke briefly with some supercilious bastard of a DC who seemed to be suffering from a severe case of vagueness.'

'What did he tell you?'

'Just that my brother is helping them with their inquiries and that he couldn't really elucidate on that. I had the feeling that he wasn't exactly going to give us the benefit of the Judges Rules. He said we'd be put in the picture soon enough.'

'So where are you now?'

'I'm actually in the office at the moment. Bert let us in.'

'All right ... I'll come down. Give me an hour and I'll meet you at Doughty Road presently, okay?'

'Thanks, Mr Goldberg.'

'Don't worry. I'll see you in a while.'

The lines clicked and suddenly the phone was purring at me. For the first time in the past few hours I felt a sense of relief. I rubbed my forehead as though it were a magic lamp containing a legal genie called Jake.

'Thanks, Bert,' I said, getting up. 'I'm much obliged to you. Come on, kid, let's get back to the Majestic and have a quick coffee while we wait for the man to arrive. Then you can drop me back at the police station.'

By the time we were back sitting at a table in the Majestic Café I had managed to pull my scattered wits back towards me. Dossers were all around us, making cups of tea last longer so that they could stay out of the shaking rain.

'Jesus,' I shook my head thoughtfully. 'I was never so relieved to hear the sound of Jake's sarky voice. He's got a lot of experience in cases like this. Apparently he's dealt with five murder trials in the past twenty years.'

'But if Tom is—well—I mean ...'

'If Tom is charged with murder—yes?'

'Well, can your firm act for him? Isn't there some rule that forbids anybody as close as you are to Tom being involved in the case?'

'No. I guess it's up to Markbyss or Jake. There's no law or rule against us dealing with it but they might not want to because of emotional involvement. I don't know. I hope Goldberg doesn't take that view. If it were me in that police station I'd want to see Jake's phizzog more than anybody else's. Come on, drink up. You can drop me at Doughty Road, then go home and get some sleep. You have to get up for your office tomorrow.'

'It doesn't matter, Nicky, I'm staying,' she said. 'Come on, then.'

The duty sergeant asked if he could help us. I told him I was waiting for my principal and he went away, leaving me to pace up and down, waiting ...

An hour had passed since I spoke to Jake. Yet again the waiting was interminable. The station house clock ticked by slowly. The muffled radio voice from a panda car called: 'Delta One to Base ...' The waiting, waiting, waiting made me increasingly restless. I was too absorbed to speak to Diane and she had run out of things to say and noticeboards to read.

The swing doors swept open. I spun around but it was only two squad-car drivers returning from a patrol. They glanced at us as though they'd never seen human beings before and disappeared into an anteroom.

'Delta One, go to 47A Old Ford Road—suspect seen climbing roof, over.'

Suddenly at twenty to three the doors swung open and my heart lifted at the sight of the arrogant Jake Goldberg, complete with his black, unbuttoned, Crombie coat.

'Hello, Nicky. Now what problems have we got here then?'

'It's still as I told you, Mr Goldberg. I've no idea what the circumstances are but I'm certain it's a mistake. I wouldn't say that my brother was a killer.'

'All right. What's your brother's name?'

He pushed past me to the counter where there was no sign of any personnel. 'Shop!' he called, rapping the counter with his fist. 'Anybody at home?' The duty sergeant appeared from around the corner with a frown on his face. 'Oh, there you are!' Jake spoke with his built-in sarcasm. 'My name is Goldberg—of Marlon Markbyss & Co. solicitors. I understand you're holding a client of mine here. I'd be very much obliged if we could clarify what the problem is.'

It had more than a salutory effect on me to see Jake take over.

'This would be Mr Delaney, would it, sir?'

'Well done,' said Jake. 'That is precisely who we are talking about. Who's the officer in charge?'

'Erm—I think we've got Chief Superintendent Balfour dealing with this one, as it happens, sir.'

'I'd appreciate it if you would tell him I am here.'

'I believe he's interviewing your client at the moment, sir.'

'That's handy! You will no doubt appreciate that I am anxious to see my client, who I understand has been here for some thirty hours,' Jake said. 'At the moment I am completely in the dark as to what the position is and don't even know whether charges are pending. I know not what allegations are being made, if any, and as Mr Delaney's legal adviser I feel that I should have a general idea, at least. Would you agree with that? Perhaps you could attract the attention of at least one of the officers involved in this case.'

'I'll see what I can do, sir.'

'I knew you would, ossifer. Thank you.'

The policeman went away and Jake turned back to us, taking out a packet of Players. He offered Diane one, saying 'Who are you?'

'This is Diane—my girlfriend. Diane, Mr Goldberg.'

'Pleased to meet you, dear,' he said as she selected a cigarette. Then for the first time ever he offered me one.

'Sorry to drag you out at this time of the night,' I said as his gold lighter clicked at the end of my cigarette.

'Don't worry about it, Nicholas. It can't be helped. You know if you've got any problems I'll help you out if I can. You know that by now, don't you?'

'Well, I'm certainly glad to hear your authoritative voice around here at the moment,' I half laughed. 'That's for sure.'

'Tell me a bit about your brother. Has he ever been involved with the police before?'

'We were both adopted by different families, he by one in Liverpool. I gather he got into minor troubles when he was a kid. Thieving and criminal damage and that sort of thing. Nothing big. He went to an attendance centre when he was fourteen but since then he's been in the clear.'

'What's his occupation?'

'He's unemployed.'

'What sort of person is he? Is he calm, placid, volatile, or what?'

'He's an easy-going sort of guy,' Diane chipped in. 'He certainly didn't kill anybody, I don't believe he could.'

'Well,' Jake blew out cigarette smoke, 'we'll see. Meanwhile, both of you take it easy. You've got to be in the office in a few hours, Nick. Did you file that affidavit for me?'

'What—oh—yes, yes I filed it yesterday.'

'What about Brelsford? Everything under control there?'

'I gave the brief to Marriott's clerk.'

'Good!' said Jake with satisfaction. 'We'll make a good lawyer out of you yet. That was a good result we got at the Bailey yesterday, you know?'

'Yes, I was telling Diane about it.'

'Hepburn was well pleased with that. Anyway, tell me, Nicky, when was the last time you saw this brother of yours? Recently?'

'Last weekend. We arranged to meet tonight—or should I say

last night? But he didn't show. Now we know why.'

'How did he seem when you last saw him?'

'Cheerful. Quite happy.'

The side door opened and a stocky treble-chinned man in a blue suit stepped into the reception. 'Hello, Jake. What are you doing out and about at this unholy hour—as if I couldn't guess! How's tricks?'

'Not bad, Mike. And you?'

'Mustn't grumble,' the detective shoved his fists deep into his trouser pockets. 'Wouldn't do me any bleeding good if I did! You're Delaney's brief, are yer?'

'That's right.'

'Ooh, 'e won' arf be glad ter see you,' chuckled Mike.

'So what's the SP on this then?' Jake asked.

'I think you better come inside, Jake.' The detective opened the door.

'Wait here, Nicholas,' Jake said and they both went out of the room and closed the door.

'They come across as though they're on the same side,' observed Diane.

'Well—that's the legal profession for you,' I took a hard pull on the cigarette. 'You are now in the land of a nod's as good as a wink. Jake knows everybody from Flying Squad officers to East End characters—from the Clerk of the Lists to the commissionaires on the door, from QCs to criminals. We flagged a cab down one time and he even knew the bloody driver!'

'A useful man to have about in a crisis then,' Diane said.

The next hour seemed like eternity. I was aware of every minute that passed by—each one seemed longer than the one before. I felt drained, tired and groggy, and depressed by the atmosphere of the station and the indifferent laughter of a couple of unseen policemen.

Then the door opened again and Jake returned.

I heard his words but could hardly grasp the meaning of them, as though I were the one concerned. 'They've got some serious charges against your brother, I'm afraid, Nicholas.'

'Oh no,' said Diane.

'It's a mistake,' I said hollowly. 'It has to be a mistake.'

'Come on.' Jake held open one of the swing doors. 'I'll buy you a drink.'

'Drink? But it's four in the morning.'

'You may have heard a rumour that God moves in mysterious ways. That is correct—I do! Come along now. We'll talk in the car.'

It had stopped raining. The three of us slid into the comfort of Jake's burgundy Rover. Within a few minutes we were speeding along the dark streets of Old Ford.

'Now listen to me, Nicky,' Jake said. 'Your brother is facing three charges. Number one: that on March 10th he unlawfully murdered a girl called Donna Maddon ...'

I heard an escape of breath from disbelieving Diane in the back seat. 'It's all bollocks!' I exclaimed, in a voice that didn't even sound like me to me.

'Secondly, he's charged with attempt to commit arson, to wit, he tried to set the girl's home alight. Thirdly, he is charged with assaulting a police officer at Doughty Road Police Station last night.'

'It's a cock-up or a fit-up, one or the bloody other,' I declared angrily.

'Steady on,' Jake cautioned. 'You know yourself we're not going to do any good by getting busy like that—what good is all that gonna do? I know you're upset and it's come as a bit of a shock, but if we want to do our best for your brother we can't go getting emotional about it, there's no value in it.'

'What have they got?' I asked with more restraint. 'What's the evidence. They didn't knock a statement out of him for Christ's sake, did they?'

'He's signed nothing, which is sensible, and I've advised him to keep it that way and not to answer any more questions, now that he's been charged, in my absence. I'll wait and see what the DPP delivers before I draw my conclusions from their evidence. Your brother will appear before Thames Magistrates in the morning and he'll be remanded. We'll apply for legal aid and when the certificate comes through we'll make an appointment to see him in Brixton.'

'How did Tom take it, is he okay?'

'He's all right. A bit tired, that's all. He feels better now that he knows he's got help out here. But you know yourself, Nicky, it's going to be a long fight. For the next year or so he's gonna be a client more than a close relative, and there's no two ways about it.'

'You will handle the case then?'

'Of course. No problem.'

We left the car in a dark, empty side street, street lights reflected in the shivering puddles. Great depressing Victorian walls stood all around us. It would not have been surprising to see Fagin or Quilp scuttling along. Instead, we passed a grey dilapidated vagrant man sleeping in the doorway of a dress factory. It seemed strange to think that beautiful girls' dresses were born in a gloomy pisshole of a building like that.

Soon we were in Spitalfields Market. To add to the unreality of the night, it was just turned 4.15 am and the streets and warehouses were like a beehive of market porters humping, fetching, carrying, loading and unloading, as though it were the middle of the day. The cafés and the pubs were all open as well, and Jake took us into the comfortable pink-lit saloon bar of one public house that was doing fair trade. Walking into a pub at this time of the morning, smelling the malt and hops, hearing the song 'Desirée' playing from the jukebox, gave me a weird, disorientating feeling. Jake bought the drinks and we went to a corner table and sat down.

'Did you speak to Tom alone?' I asked.

'Of course. He denies all the charges. He told me that on the night of the murder he was at a Jamaican drinking club in Stoke Newington until ten o'clock, and then he came here to the market, where he told me he had a drink and got talking with a vagrant.'

'He's got an alibi then?' said Diane.

'Well, that depends,' Jake said. 'I've yet to see the medical evidence confirming or estimating time of death. If she was killed early in the evening the chances are we can find alibi witnesses from this club to verify your brother's story. But if she was killed later we need to find this vagrant, which is hard, Nicky, because how do you find a vagrant in London. They all look the same and they're always on the trot. Keep your fingers crossed that it all happened early in the evening.

'My God, poor Donna,' said Diane. 'What's happened to her children?'

'Yes,' I said. 'Weren't they there. Didn't they see something?'

'All I can tell you at this stage is that somebody has ID'd your brother and marked his card,' Jake took a sip of his red wine. 'The

113

police also went to his address, as you correctly told me, and took away various articles of clothing and a hammer. The girl was apparently bludgeoned with some sort of blunt instrument and at the moment they are saying that her injuries could have been inflicted with a hammer. The articles that the police took from your brother's address are now destined for the laboratories for examination. We'll just have to wait and see what the results are when the police deliver. In the meantime, you and I, Nicholas, shall attend this Cat O' Nine Tails Club in Stoke Newington and take some statements of our own. But before we do any of that— I'll give you a lift back to your car, then you can get some sleep. You both look tired. You might as well have the morning off, Nicky. I'll speak to Mr Markbyss at the office when I get in. Don't worry. You know I'll do my best for you. Leave it to me,' he said.

At 5.00 am I closed the flat door. Diane threw her shoulder bag on the armchair. 'D'you want coffee, babe?' she asked.

'No. Let's get some sleep. You look how I feel: shattered.'

'I am.'

We went into the bedroom, stripped our clothes off, and crawled under the sheets, where we found each other again, warm skin against warm skin and nothing but darkness and breathing.

'Don't worry, Nick,' she said softly. 'It's all a mistake. A terrible mistake. They'll sort it out.'

'You've got more faith in the legal system than I have then,' I admitted suddenly. 'Blokes like Jake are good—but nothing is certain, least of all justice, huh! If only the best legal system in the world were perfect.'

Time wore on and when I spoke to Diane again I got no answer, just the sound of her unconscious breathing.

114

Chapter Twelve

So began a long summer for Tom, remanded in custody at Brixton whilst waiting for the police to assemble their case and for the courts to slowly work their way through the great backlog of cases all breathing down their necks, anxious for their turn. I'll never forget that first Saturday afternoon Diane and I went to visit him. It was a real spring day bringing the first warm sun of the year. Diane wore a cool summer dress and sandals and I had my sunglasses at the ready. Even the dull emptiness of London south of the river was dressed up by the generous sunshine as we drove through Kennington. Leaving the car in a side street just off Brixton Hill, we walked along Jebb Avenue past the perimeter walls and barbed wire to the great wooden doors. It seemed odd to be visiting the place as a private caller rather than a legal rep. A warder opened the door for us and we stepped into the daunting precincts of this palace of fun and colour TVs, and we were directed into a room which was crowded with men, women and children waiting to see somebody.

The officer behind the desk took our names and entered them in a book, tearing out a slip to be given to a warder, who would go off to find the prisoner.

We were then ushered to another section where Diane handed over the bag of treats for Tom: four ounces of tobacco, forty French cigarettes, sweets and books. A cheerful old warder took them from her and handed her a receipt, instructing her to give it to Tom when we saw him.

The next hour was spent sitting on a bench in the crowded smoky waiting room. Diane had never been in a prison before. She stared at snotty-nosed little toddlers rushing around the room, whilst I looked at the crowd of weathered faces from another world, faces that were always or often up against the law. This place wasn't new to some.

'Jesus,' Diane fidgeted uncomfortably. 'This place is so oppressive.'

'No, it isn't,' I scoffed. 'It's a four-star hotel! It's the Brixton Hilton. See that bellboy over there in the uniform! Very efficient. You don't get big strong bellboys like that at Claridges.'

A warder came out of a small doorway.

'Delaney!' he called above the hubbub of waiting room conversation. He took Diane and me through several doors before we came out into the visiting room. Unlike the legal visiting booths this place was far from private. It was a large smoky room full of people talking, talking, talking, with the prison walls and uniforms lowering over every conversation. A warder sat at a desk at one end and there was a steaming tea stand at the other. I think both Diane and I felt a little disorientated for a moment and at first we couldn't see Tom among this crowd.

'Nick! Diane!' a voice called, and there he was, sitting alone at a table. We weaved our way down the various aisles and sat down across the table from him.

'Have you got a cigarette, kid?' he said. 'I'm gaspin' for a drag.'

Diane offered him a Dunhill and he almost knocked the packet out of her hand taking one. 'I'm sorry,' he blushed. 'I don't know whether to smoke it or make love to it. I haven't had one since I was at the pleece station.'

Diane pushed the receipt across to him and said, 'We've brought you these things, Tom.'

'You'll be allowed to pick them up when we leave,' I said. 'Make sure they give you everything that is on that list.'

His face was a strange mixture of relief and emotion. 'Ah, Jesus, thanks youz two,' he said rubbing his forehead. 'I don't know what to say ... Hey, d'yer want a cup of tea? I could do wid one mesself, but you'll have to get 'em in. I'm not allowed to stir from here.'

'I'll get them,' Diane looked around nervously, and got up. She walked away, past the straying eyes of men who no doubt fancied her for a cellmate.

'How are they treating you?' I asked.

'All right, I guess,' he shrugged, more absorbed in his nicotine fix. 'There's three of us cramped up in this poxhole cell and it's

116

getting on me neerves. Banged up together in a small cell, sleepin', pissing and shitting together, it's driving me up the fucking wall. One of the guys is in for murder for the second time in fifteen years and he's a real headcase, screaming at night and threatening to smash everything up. The other guy is dead scared. He thinks he's banged up with two murderers all night. Guess what he's in for? Nickin' fucken cars!'

'Well, look, Tom, in a few weeks Goldberg will be here to see you and you'll be able to get things off your chest about what is happening. In the meantime, give me some idea of how it all came about.'

'Last Wednesday these two detectives came round,' he said. 'They wanted to know when I last saw Donna and when I was last round her way. They wanted to know where I was on March 10th, and I honestly couldn't remember. Then they asked me about my criminal record and I came out and told them there's been notten on me since I was a kid. So they asked me to come to the station. Now, at that time I didn't know what it was all about and I certainly had no idea that Donna was dead. They took me down to Doughty Road and they left me in this interview room for ages before they came back and told me to take me shoes off … From that moment on I had three of 'em on me back all night, the next day and the following evening, when they took all me clothes away. I was dead scared, started gettin' confused, and I didn't feel too clever half the time without the clothes. I couldn't believe it when they told me that they suspected me of killing Donna and thatt somebody had witnessed me leaving the house soon after she was killed. They said that somebody heard me having a row wid her, but it's all shite, Nick, you've gorra believe thatt. I haven't been up there since before Christmas.'

Diane sat down with two cups of tea, for Tom and me.

'Who ID'd you?' I asked.

'They wouldn't tell me and I assumed they were bluffin',' said Tom. 'It wasn't til the followin' night I realised they were talkin' about one night I was up at Jimmy Mingo's club.'

'You're sure that was the night Donna was killed?'

'Dead sure. It was a Friday night a few weeks back and the' was a film on telly I wanted to see but I forgot about it til it was too late. A Woody Allen picture, *Take the Money and Run*.'

'Christ,' muttered Diane. 'We saw it.'

117

'I wish I'd been sittin' there watchin' it with you,' Tom nodded.

'Okay—I'll double-check the date that that film was transmitted. On Monday Jake and I will be visiting Jimmy Mingo for a talk—this tramp business in Spitalfields is much more difficult. But we'll have to see what the police come up with.'

'They cahn't stick this shite on me, our Nick. I didn't do it—why should I fucken kill the geerl?'

'Try and take it easy, Tom. I just want you to know that we'll be pulling the fucking stops out on this and that's a fact.'

'I'd appreciate it, kidder. I don't wanna do a life sentence for sumpin thatt's not down to me in any way at all.'

'How do you feel at the moment?'

'Numb.'

'Goldberg is one of the best criminal lawyers I've ever seen and we can get a good QC, so everything is under control at the moment.'

'I tell yer, Nick! I was glad to see thatt guy Goldberg walk in the other night like a fairy godmother, no doubt about it. I'm very much looken forward to meetin' him again. When will that be?'

'Your legal aid certificate will come through quickly,' I told him. 'But there's no point in rushing up here until we've had a chance to consider police evidence and assess their case.'

The twenty minutes allotted for the visit disappeared before we knew where we were. It was time to go. 'I'll be back to see you next weekend,' I said as we got up. 'Keep your chin up, mate.'

'And I have a day off on Wednesday,' Diane said. 'I'll come and visit you in the afternoon.'

'Ah thanks,' he managed his first smile. 'Hey look, do us another favour, will you? When you gerra chance pop down to the house and see if you can find the photo of our Sandie and Damien. I'd like to have it and all thatt.'

'We'll go and pick it up now,' I promised. 'Diane can bring it when she comes on Wednesday.'

Tom was told by the warder to wait while Diane and I were herded out with another group of departing visitors. We were then escorted back to the main gate by a condescending screw who let us all back out into the bright sunshine.

Chapter Thirteen

As far as the office was concerned only three people knew of my connection with the new client.

'We must do all we can on this, Jacob,' Markbyss said as he sat back in his black leather chair on Monday morning.

'Of course,' Jake said, leaning against the filing cabinet.

'Which counsel are we thinking of employing on it?' Markbyss wanted to know.

'Well, it's got to be Duvalier or somebody of that calibre,' Jake said, inspecting his fingernails. 'I'll be phoning Julian Reeves when the time comes to make sure that one or the other is available. And I'll get Purnell or Hilliard as a junior. They're all good, intelligent counsel. We don't want some schmock like Geraint Everard, let's face it!'

'Good,' said Markbyss, then turning his smile at me, 'Don't worry, young man. We'll look after it. You know it's all in Mr Goldberg's capable hands and I shall be keeping abreast of any developments as well.'

'Thank you both for your support,' I said.

'Not at all,' said Markbyss.

'Of course not,' said Goldberg, straightening his tie.

It was back to business as usual, with plenty of boring routine paperwork and procedures. But I didn't mind taking on all the outdoor work, not being in the mood to sit behind my desk all day. Travelling around the City and WC2 and EC4 would help my mind keep pace with my adrenalin.

Among the girls in the office there was a certain amount of curiosity about Tom's case. Murder stimulated their interest more than the common or garden bank robberies and frauds that kept Goldberg's filing cabinets full to capacity. The last murder case Markbyss & Co had dealt with was in the early seventies when one of Jake's clients was aquitted of murdering a cousin outside a pub in the East End. The dusty files were still in the dark filing room, among all those of the others who went down to prison and of those who did not. For the first time for years I could see how strange our profession must look to outsiders.

I set out for the Law Courts and lodged some papers with a clerk in the Chancery Division, then went down the ancient steps, along the dull red-floored corridors and yellow walls, past the mysterious doorways labelled Master Dazzle or Master Clarnico, to issue a dozen writs, two of them on behalf of John Sinclair.

At quarter to eleven I stepped into the Bear Garden. My summons before Master Jager was at eleven. The Bear Garden was full of solicitors' clerks conferring with each other in a hubbub of noise, waiting their turn to go before the fattest and most belligerent Master of the Queen's Bench Division. I handed my summons to the messenger and he checked his list. 'The other side hasn't arrived yet, sir. I'll point you out to him when he gets here.'

'Cheers.' I walked across the floor to one of the heavy tables under the large gilt-framed portrait of the late lamented Lord High Chancellor Grim Phizzog. I opened the file to look at some of the correspondence when suddenly a female voice exclaimed, 'Nicky!' I looked up to find that one of the clerks sitting around the table was a blonde-haired girl that I had been at university with and hadn't seen since we graduated.

'Kim! How are you?'

'I'm fine! And you? You look well, I must say. For a second I wasn't sure that it was you. I remember you as a sweater-and-jeans man and here you are in pinstriped sartorial elegance, looking the proper legal young gentleman.'

'Christ, you're the first person I've seen from the university slumming it around here.'

'Really? I've bumped into a few of them. But it's good to see you. Who is your summons before.'

'Jager.'

'Oh shit! I don't envy you that.' She pulled a face. 'I go before Master Tucker in a moment. He's almost sweet. I simply hand him the form and say, "Master this is my summons," flicker my eyelashes at him, and I normally get what I want.'

'Equality of the sexes! I'll be lucky if Jager doesn't boot my arse out of it.'

'Everybody is lucky if Jager doesn't boot their backside out of it. He doesn't succumb to eyelashes. I've seen many a solicitors' clerk come out of his chambers rubbing their arses with tears in their eyes.'

'How are you fixed for a cup of coffee afterwards?'

'Okay. I've got to go down to the Crown Office when I've finished with Tucker but I could meet you in the ABC in, say, an hour?' She got up and picked up her attaché case. 'I'd better tiptoe in now.'

'Good luck. I hope your eyelashes don't fall on his desk.'

'Cheeky.'

Ten minutes later I participated in a procedural and almost civilised dogfight with my opponent solicitor over some matter that I have long forgotten about, before the ascetic Master Jager, all jowl and snarl, his chins doing a curious impression of a belly-dancing competition. After arguing the toss about something and nothing for ten minutes the Master made an order in my favour and thrust the summons back at me aggressively, as though it were a writ he was serving on me, or as if he was having me arrested for farting in court.

I was glad to get out of the absurd place. I'm sure we had High Court actions in our office that started before I went to university and might not be settled until after I qualified. The lifespan of some actions is comparable to that of some parrots—what with all the wrangling, summonses, directions, bullshit and piss-taking, before the action finally crawls into open court, suffering from fatigue and nervous exhaustion, and a High Court judge puts it out of its misery once and for all.

Kim was sitting at a table at the back of the orange-lit ABC when I joined her with a cup of coffee and a Danish pastry.

'How did you get on?' she asked.

'I got a result, believe it or not. Only just, though. And you?'

'Yes, the old dear came through once again and gave us extra time,' she smiled. 'My principal will be pleased because he forgot all about it and we're well out of time. Our opponents wanted to get the action struck out altogether but the Master gave me another chance.'

'Well done! Who are you articled to?'

'Abel Blackman & Co., Quality Court—it's just off Chancery

121

Lane. Where are you?'

'The City. A firm called Marlon Markbyss & Co.'

'Any good?'

'Not bad. They're small but lively. We just did the Hepburn fraud trial at the Bailey.'

'Oh yes, I read about that. I'm impressed. Do they do a lot of that kind of work?'

'We do a lot of all kinds. The legal executive specialises in large criminal cases—he's just acquired a murder case in fact.'

'Sounds interesting,' she said. 'The best we can do is sue somebody whose horse keeps shitting on our client's property.'

'Fascinating stuff.'

'We have two equestrian cases going at the moment,' she inhaled cigarette smoke. 'One of our clients sold a horse to a woman who bought it for her young daughter to ride, on the understanding that the animal was a gelding. While the girl was out riding one morning this "gelding" espied a mare in the next field and became overwhelmed with wanton passion, lust, desire, and made a beeline for the mare's feminine charms, with the terrified girl on its back. So her mother sued and a legion of vets are being called in to argue whether the horse was actually castrated or not.'

'Why don't you save time and money by calling the horse into the witness box to give evidence,' I suggested. 'After all, I would imagine that the horse would be the best source of information.'

'I'll suggest it to counsel,' she laughed.

'What are your plans when you qualify?' I asked.

'Originally I wanted a partnership,' she said. 'Now I don't think I could be bothered with all the hassle and responsibility. Too many worries. I'll just get a salaried position if I can. The trouble is that things are not too good at the moment. Too many people are qualifying for too few jobs. My brother has been qualified for five years. He works at Limehouse Legal Aid Centre. I might actually try something like that for a while. I haven't made up my mind yet. Have you ever thought of doing that, or are you going into the more lucrative company work?'

'I guess so. I suppose I suffer from great ambitions.'

'Great ambitions often lead to small achievements for most of us. Though I think my brother enjoys and gets more out of what he's doing than he did when he was working for a swish Marble

Arch practice.'

'We have all sorts of options open to us. My major concern at the moment is to get through Part 2 and qualify.'

'Oh, mine too. I should think you'll be okay, Nick. You were always very studious.'

'Don't count your eggs before you've laid any,' I scoffed.

After a while she got up to go. 'I'd better get back to the office,' she said. 'Give us a ring sometime, Nick. We're in the Law List— just about. If you feel up to it we'll have a drink some time.'

'I shall,' I promised. 'Take care.'

What busy people we are, I thought, when she had gone. I was sorry in fact that she'd had to rush off—her sense of humour appealed to me and I was in need of it.

I willed myself back towards the traffic growl of Temple Bar where office girls filled the pavements queuing up for lunch-time sandwiches. I walked past the Wig and Pen Club, stopping for a moment to look at caricatures of obese barristers, and thought about the Law, and my self-important feelings about my role in it—which now seemed to take on a new meaning, a new importance.

'Is there any sort of case you wouldn't accept?' I asked Jake, mostly just for something to say, as he drove up Kingsland Road from Shoreditch calling the slow driver in front of him 'a ponce'.

He thought about it for a minute or so then took his chance to overtake the car.

'I wouldn't like to take a rape case on,' he answered finally.

'How come?'

'It's a personal thing,' he shrugged. 'I think it would worry me. It's not something that I'd like to be wrong about.'

It seemed strange to reflect on the fact that six months ago I did not like Jake and his offhand arrogance and sarcasm. Now he was a friend in need indeed.

We pulled up outside the alleyway in Stoke Newington, and I led him along to the front door of the Cat O' Nine Tails Club. Suddenly a tall dreadlocked West Indian appeared in the doorway. Jake introduced himself as a solicitor. 'We act for a chappy by the name of Tom Delaney,' Jake advised him, 'and we understand you can help us with inquiries on his behalf.'

The man's face relaxed. 'Well, woss the problem then? Tom in some sort of bovver?'

'Can we come in and discuss it, er, Mr Mingo, is it?' Jake asked.

'Yeah, Jimmy Mingo.'

Mingo brought us in and led us through the Jamaican music and into a scruffy-looking kitchen at the back. He invited us to 'park at the table', which we did.

'So woss the score then?' he asked, locking his fingers together. 'Solicitors? Woss ole Tom been up to then?'

'Can you cast your mind back about three Fridays?' Jake asked. 'March 10th is the night we're looking for.'

'I could have a go, I s'pose,' said Mingo. 'What am I casting it back for?'

'I want to know if you saw Mr Delaney that night,' Jake told him. 'I want you to think hard on the matter—it's extremely important.'

Mingo rubbed his chin and thought hard. 'Three weeks ago, eh? I s'pose it was about then. Tom came up 'ere one Friday night. His Giro hadn't come and he was a bit stony. He wanted to put hisself in the vicinity of a friend's earhole, or something, but the guy didn't show. I was a bit low on funds messell but I lent him a spanner and some chick I know lent him a couple of notes.'

'What time did he arrive?'

'I dunno. 'Bout seven, I think.'

'Did you see him leave?'

'He had it away early that night. He was gone no later than arf ten.'

'Were there many people here?'

'On Friday nights this place is really at it, mate.'

'And you'd be willing to give evidence in court if necessary,' Jake assumed.

'Woss this all in aid of, man?' Mingo wanted to know.

'Mr Delaney has been remanded in custody on a murder charge,' said Jake.

'What! Tom? Turn it in, mate, is this a wind-up?'

'I'd hardly spend time driving up from the City for the purpose of a wind-up,' Jake said, taking his notebook out of his case.

'Well,' Mingo shook his head slowly. 'Your man was here that night and that is a fact. Twenty people musta seen him. Kim Sowah laid a couple o' quid on the cunt!'

124

'Let's get some of that down in writing then,' Jake said, opening his book ...

We spent a couple of hours in the club, taking statements from the various people who remembered seeing Tom there that night. One guy in particular remembered it because it was his wife's birthday and he promised to get her to ring the office. When we had finished we left Markbyss's business card and asked Mingo to urge anybody else who was around that night to come forward.

'Well,' I said, as we strolled back to the car. 'What do you think?'

'Some of it's good,' he said, 'and some of it is a bit iffy. Four of them have got form and come across aggressively—black people with white chips on their shoulders. If we have to call Mingo, for instance, the mere appearance of the man is going to frighten the life out of the jury. Anyway, we've got much to work on ... It's been a long day, Nicky. I'll give you a lift home.'

It was about ten days after the arrest that I received a telephone call at home during the middle of the evening. A man asked for me by name and I could tell by the echo on the line that it was long distance. Having made sure he was talking to me, he identified himself as Tom's father. Tom had told Diane that he would write to his family and asked her if it was all right to hand out our number and address in case they wished to come and visit him. They would need a cheap place to stay in London. 'The old feller won't fancy the Savoy, he'd sooner have Nick's home cookin',' he had joked.

'Our Tom has written us a letter from prison,' his father said. 'It came as a bloody hell of a shock—we're dead wurried. His mam is in a right state, I can tell yer. We want to see him and we want to come down there and find out what's goin' on. Well, the thing is, our Tom reckons you'd be able to put me and the missis up for the night. Is thatt right?'

'Of course. When are you thinking of coming?'

'Well,' said Mr Delaney. 'We don't want to put you to too much trouble. Would the day after tomorrow suit?'

'Yes, fine. How will you be travelling?'

'A coach gets into Victoria Station at about one o'clock. That's the one we want to be on.'

'I'll be there to meet you,' I promised.

125

The following day we made preparations for their arrival. I arranged with Markbyss to take the afternoon off to meet them and Diane did her housewifely bit by getting in extra provisions.

Then at lunch time on Thursday I left the office and went to Victoria Coach Station, where I stood at the bay waiting for the Liverpool coach to come in. It arrived about twelve minutes late, a great gleaming shuddering machine that had hauled itself away early that morning from the dark northern streets and skies. I thought of Tom and his girlfriend Sandie travelling to London for the first time, looking forward to all the things the capital had to offer.

I watched the people filing off the coach, hoping to recognise the couple from some of Tom's photographs, and I did. Mr Delaney was a big broad-shouldered man with frazzled steel-grey hair and a craggy square-jawed face. He wore a coat of Donegal tweed and carried the one suitcase between them. His wife by contrast was small and frail-looking, with dyed-blonde hair and glasses. They both looked a little lost as they stood there gazing around at the people rushing to and fro.

I stepped forward and walked up to them. 'Mr and Mrs Delaney? I'm Nicholas Heyward.'

They both looked at me as though they were surprised to see me or had expected someone else. 'Pleased to meet yer,' he held his hand out for a firm handshake. 'Our Tom has been telling us all about yer. We've been looking forward to meeting you but I hoped for better circumstances than these, I might just as well tell you the truth.'

I shook hands with Mrs Delaney who stared at me in such a way that I knew she was looking for Tom. 'I hope we're not putting you out too much,' she said.

'You won't be putting us out at all,' I assured her. 'It's not a big flat but you're quite welcome, as long as you don't mind.'

I managed to flag a taxi down in Buckingham Palace Road and we climbed into the back and set off for Kentish Town.

'How is Tom then?' Mr Delaney wanted to know.

'Pretty well. He's over the initial shock now and is just biding his time.'

'Happen there's not much else he can do,' nodded Mr Delaney. 'I'd like you to tell me what happened.'

'Well,' I offered them both a cigarette which they declined.

126

'Tom got to know a girl called Donna Maddon and became friendly with her. Not close, but for a while they were in each other's company—that is a fact which is not in dispute. Tom says that this relationship started phasing out around Christmas time and that he hasn't seen her since. On March 10th she was murdered at her home and, although I have no details as yet, I gather certain witnesses claim to have seen Tom about the house that day.'

'What does our Tom reckon to dat?' Mr Delaney asked sharply.

'He categorically denies it.'

'Dat's good enough for me!' Mrs Delaney said.

'Our Tom didn't kill no one, datt lad!' Mr Delaney affirmed, almost aggressively. 'He goes out of his way to avoid trouble and there's no way he'd so much as raise a fist at a woman, dat I do know.'

'He went through a lot with young Sandra.' Mrs Delaney shook her head. 'Screaming at him to help her or get her more drugs and all sorts. He never gave her so much as a belt although there's plenty as would. But our Tom was always a bit on the soft side where women are concerned.'

'So what happens nah den?' demanded her husband.

'Now is a time for preparation and waiting,' I told them. 'The police are garnering their case, which they will present before Thames Magistrates. If the magistrates decide that there's a case to answer, Tom will be committed for trial in a higher court. We then prepare our case and after that it's a matter of waiting until it actually comes to trial.'

'Your boss is doing the case, is he?' said Mr Delaney. 'I hope he's good. I want to see some bloody justice done here.'

Back at the flat I took their coats and told them to make themselves at home. They sat in the armchairs looking around uneasily while I went into the kitchen and fried up some food.

As we sat at the table over lunch I told them that I had made an appointment for them to visit Tom at the prison tomorrow afternoon. They had come a long way at much expense, despite their meagre income, just to see their son for twenty minutes, and would have to roll back North tomorrow night, leaving him behind bars. I could only imagine the anguish they must have felt. Throughout their stay they never lost their incredulity that this could be happening to them. And their main anxiety was that Tom would have to remain in jail until his innocence could be established, until he was inevitably vindicated at the trial, for they were certain he would be.

'We shall be making an application for bail at the committal proceedings,' I said. 'But I warn you not to be very hopeful. It's highly unlikely that we shall succeed.'

As the afternoon wore on they relaxed a little more. I listened as they both thought back over the years of bringing Tom up, going right back to the beginning. They were married for ten years without children. 'I always wanted a son,' Mr Delaney said. 'We thought that for some reason we might not be able to have kids.'

'It was a bad time,' his wife chipped in. 'I'd always wanted a family life, so we were really made-up when the adoption came through.'

'Then you had a daughter of your own,' I said.

'Yeh,' nodded Mr Delaney. 'Our Kathleen come along afterwards. She wanted to come down today—she thinks the weerld of our Tom. But the finances wouldn't allow for it.'

Mrs Delaney went on to ask me about my adopted background. It all seemed so different from their lives that once again it was hard to believe that Tom and I originated from the same hazy and muddled background.

'How long have yer been training to be a lawyer?' he asked.

'This is the fifth year,' I said.

'You must know all about it den,' he said. 'When will you be a finished lawyer?'

'In about a year's time, with luck.'

'Your mam and dad must be real proud of yer, Nicholas,' said Mrs Delaney. 'They've done well for yer and you've done well for them. I wish our Tom had found himself a career. It's not as if he isn't bright enough.'

'There's notten goin' for a young feller up North these days,' scoffed her husband. 'They mek 'em redundant and then call 'em social security layabouts and scroungers, but don't have the jobs to give 'em to be otherwise.'

Diane let herself into the flat at about six o'clock, just as the portable television was bombarding us with news of doom, but Diane was able to dilute all that with two bottles of cheap plonk

128

she'd brought in with her. Mrs Delaney insisted on cooking dinner. 'It'll keep me busy,' she explained. 'It'll be good to have something to do, instead of sitting here mithering.'

She served a delicious meal of liver cooked in cider, and the wine helped to pacify her tense nerves.

The conversation never strayed far from Tom.

'It's strange to think that you two brothers don't meet up for years and den when you do you wind up being called on to defend him like this,' said Mr Delaney.

'I'm glad it's somebody in a position to help,' his wife remarked. 'At least we can go home tomorrow knowing that our Tom's lawyers really care and are not in it just for the money they can get out of it.'

'It's more than strange,' I said, taking a sip of wine. 'I had no intentions of getting too deeply involved in criminal trials. I intended to specialise in chancery and company law. I find myself in a different situation these days.'

'Your job sounds interesting,' Mrs Delaney said.

'It has its moments,' I nodded. 'I never expected to feel as passionately about criminal work as I obviously do now. Thoughts of my exams have taken a back seat now that Tom is on trial. I'm beginning to see and feel the harrowing experience of being arrested, charged and remanded. It's brought it all a lot closer to me. I suppose there'll be a lesson in it somewhere.'

'You might be a better lawyer for it,' Diane suggested. 'The night we met in Leicester Square you and Tom had just discovered each other. You were a little dazed and disconcerted. I had this weird feeling then that Tom was going to be some sort of lightning conductor for your future. I had the feeling all the more when I met him myself.'

Later I invited them all out for a drink. Mrs Delaney didn't like pubs and declined the offer but I talked her husband into joining me. 'Go on, Joe,' his wife urged, 'go out and have a drink, for bloody hell's sake!'

I took him for a walk up Brecknock Road to a quiet pub where a colour TV showing a football match had all the men in the pub mesmerised.

'What will you have to drink, Mr Delaney?'

'Call me Joe, lad, for Chrissake,' he said. 'And I'll get these.' We sat on stools at the counter and he bought two pints of bitter.

129

'This London ale is not much cop,' he complained dispassionately. 'You need fucken courage ter drink it. Still, it's better than notten. How long you known young Diane, then? She seems like a nice gurl, friendly, like. A lot of 'em down here are a bit on the stuck-up side.'

'It must be getting on for two years now, though we've only been living there for about six months. Doesn't time fly when you're having fun?'

'How much d'you pay for dat place? If you don't mind me askin'.'

I told him and he whistled. 'It's dear down here, I'll say thatt. I don't think I'd like to live in London. I cahn't really understand what our Tom sees in it. When he came up for Christmas, after a few days I could tell he was a bit restless. He wanted to come back just after Boxing Day but I talked him into stopping for the New Year. But I don't think he was sorry to be wiping Liverpool off his feet. If he'd have stayed where he was he might not be in this bloody fix, though I don't suppose you can blame the lad.'

'He wants to broaden his horizons in his own peculiar style,' I said. 'Although I can't help thinking he should go a different way about it.'

'When this is all over we'll all have to get together and have a party, our family and yourn,' he said a little more cheerfully. 'We'll have to watch out for Tom, though. He can be a sod when he's pissed.'

When it's all over, I thought. He's already planning the celebration because the outcome is a dead certainty. Before any of us, he knows the verdict. When it's all over ... He hadn't yet grasped the fact that it was only just beginning.

130

Chapter Fourteen

One morning in May I arrived at the office to find a box of documents had been delivered by the Director of Public Prosecutions. I glanced down at the label which read 'Regina v. Thomas G. Delaney', then I tore open the straps and took out the bundle of papers. On the top was a copy of the indictment. Then there were statements made by a series of witnesses: firemen, policemen, doctors, pathologists, civilians; and at the bottom of the pile I came to a catalogue of glossy black-and-white photographs. They showed exterior and interior shots of Donna's house in Narrow Way. Then I turned to a photograph that turned my stomach. Donna lay flat out on the carpet, her head broken, her mouth open and the pupils of her eyes only half-visible from under her eyelids so that mostly only the whites of her eyes showed. All life had been battered out of her. The next photo was even more harrowing. It was a close-up of her face, with the wound and those grotesque dead eyes. I shuddered at the disgusting violence of it.

I carried the documents into Jake's office. He hadn't arrived yet so I sat in his chair and started reading the statements.

I was becoming more and more immersed in them when the door opened and Jake entered the room with his briefcase, Crombie and hair flattened to his head with rainwater.

'You look wet,' I said abstractedly, my real concentration still on the last statement I'd just read. 'Still raining?'

'What makes the boy think it's still raining?' Jake appealed to the filing cabinets, taking off his saturated coat. 'Don't I always swim up the river Thames to work every morning, what else? Shmock! And why are you sitting in my chair, pray tell?'

'I'm reading the depositions in Delaney,' I said. 'They arrived this morning.'

131

'Leave all that to me, Nicholas, if you please. I'll tell you when to get busy on this. In the meantime I've got a lot of other jobs for you to do. The first is that I want you to go round the corner and purchase twenty Players for me. Then I want you to instruct Susan to make me a cup of coffee and serve it together with two chocolate biscuits. When you've done that I want you to take the Buy Car file to the High Court and keep Tony Marriott company.'

So I spent most of that day sitting behind a boring old barrister waffling about damages in a civil case at the High Court. The best I could do was doodle in my notebook, wondering whether or not Jake was sitting in his office reading the police evidence against my brother.

Joe and Mae Delaney had returned to Liverpool after seeing their son in Brixton, even more convinced of his innocence. Mae was in tears but Joe was upright and defensive, as though somebody had insulted him. 'Thatt lad no more killed dis woman dan I flew about in the air,' he remonstrated with a tough don't-you-try-and-do-me-down voice. 'He's innocent and we want everything done for him, Nicholas. He shouldn't be in that prison at all.'

'When it comes to trial you'll be welcome to stay with us,' I told them. 'And feel free to come down any time you like.'

'Dat cahn't be as often as we'd like—with the work situation as it is,' he confessed. 'But we'll certainly take you up on that when the trial starts. We'll be here to stand by him then, don't worry. Nobody up our way who knows him believes he did this, and they're all rooting for him ...'

Four days after perusing the depositions Jake and I drove off to Brixton Prison. His Rover seemed to float through the London traffic, and sunlight glinted on the swirling river as we drove across London Bridge. We left the car not far from the prison and walked to the prison gate, a depressing sight that I was well used to by now. Jake rang the bell and hammered on the door. A uniformed man let us in and we marched into the reception, Jake taking the letter of authority from his inside pocket.

'Was that you banging on the door, sir?' demanded one of the warders in an aggressive tone.

'Yes,' replied Jake, a little taken aback—so was I.

'Did you have to knock as loudly as that?' the warder wanted to know.

Immediately I became angry myself, but Jake was livid.

'I wasn't aware that the Home Secretary had laid down any legislation concerning the volume of knocking on prison doors,' he replied stiffly. 'I trust that I did not wake anybody up!'

The warder's voice melted. 'Well, they're heavy doors, they are, sir. You don't have to knock hard.'

'The door is still there. I was trying to enter, not escape.' Jake threw the envelope down in front of the man. 'And I would advise you that I am an officer of the court and would be obliged if you addressed me with due respect.'

The extraordinary warder opened the envelope and made no further comment as he read Markbyss's letter authorising us to interview Tom.

We were taken across to the legal visits wing. As we walked through the hazy sunshine of the prison courtyard I felt as though I'd come a long way from my first prison interview.

Locked inside the legal block we signed in and were shown into the glass interview booth. Jake took from his briefcase his notebooks and two sets of depositions, plus a packet of cigarettes. We smoked one each before Tom was finally brought in.

They shook hands and Jake asked him how he was.

'Not too bad,' he answered. 'Biding me time. The nightmare quality of bein' here isn't as relentless as it was in the beginning. But, by Christ, I'll be glad when sumpin happens. I feel suspended from life in here.'

'Well, take a seat there and we'll get started on these depositions,' Jake said as we settled down around the table. 'Cigarette? ... Now, I've got here two sets of depositions, which the Director of Public Prosecutions have furnished us with. I'll be leaving one set here for you to read at leisure and of course we'll discuss at a later date any points that you subsequently have to make. But meanwhile I want to take a preliminary statement from you for our own purposes.'

Jake headed the first page of his notebook: 'Statement of Thomas Gerard Delaney who will say as follows'. In response to Goldberg's questions Tom gave him details of his juvenile criminal record, his employment status, and his relationship with Donna and her common-law husband, who Tom wanted us to check out. 'This guy has got a history of violence. Donna was dead scared he'd find her. He loved his kids and she was worried

133

he'd want to get back at her for takin' them away from him. I'd like all tha' checked out.'

'I want you to turn to page 33 in your bundle and read the statement of Kevin Galveston, who apparently lives in the basement of 22 Narrow Way,' said Jake. 'Do you know this man?'

'I've met him a few times,' Tom said, turning to the relevant page. He read the statement of Galveston, who had told the police that around tea time he heard what sounded like Tom arguing with Donna in her room and he claimed to have seen Tom leaving the house about an hour later. He also discovered the fire in the house, although that was much later in the evening.

Tom was incredulous. 'Why is the guy sayin' all thatt? It's a load of shite—he never saw me there or anywhere near the place. Like Donna, I haven't seen this bastard since before Christmas.'

'Why do you think he told the police otherwise?' asked Jake.

'I've no idea but it's a load of fucking lies!' he thumped the statement down on the table. 'What's going on here? I don't understand what they're trying to do.'

'This man has positively identified you as being there at around six o'clock in the evening,' said Goldberg. 'The medical evidence has indicated that the girl died between 6.00 and 10.00 pm. If this man is lying why has he chosen you as a scapegoat? Had you ever argued with him over anything?'

'No,' said Tom. 'I didn't know the guy all that well. When I used to call up and see her last year he'd often be in her living room, sitting there smoking dope and chatting her up. Donna and me would be going out for a drink and he'd sometimes invite himself along.'

'Did that annoy you?'

'Not at feerst. There was notten between me and Donna so it didn't matter a damn to me whether he got into her pants or not. He just got to be a bit of a bore, thatt's all. He was a fantasy artist. He'd been around the world, roadying for the Beatles and Rolling Stones and every famous rock band you could name from the sixties til now. He'd knocked off dis, dat and the other tasty lady, and he'd done everything. He was the kind of dreamer thatt had done everything and couldn't see how ludicrous and unconvincing he sounded. I felt sorry for him more than anything else but in the end we started avoidin' him. He seemed harmless

134

and he had this thing about Donna, which she just laughed off. She said, "His heart's in the right place. His brain I'm not so sure about." And there's no way I could get from Old Ford to Stoke Newington thatt quickly unless I had a car which I haven't got.'

'Why did you stop seeing the girl?'

'There was no mileage in the relationship. We were friends, thatt was all, there was no heavy scene. I went up to Liverpool at Christmas and didn't see her again. I went around a couple of times in January but she wasn't there. Then I heard thatt she'd started a scene with some guy so I didn't go round there again. I didn't have much money anyway.'

'You arrived at the Cat O' Nine Tails Club at seven, stayed until ten and then you left for Spitalfields. That was early to leave on a weekend evening, why did you?'

'Like I said, cash problems. I only went up to the club to collar a guy who owed me some money, but he didn't turn up so I had to borrow some instead. Then I was feelin' restless thatt night and didn't want to go home, so I walked back to Bethnal Green, had a coffee in the Majestic Café and then took a stroll up Spitalfields, via Brick Lane. But at the time this mysterious bastard was topping Donna I was in Stoke Newington—I'm well covered for thatt!' he waved his cigarette over Galveston's statement.

'Let's turn to the police statements,' Jake said. 'You've given me your account of what took place in the police station and it differs in many respects from the statements made by these officers themselves. That's to be expected. Let's just see how they differ.'

'If this Haskins guy reported that he kneed me in the bollocks and twisted me fingers then he'd be tellin' you the truth,' Tom snarled. 'But if he hasn't mentioned it he's a lying double-faced clone. I guess everybody'll believe him over me.'

As expected, nearly all of the police statements differed in most respects from the one that Tom had given us an hour before. DI Haskins, DS Meade and TDC Villiers all offered identical statements that contradicted Tom's. Tom challenged these statements word for word although he accepted that Chief Superintendent Balfour's impressions of his interview with him was only slightly inaccurate.

Tom explained that he was scared that night. Apart from the police, nobody knew where he was. Once inside the station he felt as though he was never going to be free again. At various points during the first twenty-four hours his clothes were taken away and he was questioned relentlessly by Haskins and Villiers and then the others. He realised that they were out to trap him and he was on his own against them. On the second day he was so tired and harassed that he wanted to give himself up just to get them off his back, so that he could sleep or have a cigarette. The psychological warfare, the taking of his clothes, the walls that sealed him off from the rest of the world, the double act of Mr Nice and Mr Nasty conducting interrogations, their conviction that he was guilty all made him feel condemned already and it seemed that this experience would not end until they'd heard what they wanted to hear. The fact that they could not legally hold him for longer than forty-eight hours was lost on him in his confused and bullied state. In a moment of desperation and disorientation he nearly gave in to them, then an hour later retracted the verbal statement now recorded in the police statements.

It took Jake two hours to go through these verbals, making notes of Tom's dismissal of much of the dialogue, which he claimed never took place. By the time we had finished he had almost rewritten the three statements made by Haskins, Meade and Villiers.

'We'll finish here for the time being.' Jake closed his notebook. 'I want you to take these deps back to your cell and read them carefully, as I know you will. No doubt we'll have more to talk about when I see you again.' He stuffed his papers back into his case as we stood up. 'One more point, Tom. The hammer that killed Donna had your name scrawled on the handle and the police have taken away from your home a selection of tools with similar marks notched on them.'

'I forgot all aboutt thatt,' Tom tensed up again. 'It was a bit of a shock when the pleece showed it to me, I left it at Donna's gaff after doin' a job for her last summer, like. I just forgot all aboutt it.'

'All right. We'll go into that a little more the next time I see you. Try not to worry too much.'

'Thatt's not easy,' Tom seemed agitated again, now that the afternoon away from the cells was gone and we were about to leave him behind.

'We'll be in touch soon,' Jake shook hands with him again.

'T'anks Mr Goldberg. It's a relief to see some of the wheels goin' round at last.'

'I'm sure it is,' Jake smiled.

'I'll see you at the weekend,' I gripped his arm as Jake opened the door. 'Diane and I will be up as usual.'

'I'll look forward to thatt,' he smiled.

'I've just been thinking—would you like me to get in touch with Rendezvous House?'

'No. I don't want her to know anything about all this. If she knew she'd leave Rendezvous House and try to get to see me. It would fuck both our heads up and neither of us need thatt. It's best to leave thatt alone.'

'Okay,' I nodded. 'See you on Saturday then.'

Jake and I signed out and as we were getting our passes back I looked up to see the large warder leading Tom back into the prison.

Chapter Fifteen

One afternoon in August I came into the general office from lunch and Greta handed me the two briefs that she had finished typing and asked me to deliver them to the Temple.

REGINA *v.* DELANEY

BRIEF TO COUNSEL

To Mr John Faconti QC
  2 Pump Court,
  Temple EC4

               (with you Mr Scott Hilliard)

Instructing solicitors are concerned on behalf of the defendant Thomas Gerard Delaney, an unemployed labourer aged 22 who resides at 450 New Road, London E1.

The Defendant is charged on an indictment containing three counts:

Count 1: That on 10 March 1981 he unlawfully murdered Donna Maddon at 22 Narrow Way, London E3, within the jurisdiction of the Central Criminal Court

Count 2: That on 10 March 1981 he did commit arson with intent to endanger life at 22 Narrow Way, London E3

138

Count 3: That on 1 April 1981 he did assault Detective Inspector Michael Haskins at Doughty Road Police Station.

The brief ran on for some fifty pages, relating the prosecution case and then providing the answer to it, regularly referring to all the statements on either side. The statement by Tom challenged the police, fifteen statements from the Cat O' Nine Tails Club challenged the statement of Kevin Galveston. Paragraph by paragraph, allegation by allegation, Jake dealt with each statement.

'... it would seem that the witness Galveston had taken a somewhat more than passing interest in Donna Maddon. Instructing solicitors take the view that it would be useful to explore this relationship in view of possible animosity that may have existed between this witness and the defendant. Counsel will note that although Mr Galveston told the police that he had seen the defendant at 22 Narrow Way during the last two weeks prior to the murder neither Mr and Mrs Taylor nor the dead woman's children are able to confirm this ...

'... The defendant does not dispute the fact that the hammer belongs to him. In view of the fact that no fingerprints were found on the weapon counsel may think it unlikely that the killer would have left behind such incriminating evidence, locking himself out of the room, after having taken the trouble to wipe the hammer clean. The defendant's explanation seems much more feasible ...'

The brief went on, finally ending with the words: 'Will counsel please attend the Central Criminal Court and obtain an acquittal.'

I took both copies of the brief and stepped out into Gracechurch Passage, carrying the bundles of red-taped documents under my arm, and walked through Leadenhall Market. The August sunshine beamed as far as it could into the alleyways and passages of the Market. I remembered the evening last autumn when a raggeddy-arsed devil had walked through here with me, claiming to be my flesh and blood.

I flagged a cab down in Cornhill and sat in the back, loosening my tie as I watched the City spin past in the heat. Office girls walked along in summery dresses, reminding me of the freedom that I hoped would be Tom's. As the cab drove along Queen Victoria Street I recognised the sense of anticipation and the rush of adrenalin that I'd experienced on the night all this began. We were getting closer and closer to what could be the turning point of Tom's life and the climax of my career so far.

I looked out at the river Thames, sparkling and swirling in the sunlight, before the taxi turned into Middle Temple Lane.

It's a vision that sticks in my memory, climbing up the musty staircase to Faconti's chambers and handing the brief to his clerk, before delivering the copy set to Scott Hilliard in Essex Court. Back out into the sunshine of the Temple I strolled past the fountain, feeling at once light-hearted and apprehensive, uncertain as to how things were going to turn out. There was nothing to do but wait. All that could be done had been done. And yet had it? I wondered as I gazed at the fountain. I could see nothing that Jake or I or anybody else could do. From now on it would be a battle of the barristers, jumping up and down like a black-and-white Punch and Judy show in the wooden theatre of the court.

There was a certain judge who often presided over trials at the Bailey who was considered an out-and-out bastard. I reckon there must be many a lawyer and client whose hearts must have sunk when told that their trial was to go before him. Most of his career had been spent prosecuting and now that he was on the bench most of his sympathies lay with the prosecuting counsel. He was an old stickler for law and order, and even in these days of headlines about corrupt policemen he did not take kindly to allegations made against them. Some time during that summer Jake had lunch in Ludgate Hill with a shadowy figure from the Clerk of the Lists office. They had known each other well over the years and Jake brought this man's attention to the case of Delaney. The upshot of the meeting was that the man promised to do what he could to keep Regina *v.* Delaney out of this judge's list.

140

Chapter Sixteen

Jake and I arrived at the Old Bailey at 10.15 on a Monday morning. Court number one was full of strange impartial faces preparing for the proceedings. Barristers were undoing their red-taped bundles and spreading their papers out in front of them, chatting and joking amongst themselves. The shorthand writer was taking her place, the Clerk of the Court was flicking through bundles of paper and the court usher was flitting in and out trying to look important. At the centre of the court room, between the barristers' benches and just under the clerk of the court's desk, was the solicitors' table, where Jake and I seated ourselves opposite a rather attractive blonde lady from the DPP's office.

I looked around and looked around twice as Tom came up into the dock accompanied by a warder. For a moment I hardly recognised him. He was wearing the burgundy suit and white shirt that I had loaned him, his long dishevelled hair was cut short and looked tidy, and his chin was smooth and clean-shaven, making him look younger than he was rather than older as before. He looked like a clean-cut boy instead of a stray. It was a suggestion that Faconti had made when he, Scott Hilliard and Jake had gone to see Tom at the prison.

The rustling of papers and the hubbub of unconcerned conversation ceased abruptly at the sound of knocking on the door and the call to 'Be Upstanding!' Mr Justice Cassidy entered the court as the bailiff bellowed out to all those who having any business before the Central Criminal Court on this day should draw near and give their attention. Everybody in the court except Tom bowed to the judge, who bowed back and sat down and so did the rest of us.

The Clerk of the Court stood up and Tom was told to stand, then the Clerk read the indictment to him and took a note of his

141

answers: Not Guilty.

Matthew Wetherby QC got to his feet. 'M'lord, I appear for the prosecution in this matter, assisted by my learned friend Miss Cavendish. The defendant is represented by my learned friend Mr Faconti, assisted by my learned friend Mr Hilliard ...'

And the rest of that morning was consumed by jury selection and the taking of oaths and undertakings to try the issue before them fairly. Mr Faconti called, 'Challenge!' twice, and the prospective jurors, both middle-aged men of the old-school appearance, stepped down and were replaced by two women in their early thirties. By the time the jury of three women and nine men were assembled it was one o'clock and the judge adjourned the court for lunch.

At two o'clock Mr Wetherby opened the prosecution's case by introducing himself and his learned friends to the jury and informing them as to who the defendant was and what he was charged with. Joe and Mae Delaney sat up in the gallery and looked down on what to them was a remote and alien scene with characters in absurd costume about to debate their son's fate.

'Members of the jury,' Wetherby went on, 'it is my job to present to you the facts of this case upon which you will hear evidence from a number of witnesses. During the course of this trial you will hear that at some time during 1979 the defendant Delaney made the acquaintance of a woman called Donna Maddon. Miss Maddon was the 29-year-old unmarried mother of two young children—Tracy aged eleven and Steven aged four. At the time she met the defendant she was living with the father of her children in the Spitalfields area of London. Her common-law husband was a man known to the police as a drug dealer, and he was also an acquaintance or contact of Mr Delaney. Miss Maddon was known to be weary of her boyfriend's lifestyle and wished to remove her children from such an environment. She wished to find alternative accommodation and provide a better life for her family but this proved easier said than done. This unfortunate young mother was faced with a choice between the devil and the deep-blue sea. In her desperation she turned to Mr Delaney for help. Delaney himself resided in a house in New Road, Whitechapel. It was an illegal occupation commonly known as a 'squat'. He had neither the landlord's permission to be there nor

142

that of the landlord's agents. He shared this property with several people, including his common-law wife and mother of his child, who was a barbiturate addict and had often bought drugs from Miss Maddon's boyfriend, as had Mr Delaney. In fact it was no secret that in some circles Miss Maddon's boyfriend had sold Mr Delaney's girlfriend some dud drugs and it was known that Mr Delaney was very angry concerning this. The defendant himself has not disputed this but has in fact confirmed it.

'The help that Mr Delaney offered Donna Maddon was to "open up a squat" for her until "something could be sorted out with the council". Mr Delaney after a short interval found an empty house which was 22 Narrow Way near Old Ford. Together with a friend he broke into the house and replaced the lock the same day with a Yale lock of his own. Within that day Donna Maddon and her children had moved into the house and settled in the rooms on the first floor of the house. Over the next few months a young married couple by the name of Taylor were invited to move into the ground-floor rooms and then later a man called Kevin Galveston took possession of the top floor.

'You will hear that during the afternoon of 10 March 1981 Mrs Taylor met Donna Maddon leaving the house. Donna Maddon told Mrs Taylor that her children were staying the weekend with her mother in Dagenham and that she was just going down to Whitechapel to pay Tom a visit. Mrs Taylor did not see Donna Maddon again but at five o'clock that evening she and her husband both heard voices from Miss Maddon's room above. They were able to identify Miss Maddon's voice but not that of the man she appeared to be having an argument with. After something like half an hour the voices died down and there was some door-slamming. No more voices were heard but much later, at eleven o'clock, they heard a bumping sound on the floor. That was the last sound they heard that night from Donna Maddon's flat.

'You will also hear evidence from Mr Galveston, a GPO telephone engineer, who had a room upstairs. Like the Taylors and the Maddons, he had resorted to squatting because of difficulties in finding accommodation in London within his price range. He also heard the sound of an argument or raised voices coming from Donna's rooms, but he, having made the defendant's acquaintance during the period that Donna and Mr

Delaney had been seeing each other, was able to recognise the defendant's voice. He places the argument at about 5.15 in the evening. Later, at 6.15, he heard the front door slam and happened to glance out of the window. He saw the defendant Thomas Delaney leaving the house and walking down Narrow Way towards Bethnal Green. When Mr Galveston comes to give evidence you will hear that he is quite clear about that.

'Members of the Jury, it was at about 11.30 pm that Mr Galveston returned from an evening out. He felt sure that he could smell burning. He decided to investigate and a few minutes later discovered smoke pouring out of a disused airing cupboard on the first-floor landing. Immediately he knocked on Donna Maddon's door in order to alert her to the fire. He received no response and when he tried to open the door he discovered it was locked. He went downstairs to warn the Taylors and then dashed out of the house and ran to a public telephone box where he made an emergency call for the assistance of the fire brigade. You will hear that this call was logged at 11.40 pm.

'The fire brigade arrived at 11.45 and were told by the Taylors that there was a woman on the top floor who might have taken sleeping pills and could not hear the attempts that had been made to warn her of the fire. Mrs Taylor was sure that Miss Maddon was there because of the sound she claimed to have heard earlier.

'When the officers reached the first-floor landing the smoke was already dense and when Fire Officer Walker banged on the door he received no response. He decided to break the lock off the door. He entered the smoky room, and discovered Donna Maddon lying on the floor. She was clearly dead.

'At 12.00 Detective Inspector Michael Haskins, Detective Sergeant Meade and Temporary Detective Constable Villiers arrived at the address. They interviewed the occupants of the house and soon after, the Divisional doctor, Dr Greenwood, arrived and examined the body. His preliminary examinations showed that Donna Maddon had died as a result of blows to the head caused by a blunt instrument and he estimated the time of death as being between 6.00 and 9.00 pm.

'A murder inquiry was underway, supervised by Chief Superintendent Angus Balfour, who set up a murder incident room at nearby Doughty Road Police Station. The police set about trying to contact as many of Donna Maddon's associates as possible. During the course of their inquiries they heard that Miss Maddon's recent male companion was one Thomas Delaney. They discovered Miss Maddon's connection with drug dealing. They heard about the occasion on which Mr Delaney bought some drugs from Miss Maddon and her boyfriend and discovered that the capsules contained nothing but talcum powder. At the time Miss Maddon was murdered her boyfriend was serving a six-month prison sentence at Wormwood Scrubs Prison, and this effectively eliminated him from police inquiries. They then became anxious to interview Mr Delaney himself.

'Mr Delaney was interviewed by DI Haskins and DS Meade at his home in New Road at 6.30 pm on March 30th. He was asked of his whereabouts on the night of the 10th. He replied "I don't remember." He was urged to think hard but was still unable to recall his whereabouts or activities of that night. He was asked when he last saw Donna Maddon. He replied, "Just before last Christmas." DI Haskins said, "We have been given information by various members of the public that you have seen her more recently than that." Delaney said, "They're mistaken. I haven't seen her for a few months now." Haskins said, "You are quite sure you have not been near 22 Narrow Way recently?" Delaney said, "I called there two or three times in January but she was never in and I haven't been back."

'DI Haskins concluded his interview and asked Delaney if he would continue to help them with their inquiries at Doughty Road Police Station. The defendant agreed.

'At 8.30 that evening he was interviewed by Chief Superintendent Balfour in the presence of DI Haskins. Chief Superintendent Balfour said, "Witnesses have told us that Donna Maddon left the house on the afternoon of the 10th saying that she was on her way to pay you a visit in New Road. Did she arrive?" Delaney said, "No," and repeated that he hadn't seen her lately. Balfour said, "Where were you at about five o'clock that evening?" Delaney said, "I think I was at home reading. I didn't go out that day as far as I can remember." Balfour said, "Is there anybody who can corroborate that?" Delaney said, "No, I was alone, everybody else in the house was at work during the day and out during the evening."

'During the night of the 30th March and 31st March Delaney

145

was interviewed again at various times, and at 2.15 am on 1st April he was again interviewed by DI Haskins, DS Meade and TDC Villiers who took the notes of the interview. Haskins asked Delaney to think again about his whereabouts and activities on the night in question. It was suggested to him that he had actually been at Narrow Way that evening. He replied, "No way." It was then put to him that he had been identified by a witness as leaving the house at about 6.15. Delaney said, "Whoever told you that is a fucking liar." Haskins then said to Delaney, "I believe you know something about this murder," at which point Delaney became excited and lashed his fist out at Haskins, catching him on the jaw. He was restrained by officers Meade and Villiers.

'During the following day Delaney was shown the murder weapon—a hammer with a notch carved on the end of the handle with the name Tom inscribed in indelible ink. Balfour asked the defendant, "Have you ever seen this before?" Delaney said, "Yes. It belongs to me." Balfour said, "It was found on the floor under a chair in Donna's room. It was used to kill her. How do you think it came to be there?" Delaney said, "Before Christmas I took some tools over to her place and put some shelves up for her. I left the tools there because we were going out and I didn't want to drag them around the pubs with me. Afterwards I just kept forgetting to pick them up. I meant to but always forgot." Balfour said, "Why didn't you use the tools that were already there?" Delaney replied that Miss Maddon had no tools of her own. Balfour said, "But we found a tool box that contained at least four hammers of various sizes as well as a number of other tools." Delaney said, "She told me she had no tools."

'During that afternoon officers returned to the defendant's *squat* in New Road and took away certain articles of clothing and a number of tools. Among the tools were several with the name Tom marked on the handles in the same way as it is on the murder weapon.

'On 2nd April at 3.30 am Chief Superintendent Balfour charged Mr Delaney in the presence of his solicitor, and then cautioned him. He told the defendant, "You are not obliged to say anything but anything you do say will be taken down and given in evidence." As was his prerogative entirely, Delaney made no comment.'

146

The ten-day procession of prosecution witnesses began. They were sworn in, examined-in-chief by Mr Wetherby and cross-examined by Mr Faconti, who had a loud, clear and almost amiable voice. The fireman said that the airing cupboard was nearly gutted, having caught fire from smouldering rags. The fire had not spread any further. His evidence was followed by that of the doctors who had examined the body. They described the multiple fractures of the skull, plus bruises and serious damage to the right eye. Then the detectives were called. DI Haskins was given leave to refer to his notebook and to the notes he made at the time of the arrest. For an hour or more Wetherby took him through his notes and statements; Haskins' account was of course still at odds with Tom's.

When Wetherby finally sat down Faconti got to his feet and another hour and a half's worth got underway as Faconti tried to pick the bones out of three-quarters of the statements.

'Could you please turn to page 5 of your statement, which is page 40 in everybody else's bundle, I think,' Faconti said. Everybody in court turned to the relevant page. 'Now here you say, "I said to Delaney: I urge you to do yourself a favour and think hard about that night. Witnesses suggest that you were in Narrow Way around the time of the murder." In fact you had only one witness who had made a statement to that effect, I think?'

'Yes, sir.'

'And not witnesses in the plural?'

'That is correct, sir.'

'Your statement goes on to say that my client responded, "Whoever told you that has either dropped a bollock or is an out-and-out fucking liar." You replied, you say, "I believe that you know something about this murder." This was the prelude to the alleged assault on you, is that correct?'

'Yes, sir.'

'But were these the exact words used?'

'Yes, sir.'

'Did you not say to my client, "If anybody is a fucking liar it is you"?'

'No, I did not, sir.'

'And then did you not say, "Why should we believe you scrounging, social security layabouts that come down here

147

poncing off the state? You northern layabouts are all the same. We work day and night so the likes of you can sleep all day"?'

Haskins shook his head and smiled. 'No sir, I said nothing that was remotely like it.'

'And was it not at this point that my client, who had been in custody for over twenty-four hours, being questioned by high-ranking police officers about the death of a friend of his, and was therefore upset and under a lot of stress, was it not then that he became excited and had to be calmed down by the other two officers?'

'He got excited all right,' nodded the witness.

'I put it to you that his hands came nowhere near you and that he merely started shouting about the injustice of your comments in the light of crippling unemployment and its hardships, not to mention the injustice of your accusations.'

'That is incorrect, sir. He lashed out at my jaw. Later on he ...'

'Just a moment, officer. I know you want to get to the bits you like the best but do bear with me for the moment.' The judge gave Faconti a stern look but said nothing, although the jury seemed amused. 'Did you at any time strike my client?'

'No, sir.'

'Did any other officer strike him?'

'Not to my knowledge, sir.'

'My client's outbursts did not inspire you to knee him in the groin perhaps? Or twist his fingers a little?'

'Certainly not!'

'And then did you not say, "You're shaping up very nicely, Tom. We're gonna have you for breakfast in the morning."'

'No, sir.'

'Who took the notes of this interview.'

'TDC Villiers, sir.'

'And you made up your own notes afterwards? How long afterwards?'

'Ten to twenty minutes.'

'And you have the infallible memory of a police officer of twenty years' experience—who never forgets a word spoken in a police interview, no matter how long afterwards the notes are made up!'

'A police officer may not be infallible, sir, but he's different from other people in that he's trained to remember things,' said

148

the detective.

'Indeed,' said Faconti. 'Did you, DS Meade and TDC Villiers make up your notes individually or collectively?'

'We discussed them afterwards.'

'You conferred with each other, jogging each other's memories?'

'We certainly discussed things to make sure nothing had been left out.'

'My suggestion is that many things were left out,' said Faconti. 'Would it be true to say that the three statements by Meade, Villiers and yourself come out of a sort of boiling pot stirred by the recollections of the three of you?'

'No, sir, that would not be true.'

All of the policemen came and left the witness box after hours of examinations-in-chief, cross-examinations and re-examinations on the content of the verbal statements. Mr Faconti was an attacker but the experienced officers would not be browbeaten.

During the second week of the trial Mrs Taylor, a teacher, was called into the witness box. Wetherby elicited from her the information she had given in the statement which he had mentioned in opening the case for the prosecution

In cross-examination Mr Faconti asked her, 'So apart from Donna's allusion to seeing Tom in Whitechapel that afternoon you had not heard anything about my client since January?'

'That's right.'

'And she gave you no indication as to why she wished to see my client?'

'No, she didn't say.'

'Are you in a position to say that the man she later argued with was my client?'

'No. I couldn't say that it was him.'

'And neither you or your husband saw Tom there that day or even that month?'

'No, we didn't.'

'Thank you, Mrs Taylor.'

The prosecution case lasted for two weeks. I sat in the middle of it, my adrenalin heating me up like a kettle, dying to get to the defence. I admired Faconti's deportment and slight flamboyance, the ability to think and argue on the spur of the moment. His voice was full of life and if anybody was nodding off he was out to wake them.

Jake looked in from time to time to see how things were developing. One morning, when Kevin Galveston, the last of the prosecution witnesses, was giving evidence I looked up to see the swing doors open and Jake tiptoed in. He bowed slightly to the bench, then tiptoed to counsel's bench and handed a document to Scott Hilliard. He tiptoed back to the door, bowed again and was gone. Mr Hilliard leaned forward again and handed the documents to Faconti.

After some time Galveston finished giving his evidence-in-chief and Faconti rose to the occasion.

'Mr Galveston. You told my learned friend that you heard Donna quarrelling with a man in her room and you say you recognised my client's voice!'

'Yes.'

'But you were not able to hear the individual words that were being shouted?'

'No.'

'Where were you when you heard these voices?'

'I was in the bathroom.'

'That is on the ground floor, the floor below Donna Maddon's flat?'

'Yes.'

'How well did you know my client?'

'Not very well. I met him a couple of times when he came up to see Donna, when they were going together. We had a drink once or twice.'

'And when would you say was the last time that you were in each other's company?'

'Last November or early December I should think.'

'Quite a period in time in fact. So let us pause and clarify a point. You are telling the court that on March 10th you were in the bathroom on the floor below Donna Maddon's flat. Two people, Donna and my client, were arguing. You were not able to hear their words but you were able to identify the voice of a man you had met only a few times, and even then not since last November, not for some three or four months.'

'Yes.'

'But if you were close enough to identify the voices which

150

were shouting, how is it that you were not close enough to hear what they were shouting about?'

'I recognised his tone of voice, that sort of lilting Liverpool accent. I wasn't really interested in what they were arguing the toss about.'

'Indeed?' Faconti shook his head sceptically. 'You have told us that an hour or so after the argument you looked out of your basement window and saw my client leaving the house looking a little ruffled, as though he had been in a struggle.'

'That's right.'

'I think,' said Mr Faconti, 'that it is an established fact that however Miss Maddon came to her death there was no sign of any struggle. You also told the police that you had not seen Miss Maddon for about a week prior to the murder—Saturday, 4th March in fact.'

'Yes.'

Mr Faconti picked up the document that Jake had just brought in. 'Mr Galveston, do you know a public house called the Four Lanterns, in Wapping?'

'Yes.'

'You know this pub well in fact!'

'Not well. I have a drink there from time to time.'

'Did you ever go there with Donna Maddon?'

'I think so. Yes. Yes I did, now I think about it.'

'How often would you say? Regularly?'

'From time to time,' the witness shifted a little in the witness box.

'When was the last time you took Miss Maddon to the Four Lanterns?'

'Er—February, I think.'

'February! Not March?'

'No, not March.'

'Did you go to the Four Lanterns yourself at any time during the week of the murder?'

'It's hard to remember that far back. I might have called in there for a drink on the Tuesday night.'

'What about Friday lunch time. Did you not call in for a drink at Friday lunch time?'

'No, sir.'

'You are sure of that?'

151

'Yes.'

'Mr Galveston, I must put it to you that at lunch time on Friday 10th March both you and Donna Maddon went to the Four Lanterns together.'

'That's wrong.'

'And that neither of you were in the best of tempers.'

'That is also wrong.'

'And that you were seen there by a number of people who overheard you and Miss Maddon arguing at a table on the verandah overlooking the river.'

'I wasn't there.'

'I see,' Mr Faconti said facetiously, before allowing a pregnant pause to be absorbed by the court.

'How would you describe your relationship with Miss Maddon?'

The witness shrugged his shoulders. 'Friendly.'

'Did you ever sleep with her?'

'No.'

'Did you ever boast to a man called Robert Wallace that you had slept with her and that you were, quote, "getting it on with her," unquote?'

'What does that mean?' the judge asked, pretending that he didn't know.

'Developing a relationship of an intimate nature, m'lord,' Faconti explained.

'One hears such extraordinary vernacular in court these days,' waffled Mr Justice Cassidy. 'Yes, yes, go on. Answer the question.'

'No, I never said that to anyone,' said Mr Galveston.

'Give the jury some idea as to how many times you took Miss Maddon out.'

'A few times. About half a dozen, a dozen.'

'Over a period of how long?'

'January and February.'

'Perhaps a dozen times in two months then. Quite regularly. What were your reasons for taking Miss Maddon out so often?'

'I don't know.'

'Come now!' demanded the QC. 'Are you in the habit of doing things without knowing the reasons?'

'No, sir.'

'Then why did you take Miss Maddon out for drinks perhaps a dozen times over a period of two short months?'

'I dunno. I suppose we were a bit lonely.'

'A bit lonely,' echoed Faconti. 'How long, Mr Galveston, had you been entertaining designs of your own on this unfortunate young woman?'

'I don't know what you're getting at.'

'How long had you been interested in starting a relationship of some sort with her?' Mr Faconti demanded impatiently.

'I never thought about it.'

'I suggest that you did sir. It is my contention that you made advances to Miss Maddon on many occasions and that late last year you were discouraged by the presence of my client in her life.'

'No way,' the witness shook his head adamantly.

'You have told us that you saw Donna Maddon regularly during the first two months of the year but in March you did not see her during the week of the murder. Why was this?'

'She told me she had to go and see Tom because she thought she was pregnant. I just didn't see her about after that.'

'In fact, as the post-mortem report shows, she was not pregnant.'

'That's what she told me.'

'Why did she confide in you when it appears that she confided in no other person on this matter?'

'I don't know, sir.'

'Was it not because at the time of the murder you were Donna Maddon's lover?'

'No, sir!'

'I suggest that for reasons best known to yourself you have told a series of lies ever since the murder investigation got underway. The truth is that you have not seen Thomas Delaney since last November until today!'

'I have!'

'And the truth is that you certainly did not see or hear him at 22 Narrow Way on the tenth day of March at any time.'

'He was there, I'm sure of it!'

'You have lied about the nature of your relationship with Donna Maddon and your claim that you did not see her during the week in question is another nonsense, isn't it?'

153

'No,' Mr Galveston almost gasped.

'I have no further questions for the moment,' Mr Faconti threw his papers down in affected contempt and sat down as Mr Wetherby rose to his feet to re-examine the witness and attempt to restore his credibility.

'That is the case for the prosecution, my lord,' Mr Wetherby concluded, and sat down. It was nearly four o'clock on the Friday afternoon. The judge adjourned the case and I accompanied John Faconti and Scott Hilliard down to the cells where the now clean-cut Tom was pacing to and fro in restrained anger and frustration.

'Thatt Galveston guy is lying his poxy rocks off,' he growled. 'It's all bullshit! I felt like jumpin' over to the witness box and shaking the truth out of the lying double-faced bastard. He's spewing lies out of his arse!'

'I'm very glad you were able to control your feelings,' Mr Faconti raised his eyebrows, clutching his bundle of papers against his waistcoat. 'It would have done no good. You would have antagonised the judge, made an unfavourable impression on the jury and wound up spending the remainder of the trial down here. I understand that it is an infuriating experience sitting in the dock for two weeks listening to the prosecution but at least that part of your ordeal is over. On Monday morning we start putting *your* case to the jury and we shall begin by calling various members of the Cat O' Nine Tails Club.' Turning to me Faconti said, 'You must make sure those witnesses are outside the court by ten o'clock on Monday morning.'

So the court was adjourned and Tom was returned to Brixton for the weekend whilst the rest of us went home. Joe and Mae were very excited about the information Jake had dug up. Jake had unobtrusively made inquiries among Galveston's workmates at the telephone exchange and had compiled a list of pubs that he was known to frequent. He had then gone from one to the other with a photograph of Donna until the manager of the Four Lanterns recognised her as being Galveston's girlfriend.

We spent that weekend in Wichfield as guests of Gareth and Alison, who now met Joe and Mae for the first time. Diane and I slept in the attic while Joe and Mae had my old room. We showed them the photographs we had taken of Tom last year. The film had not been wound on so that a photograph of me had

154

been taken on top of a photograph of Tom and in the developed frame his ghostly transparent figure loomed up behind me.

Chapter Seventeen

When the trial resumed on Monday morning a more active and hectic phase began for me. Faconti or Hilliard would alert me as to which witness they would require and it would be my responsibility to make sure that the witness was sitting outside the court at the right time. I would be zapping about looking for a vacant public phone box arranging for them to be there, and at other times I would be taking hurried statements from them outside the court on points that had unexpectedly cropped up at the trial. A lot of energy was required and I was glad that I had it.

Faconti made his opening remarks to the jury and then began calling the alibi witnesses. Jimmy Mingo was the first, and the suit that he wore seemed to emphasise his dreadlocks rather than detract from them. But he spoke up well in the witness box, insisting that at the relevant time on 10th March Tom Delaney was at his club in Stoke Newington borrowing fifty pence from him and therefore could not have been at Narrow Way. Indeed, Tom had told him that he had walked from New Road and had not even been able to afford the bus fare. 'But who can these days, man?' he added with a shrug. As for the girl, Tom had certainly never brought her to the club and he, Mingo, had never even heard of her until after Tom was arrested for 'killing the chick!'. He said he knew Tom quite well and would have known if Tom was into a 'heavy thing' with her, an answer that had to be translated for the judge, who was again confounded by the slang expressions that he was hearing. 'What is a "chick" and what is a "heavy thing", pray tell?'

'It is suggested that my client was involved in the black market trade of drugs. Do you know whether or not my client bought any drugs at your club?'

'He never did.'

'Did he sell any?'

'I'd'a booted his backside out of it if he had done.'

'Did you ever see or hear my client buy drugs or sell them anywhere?'

'He was living with this chick called Sandie. She was a barb freak. She'd do nearly anything for a Tuinal capsule. So to keep her off the street he put hisself on the street so that she could have the stuff and get some help, without dealin' with the dregs who are in the habit of taking over young chicks in need and winding 'em up into prostitution and scenes like that.'

'To your knowledge did she receive any help?'

'She went into a rehabilitation centre in the end.'

'And how would you describe Mr Delaney's interest in drugs after that?'

'He didn't want to know,' said Mingo. 'He was more of a boozer than anything else. He'd seen too much of drugs and what they can do, by living with the bird.'

Ten more alibi witnesses were called over the next few days. Some were articulate, others were not. Some stood their ground while others were confused by Wetherby's browbeating and accused the prosecuting counsel of giving them 'brain trouble'. Wetherby attacked the reliability of their memories, reduced one or two of the girls to the verge of tears, 'as though he's got some sort of personal vendetta against our Tom,' as Mac put it incredulously.

Tom was still very tense. The QC managed to arouse doubts in too many minds about whether they were sure that Tom had arrived at seven o'clock, 'or could it have been some time after?' Few of them could remember exactly when Tom had walked in, it was too long ago, how could they be expected to remember?

Tom sat in the dock, sometimes making notes on bits of paper, picking up points he saw as important, then he would watch for his chance to attract my attention so that I could come and get them. Often these points were not rational, born of the restrained compulsion to say his piece before his turn came round. It was not easy to just sit still and quiet, especially with his own witnesses not always coming across. I would hand the most relevant of the notes to Scott Hilliard, who would correlate them with his own bundle of documents.

When Wetherby had finished with each alibi witness, Faconti

157

re-examined them on the doubts that had been raised in the minds of the jury and witnesses. He was trying to re-establish the fact that Tom had been seen at the club at various stages between 7.00 and 10.00, as Mingo and several others had attested a few weeks after the event when it was fresher in their memories.

Then the four witnesses from the Four Lanterns were called one after the other, the manager and three of his customers. They had all seen Galveston and Donna together in the pub regularly over the past few months prior to the murder. Galveston had told the manager that they lived together, and the manager understood this to mean on a common-law basis. They had been in his pub during the lunch time of the day of the murder. The manager remembered it because he read of the killing and saw her photograph in the newspaper early the following week. All of the four witnesses heard the couple having harsh words with each other and at one point Donna told Mr Galveston to 'piss off and leave me alone, for Chrissake'. They left the pub separately— Donna first, then ten minutes later Galveston.

It was good to hear these impartial witnesses spread a bit of reasonable doubt about, and just as I was expecting Faconti to call Tom into the witness box a surprise came. The last Lantern witness had left the witness box and Faconti was on his feet. 'I now call Sandra Ford,' he said. I looked up at Tom who seemed stunned by this announcement and we both watched the girl walk in. I recognised her immediately from Tom's photograph, although she looked better. Her skin was clear and fresh, her long black hair healthier, and she wore a white dress. Tom stared at her from the dock as she took her place in the witness box. She looked healthy in body but in spirit she seemed slightly daunted by her surroundings.

'You are Sandra Louise Ford?' said Faconti.

'Yes.'

'And you reside at Rendezvous House, Bank Hill, Caulton Park, Surrey?'

'Yes.'

'This is in fact a rehabilitation centre for people with drug dependency problems? Miss Ford, how long have you been undergoing treatment there?'

'Just over fourteen months.'

'And before that you were living with Thomas Delaney as his

158

common-law wife and the mother of his child for some three years?'

'That's right.'

'During those three years you become dependant upon the drug Tuinal? This is a trade name for a barbiturate capsule? Could you please tell the court how this came about?'

The girl pushed her hair past her shoulder and glanced at Tom as though she was not surprised to see him sitting there—and looking so different. 'It started about three years ago—after I had my baby. I had post-natal depression and everything was getting on top of me. Tom was having trouble finding a job and we couldn't afford the place we were staying in at Earl's Court. So we had to get out. We were in debt and under all sorts of pressure and I couldn't sleep. A psychiatrist at the hospital gave me one Tuinal capsule to help me sleep one night. Then I got a prescription for thirty from my GP. They made me feel so much better that I wanted more. When I had used up the prescription I went back to the doctor but he wouldn't give me any more. He gave me a milder drug, which did nothing for me. So I turned to the black market. As time went on I found that the one or two had stopped doing their job because my metabolism had become used to them, so I found myself taking more just to get the original effect.'

'And was it by buying these drugs on the black market that you came to meet Donna Maddon?'

'That was later, but, yes, I was trying to get a deal when I met Donna.'

'How did that come about?'

'I went to see her boyfriend—Terry Coggleshaw. He was well known as a dealer and although he had the reputation of being a dubious dealer I was desperate for some barbs. All the other dealers had dried up. I'd started having barbiturate withdrawal pains and fits by then.'

'Did you buy drugs from Terrance Coggleshaw or from Donna?'

'From him—Terrance Coggleshaw.'

Faconti questioned her on her relationship with Coggleshaw and Donna, and Sandie told the court about the dud barbiturates she had been sold.

'Meanwhile, what was Tom's reaction to all this? Did he also

159

take drugs?'

'No,' said Sandie. 'He smoked marijuana occasionally. He never took any pills or anything like that. He could see what they were doing to me and he tried to put a stop to it and stamp it out. I gave him a hard time. He used reason, coercion, patience, understanding and then anger and shock tactics. But a drug addict only cares about drugs. They talk drugs when they're not taking them and they take them when they're not talking about them. They don't care about themselves or other people or other things.'

'Did he ever use violence?'

'No. Never.'

'Did he ever buy drugs for you or on your behalf?'

'Yes.'

'This may seem strange to the members of the jury, that a man who loves you and therefore would want to be protective towards you should go out and buy a quantity of dangerous drugs that could lead you further into addiction and perhaps death? Why did he do that?'

'Violent withdrawal fits can be fatal,' Sandra said. 'If you have enough of them they can kill you. We were both getting frightened and he made me promise to get help and he would in the meantime provide me with a safety net until we had that help. He was also worried about the people I was getting the drugs from.'

'Was there an occasion when Tom purchased a quantity of drugs on your behalf which turned out to be defective in some way?'

'Yes. He purchased twenty-five Tuinal capsules. Something like every third one was filled with some sort of cosmetic powder and not the drug itself.'

'What effect did this produce?'

'At first I thought my tolerance threshold was getting higher again so I took a larger dose. But when I should have been stoned on them I had quite a violent fit and couldn't speak for two days—my voice just went. Tom opened up the capsules and we found that most of them weren't Tuinal at all. Tuinal powder has a distinctive and bitter taste and this stuff didn't. I knew then that Tom had been ripped off.'

'What was Tom's reaction to this?'

'He was angry. He wanted to pay Coggleshaw a visit and have

it out with him.'

'Were all these transactions made with Coggleshaw or were any at all made with Donna?'

'They were all made with Coggleshaw.'

'So if Tom had a quarrel with anybody it was with Coggleshaw and not Donna?'

'Yes. Donna had notten to do with selling the drugs. She took them herself from time to time but not as many as I did. In fact she was really fed up with living with Coggleshaw and she wanted to leave him but she had nowhere to go.'

'Were you and Tom able to help her?'

'We found an empty house and helped her and her children move into it. It was a hole but she was relieved to get away from Coggleshaw. And it wasn't thatt much worse than the one she'd left in Spitalfields.'

'So in other words you both became quite friendly with Donna Maddon in spite of her common-law husband's treacherous drug dealings?'

'Yes.'

'When did it become necessary for you to seek help from Rendezvous House?'

'It was necessary all along but I didn't do anything until the summer before last. In fact it was Tom that made all the moves then.'

'What did he do?'

'He telephoned Release to ask for advice. They gave him the number of a drug support group in City Road. I agreed to go there for a few weeks. The idea was that you stay there and think out your next move without stepping out into the outside world that might tempt you back. In the meantime they give you substitute drugs like Valium or phenobarbitone. And advice. I got the number of Rendezvous House and arranged an induction.'

'So at Tom's instigation and with his support you managed to seek medical help.'

'Yes.'

'Miss Ford, it has been suggested that the defendant procured drugs from Terrance Coggleshaw and Donna Maddon for your use, that he was unmindful of the disastrous effects they would have on you, and that the trading of drugs was a way of life for him. Are you telling the court that this is not true?'

161

'Yes. That accusation is not true in any way. He just wanted to get on with his life, he didn't want all this. All this is my fault, not his.'

'Thank you, Miss Ford. Please stay there.' Faconti sat down and Matthew Wetherby got to his feet.

'Miss Ford. You have been in this drug rehabilitation centre for fourteen months, you say. May I ask whether or not you are any longer addicted to barbiturates or anything else?'

'I was dependent on them rather than totally addicted. I was never a hypodermic-syringe addict or anything—I never used a needle. I became dependent on them by taking them orally. The last time I took a barb was fourteen months and two weeks ago. I don't need them any more.'

'During the time that you were dependent upon them what would you say was your daily dosage?'

'About six a day. Sometimes more.'

'Six a day! Rather a lot for such a powerful drug. Would you tell the jury what the effects of this drug are?'

'It makes you drowsy and dopey, as if very drunk. It makes the world seem a bit kinder when you take it at first, then it starts getting control of you and when you fight it, it becomes nightmarish. It becomes frightening. But at the same time reality is frightening, so it becomes a choice between one evil and another. You get locked into this swooning staggering existence, with everything slowly swimming around you.'

'And this drug also impairs the faculties of concentration?'

'Yes.'

'And of the memory.'

'To a certain extent. It doesn't wipe your memory blank.'

'But it surely impairs judgment and other functions of the mind. Could one really be sure that under the influence of six or more of these capsules that what one has seen and heard has been a correct and accurate interpretation of what is going on around one?'

'It's true that I don't remember a lot of details about my life at that time,' she admitted, 'but I'm sure of the important things that happened to us. In the rehabilitation centre I have been forced to analyse my own life—that's part of the therapy. A solid year or more of notten but working on yourself like that can give you amazing insights into your past, as far back as when you were a

162

baby or even in the womb. Drug addict or not, I'll bet every person in this room or in the street outside, would more than benefit from a year or two in Rendezvous House.'

Suddenly I felt somebody tapping me on the shoulder. I looked up into the pale face of the black-gowned usher. 'Your client is trying to attract your attention, sir,' he whispered. I looked around and Tom beckoned me, so I tiptoed to the dock, where Tom leaned over to whisper to me. 'Nick—I must see her today—on me own, downstairs or somewhere. I need to talk to her, y'know?'

'I don't know, Tom—'

'I haven't seen her for ages, I need to talk to the geerl.'

'I'll see what I can do,' I said and returned to the solicitors' table.

As she was leaving the witness box I followed her out of the court room where she joined a woman of about thirty with curly blonde hair, large glasses and jeans.

'Miss Ford,' I said, and they both looked around.

I was close up to her now. It seemed strange to be standing face to face with her after hearing so much about her over the months. She certainly looked better than her photograph.

'I'm Nicholas Heyward,' I said, and I could see that she did not know the name. 'I work for Tom's solicitor. I am also Tom's brother.'

Her eyes widened with sudden amazement. 'So he found you after all that!' she exclaimed, and in the midst of the drama being played out in the court room behind us relief and happiness came into her face. 'That's really good news that he found you. It was on his mind so much throughout the time we were together. When did that happen?'

'Not too long after you went into Rendezvous House,' I told her.

'That figures,' said Sandie. 'If it hadn't been for me he might have found you sooner.'

'Self-indulgence, Sandra,' scolded her companion. 'You know better than that!'

'It's all right, I'm just making a factual statement. There was no self-pity in it. This is Valerie. She's shadowing me from Rendezvous House to make sure I don't get lost around Piccadilly

Circus or somewhere.'

'Tom would like to see you,' I said.

'That wouldn't be a good idea,' said Valerie curtly.

'Why not?' I asked.

'Sandra has made a lot of progress after a tough time,' Valerie eyed me narrowly. 'It's crucial that the past doesn't reach back into her life and undo the good that has been done. It was dangerous enough for her to come here and face this ordeal in the witness box!'

'My brother is undergoing something of a crisis as well,' I said. 'He could do with all the moral support he can get.'

'Rendezvous House has preached facing responsibility,' Sandie said. 'I had a responsibility to come here today and help Tom. I feel responsible for him. I want to see him.'

Valerie shrugged her shoulders. 'Bear one thing in mind, Sandra. You must be responsible for yourself before you can be responsible for anybody else. You'll both be on two different levels of awareness now, so don't expect the earth to move when you meet again.'

'I owe him this much. When can I see him?'

I peered through the windows of the doors to the court and saw that Tom was now in the witness box. Then I glanced at my watch. 'Tom is giving evidence now but they'll adjourn for lunch at one o'clock. I'll try and wangle a meeting for you then. In the meantime you can either wait here or go and have a coffee. But please be here at 1.00.'

They went off to a coffee bar down the road and I returned to my seat in the court. Faconti was examining Tom on his story. This would go on for the rest of the day and the following morning. Then Wetherby would stand up and attack Tom's evidence face to face. Then Faconti would counteract that. Within the next few days the jury would leave the court for the last time.

Sandie was waiting for me when I came out of court. I took her down to the cells and the gaoler let us in, then opened up Tom's cell. They stared at each other for a moment as though they were two old flames that had accidentally bumped into each other in some crowd, as though they had never expected to meet up again. Then after the first shock of being in each other's presence had passed a mutual rush of emotion brought them together, as if this meeting were a gift from the gods, bringing them a vestige of

164

hope in their respective troubles.

It seemed ages before either of them spoke, and I, the solicitor's clerk and brother, was so far away from them that I might not have been there.

'Sandie,' Tom spoke at last.

'It's Sandra now,' she half-laughed. 'Pet names and nicknames are not allowed in Rendezvous House.'

'You're lookin' well, our kid, really well,' he marvelled. 'Colour in your cheeks and shiny hair an' all tha'! Great stuff.'

'You look different too. Smart and clean-shaven. You've got rid of that lousy image.'

'Is it true—you're off the fuckin' barbs?'

'I had no fits when I went in,' she said. 'But it was hell there at first. They don't give you time to think or become self-indulgent. They worked me really hard with this heavy disciplinarian schedule. Up at 6.30, breakfast at 7.00, cleaning all morning and looking after the animals—I can milk a goat now, you know!—I also know how to use an electric drill and a blowtorch and things like that. I can do all the type of things that women usually depend on men to do. I'm much more self-sufficient. What with all that, plus daily encounter groups, dynamic meditation, sensitivity groups, slip groups, karate and dancing lessons, drama groups—by the time I get to bed I am very, very knackered.'

'I told you it was the best thing to do,' he said, a little sadly. He was glad to see her so well and ebullient but there was a look of slight defeat on his face as well. 'It's a pity we didn't meet until after you'd experienced Rendezvous House,' he said. They had relieved him of the burden of her and they had succeeded in doing what he had failed to do for her. I could guess that this was what was running through his mind. Tom suddenly looked up and remembered I was in the background.

'You've met Nick now. He's my brother. You wanted to know whether I would find him or not and I did. My long-lost brother found.'

'I'm so pleased, Tom,' she said.

'I didn't kill Donna, you know.'

'I know you didn't. When they told me about all this I was really screwed up about it, and I'm really worried about you. All the time I was in there I had no idea what you were going through. I know you didn't kill her. I couldn't believe it.'

'I couldn't believe it when you walked into court either,' he laughed. 'Are you finished with Rendezvous House or do you have to go back?'

'I'm not ready to leave yet. There's still things to resolve. But now I don't know what to do.'

'Don't you worry,' said Tom. 'By the time you get out of there I'll be well out of trouble here.'

'I hope so, Tom.'

I stepped out of the cell and pulled the door to behind me, then lit a cigarette. The gaoler looked at me curiously. 'My colleague is conferring with my client,' I explained.

Five minutes later Tom's meal was brought to him and it was time for Sandra to leave. She was very upset as I led her back up the steps to the bustle of barristers, clerks and members of the public drifting off to lunch. Valerie was waiting for us by the revolving doors that led out to the grey daylight of Old Bailey and lunch-time London.

'I'm sorry we met under these circumstances,' I said. 'Try not to worry. I'm sure this will all be over soon.'

'I'm sorry.' She rubbed a stream that was on its way down her face. 'This is enough to do anybody's head up good and proper. I wish we could talk, Nicholas. There's a lot of things to talk about ...'

But she was in no condition for talking right now. 'There'll be time for that,' I said gently. 'But this is not the right time either for you or Tom.'

'Come on, Sandra,' Valerie put her hand on her arm.

'You did well in the witness box,' I told her. 'I think you helped Tom's case a great deal. When we all meet up again it will be under better circumstances than these.'

She looked very emotional and torn between two causes at once, but I could see at a glance that she needed to be protected from all this, she was not yet strong, she was not self-sufficient enough. I saw them out onto the pavement where the buildings of indifferent London loomed over her. I walked along with them and wished her good luck, then watched them as they walked on down Newgate Street before I crossed over to the Magpie and Stump for an alcoholic booster.

Tom was back in the witness box for the afternoon, undergoing the mental strain of hours of questioning in the warm and gloomy atmosphere of the court. He had given his account of the police interviews. He had reaffirmed that he and Donna were casual friends and no more. They were neither lovers nor dealers. He admitted they both smoked grass but they did not sell it. They had had nothing to do with serious drugs other than through their connections with Sandra and Coggleshaw. He had seen the witness Galveston hanging around Donna, who liked to tease the man a little. He was good for her ego ...

The tension in Tom's face seemed to relax a little as Faconti guided him through the whole nightmare with an air of 'I'm on your side, Tom', though he still felt as though he was on a tight-rope even then. One word out of place and he would topple into a snakepit of hands, it seemed. You had to concentrate, go backwards and forwards through the things that had played on your mind for months, words gobbled up the heart and brain that wanted this all to be over in five minutes—yet where would it end? The uncertainty . . .

I watched the members of the jury as well, and they looked as weary as I felt myself before I stepped out to the public phones for a progress report to Jake, plus a cigarette to help me unwind in the quietness and peace of the vestibule.

Back in court Faconti was still examining Tom on his connections with Donna, Coggleshaw and Sandra, wanting to know about his grievances against Coggleshaw and whether or not he blamed Donna in any way for what was happening to Sandie. 'Sandie and me wouldn' have helped her when she had nowhere to go if thatt was the case,' Tom responded.

Tom was then questioned on the subject of his hammer being found near the body of Donna Maddon. 'You are telling us that at some time last October you erected some shelves in Miss Maddon's room,' Faconti said. 'But according to the police they found no shelves affixed to the wall of this room. How do you account for that?'

'I'm not much of a handyman,' Tom said. 'They could have fallen down.'

'Did Miss Maddon tell you that they had fallen down?'

'She said they were a bit precarious. She was worried about them falling on the kids. I said I'd have another go at them but we forgot all about it.'

167

'Why did you not take your tools home when you had finished putting the shelves up?'

'I kept meaning to but every time I was around there it went out of my mind.'

He couldn't explain why Donna had told him she had no tools. He could only assume that she had acquired the tools that were found by the police since he brought his own around. He said he was not in the habit of carrying hammers around London to murder people with, and he actually got a chuckle from various corners of the court over this, and a 'quite so' smile from Faconti.

He was then questioned about his whereabouts during the time the fire was started. Tom told the court that he was restless because he had little money and no prospect of a job. He described the vacancies board in the Job Centre as being half-empty. He was feeling at a loose end that night and went for a walk around Spitalfields, where he got talking to an old dosser.

'Has there been any attempt to find this vagrant?' asked the judge.

'I am instructed that the defendant's solicitors have made all possible inquiries through the Salvation Army and other agencies, my lord,' said Faconti. 'As yet the vagrant has not been traced. Understandably perhaps, searching for a down-and-out intinerant in the metropolis has proven a somewhat difficult task.'

'Understandably indeed,' muttered the judge.

The following morning it was Mr Wetherby's turn to question Tom in the witness box. The QC was in an inflexible mood of scepticism and incredulity. He went over the police statements once again, so that it was a wonder that the mere idea of this repetitive subject wasn't enough to render the jury into a catatonic state. Once again Tom was called to account for his allegations of police brutality and exaggerated browbeating. Tom was called upon to recall every word that was said but as he pointed out to the counsel, 'I can't remember word for word and I haven't got a notebook to refer to. The police took their notes but I wasn't allowed to take mine.' Wetherby baited him and sometimes Tom rose to it. With a scornful voice Mr Wetherby doubled back through the points that had been discussed so much throughout the trial. He was there to suggest that while Miss Ford was in Rendezvous House Tom has been having a serious affair with the spouse of a drug pusher. He suggested that not only did

168

Miss Ford obtain the drugs from Coggleshaw but she obtained them from Tom as well. He asked Tom if one of the reasons for having relations with Donna was to get back at Coggleshaw through her. He wanted to know why Tom had not seen her since Christmas. He suggested that the passionate side of their relationship was deteriorating and that Donna was trying to end her association with Tom as she had done with Coggleshaw. Tom answered defensively and got really angry at the suggestion that he dealt drugs to Sandra carelessly and even callously. He also became angry when Wetherby snapped: 'How long did you supplement your dole money with the selling of illicit drugs?'

'I've never in my life sold drugs to anybody,' Tom snapped back.

Wetherby attacked Tom's alibi. He made observations about the kind of people that had provided that alibi, many of whom were not without blemished records of their own. It was agreed that Tom knew the Cat O' Nine Tails Club well and also knew what Wetherby called 'the stray and wayward characters' of the Cat O' Nine Tails Club, through drug transations that were known to take place there. 'But even if we accept the evidence of these people—how is it that it would not be possible for you to get from Old Ford to Stoke Newington within forty minutes?'

'If I could run as the crow flies maybe it would be possible,' said Tom. 'If I had a car it would be possible, but I haven't. And there is no tube station link between Old Ford and Stoke Newington and no direct bus route. And as I had no money anyway I would have to have walked from there, as in truth I had to walk from Whitechapel to Stoke Newington.'

Wetherby suggested that to get himself out of the vicinity of the murder a taxi would have sufficed, but Faconti objected on the grounds that the prosecution had not produced a taxi driver to give that suggestion any credence.

Then Wetherby went on to discuss the convenience of talking to a nameless and faceless vagrant in Spitalfields at the time that 22 Narrow Way was being set on fire. 'Here we have another stray from a wayward world, who is apparently still stray and has waywardly eluded all attempts that have been made to trace him. The reason for this is, of course, because this witness does not exist, isn't that the truth of the matter, Mr Delaney?'

'He exists,' insisted Tom.

'So you say,' leered Mr Wetherby. 'Now let us turn to the question of your hammer being found that night at 22 Narrow Way. And the question of the non-existent shelves that you say Donna Maddon asked you to erect. The truth is that this story is just as ludicrous as your phantom tramp in Spitalfields. I put it to you that you carried that hammer to Narrow Way on 10th March and not before. I suggest that your intention was to use it for the purposes of threatening or violent behaviour ...'

He went on to suggest that Tom killed Donna Maddon and that later on he left the club and returned to Narrow Way, where he had left the hammer. He wanted to make sure he had left no traces of his earlier presence. 'The house was in darkness and you assumed that everybody was out enjoying the first night of the weekend. You found yourself locked out of Donna's room and you panicked because you knew that you had left the hammer with your name on it on the other side of the door. You then decided to light a fire in the airing cupboard immediately next door to her room, in the hope that fire would gut that room and destroy any incriminating evidence. You have lied and lied throughout this case, while simultaneously pointing the finger of blame at others, such as the reputable police officers and the witness Galveston ...'

Tom withstood the heat of all this though seven months of tension and agitation showed. Finally Wetherby sat down and Faconti stood up and re-examined Tom on the points Wetherby had raised. After an hour of this Tom at last left the witness box and returned to the dock. 'That is the case for the defence, my lord,' said Mr Faconti.

When the court resumed the following morning Wetherby got up to make his closing speech to the jury. It took him just over an hour to go over the likelihoods and improbabilities of the case for the defence, from the 'highly suspect allegations against the police officers who arrested him' to the 'dubious characters who had offered an alibi for the court to consider'. 'The defendant was unable to account for his whereabouts when questioned by the police on the 30th March, just three weeks after the event. Yet here, six months later, he is able to recall his whereabouts with detailed clarity. However, he is unable to substantiate his alibi for the latter half of the night during which the fire was started. And

170

you, members of the jury, must consider the facts and not the fancies of the defendant. Let me first mention the facts. The facts are that Delaney had contacts with the drug world. There is no dispute about that. The facts are that he bought drugs for his addicted girlfriend and mother of his child. There is no dispute even about *that*. An extraordinary thing for a caring spouse to do, you might think. The facts are that the defendant struck up a relationship with Donna Maddon which, we are told, petered out at the end of the year. It is a fact that Donna Maddon was murdered with a hammer that belonged to the defendant. Nobody is disputing that either. But, members of the jury, let us turn to some of the fancies with which the defendant has entertained us. The defendant says that this hammer was used to erect shelves in Donna Maddon's living room. Is that a fact? No, it is not a fact, for if it was, where are the shelves—what became of them—why are they not still on the wall? The defendant says the shelves were a little shaky on the grounds that he is not a very skilled handyman. I think you will agree, members of the jury, that if his woodwork is as shaky as his story then the shelves deserved to fall down!

'You have heard my learned friend's cross-examination of the Crown's witness Kevin Galveston. It was suggested that Mr Galveston knew more about this dreadful murder than the man now standing before you in the dock. He was no more involved with Donna Maddon than the other occupants of the house. Delaney was far more entangled in Donna Maddon's life than he, and more involved in the netherworld of drug addicts, squatters and drug pushers. There is no substance or justification in pointing the finger of suspicion at Kevin Galveston. He had been eliminated from the police inquiries before the arrest of Delaney. The police had not seen fit to charge Mr Galveston but at the end of the day saw fit to charge Mr Delaney. It is my contention,' Wetherby concluded, 'that after weighing the evidence, the facts against the fancies, you will have no difficulty in reaching a true verdict according to the evidence before you, and that verdict must surely be one of guilty.'

Matthew Wetherby sat down and rested back on his bench with satisfaction. Miss Cavendish, his junior and Scott Hilliard could now sit back and rest after the volume of notes that they had scribbled throughout the trial. John Faconti rose to his feet once more to make his closing remarks to the jury. This took two hours.

'The prosecution have tried to show that my client was wheeling and dealing hard drugs to his common-law wife. But we have heard from Miss Ford herself that this is just not the case! We have heard that my client made prodigious attempts to help her find a cure for her drug dependency. He understood the harrowing problems of barbiturate withdrawal as a close observer must, so, powerless to do anything else, he made the decision to purchase more in order to keep her in one piece while professional help could be sought. Sandra Ford told us that it was Tom who found the drug counselling organisation in City Road and it was under his auspices that she finally attended this organisation who referred her to Rendezvous House, a rehabilitation centre with the toughest programme in Europe. As a result of this, fourteen months later she stood before you in the witness box and spoke quite coherently and was most articulate. Did she look or sound as though she might once have been a drug addict? Or did it sound as though my client's insistence on taking her to City Road had worked? And does such concern and action suggest the character of a callous drug pusher? I'm sure you will agree that it suggests quite the contrary. We know that my client did not use hard drugs for his own purposes. There have been no allegations made in that direction. The prosecution suggests that it was money that was the attraction—"supplementing his dole money" as my learned friend put it. But, members of the jury, where is the evidence for this? Any bank accounts, post office accounts, building society accounts? Not at all! My client was not known as a big spender about town! You will recall that on the night of the murder he borrowed £2.50 at the Cat O' Nine Tails Club. Why bother with that if one is in the lucrative market of illicit drugs? The reason is of course that he was recently laid off from a labouring job and found himself on the rolls of the unemployed. With 7,000 people unemployed in his borough alone it was probable that he would remain in that position for a while. He would not be in a position to afford the outlay of money for drugs even if they could be later sold at a profit. So his dole money had been delayed in the post and he had no money at all. He was hungry and walked all the way from Whitechapel to Stoke Newington to try and borrow enough money for a meal

172

and some cigarettes. Would a ruthless money-mad drug pusher find himself in such a position.

'Let us look again at my learned friend's facts. My learned friend emphasises that my client "had contacts with the clandestine drug world" and "does not dispute it". This is a fact, true enough. But I urge you to consider the fact carefully, as I know you will. Where should the emphasis on this fact lie? The evidence of Sandra Ford shows that the emphasis lies on the real fact that Thomas Delaney was in a double bind, caught up in circumstances that he hated yet could not walk away from. He was trapped, almost as much as his girlfriend was trapped, against his will or inclination. You may take the view that he was unwise—that he should not have stayed with his girlfriend and put up with her addiction, that he should have walked away and washed his hands of it. You may feel that he is the author of his own misfortunes. On the other hand, you may take the view that he showed responsibility by helping her weather the storm. You may take the view that he is a young man who faces up to his responsibilities.

'The evidence against my client is largely circumstantial. His lordship, when he comes to sum this case up, will direct you on the importance of reaching a unanimous verdict beyond all reasonable doubt. When it comes to the evidence of Kevin Galveston you must consider his statements extra carefully, for his evidence is extremely important. He is the only witness who claims that my client was at the house at the relevant time. Is his testimony reliable? You must decide whether his evidence is sound enough to lead to a conviction that would imprison my client for life. If a question mark hangs over it you must put this evidence aside. If there is any doubt in your mind about the prosecution evidence it is your duty to return a verdict in favour of the defendant and acquit him on all counts.

'Concerning the murder weapon—the hammer—again it is for you to decide whether it is likely or not that my client carried it from Whitechapel to Old Ford for the purposes of committing some intimidating or violent act against Donna Maddon or anybody else. You must consider my client's account—that it was simply left there after a job he had done for Donna some months previously. Isn't this more likely to be the case?'

Faconti went on for the two hours, forcefully, I felt, countering

173

Mr Wetherby's final conclusions. 'Members of the jury,' he leaned a little towards them, 'I'm sure that you will consider all the evidence before you very carefully and return the right verdict that will say Thomas Delaney was not in 22 Narrow Way that night, he did *not* murder Donna Maddon, he did not set fire to 22 Narrow Way; he is not guilty!' With that Faconti sat down. The war of words was over. It was nearly one o'clock and the judge adjourned the court for lunch.

I think the heavy tension was back with a vengeance as Mae, Joe and I sat in the Magpie and Stump eating shepherd's pie lunches and drinking lager. The pub was slightly smoky and buzzing with conversation as lawyers and officials filled the bar for their luncheon sessions, some in stiff collars yapping in Etonian to clients buying them thank-you drinks.

'He's good thatt Mr Faconti is,' Joe asserted, tucking into his food. 'He's got some voice and comes across—I think the jury like him as well. I like him—he's just the job. He'll gerr our kid off all right. It's made me dead 'ungry just listening to him.'

'It's the other feller thatt's made me just the opposite,' Mae pushed her plate aside. 'He seems so determined to put our Tom away for good. He doesn't know our Tom did it! What makes him so sure? It's like an obsession with him.'

'He's wrong, dat's all,' said Joe. 'And he's getten paid well for bein' wrong!'

'I don't know 'ow the feller can sleep at night,' Mae rubbed her wrists nervously.

'Not long now, eh, Nick?' Joe winked.

'No. Not too long now.'

Mr Justice Cassidy started summing up that afternoon. He began by directing the jury on all the evidence that they had heard—it took all afternoon and the first hour of the following morning—emphasising all the time the choice between one account or the other and stressing how the jury must weigh the evidence and probability in the balance. 'It is not unusual in a criminal trial to hear allegations made against the police,' he told the jury. 'In most cases these allegations are often unfounded and have no truth in them. But what about this case? Mr Delaney claims that a high-ranking police official kneed him in the groin and then twisted his fingers. It is for you to decide whether it is probable or likely that a police officer would do such a thing,' the judge threw his pen down. 'Would a police officer behave in this manner on a murder inquiry? It is for you to decide whether the defendant is telling the truth about that ...'

The following morning he directed the jury on points of law and they were then asked to retire and consider their verdict. At this point I sought out a public phone and called the office. Sue put me through to Jake and I told him that the jury had just gone out.

'What was the summing up like?' he asked.

'He didn't actually say anything prejudicial that I could pick up,' I said. 'But it was the way he said one or two things—the tone of his voice and the incredulous slinging down of his pen at one point. That kind of thing disturbs me.'

'All right. I'll be along in a short while. They'll be out for a while yet, I should imagine.'

I took Joe and Mae into the lift and whisked them up to the canteen. Nobody knew how long the jury would be out, of course. The waiting would be excruciating. As the day wore on court number one was the quietest it had been during the day for the past month. After all these months of waiting we were now on a knife edge. It seemed hard to believe that all this could be over soon.

Then at 2.20 the usher emerged from the court. Counsel were sent for and people began hurrying back to court number one. They jury had returned.

Chapter Eighteen

Mr Justice Cassidy took his place at the bench again. A few minutes later the jury filed in. I stared at each face as if to get some idea of the verdict they had reached. The jury sat down. The Clerk of the Court called for the prisoner to stand and then for the elected foreman of the jury to stand. My own heart was thudding away like merry hell, so God knows how Tom was feeling. 'Have you reached a verdict on which you are all agreed?' the Clerk asked.

The silence in between the question and the response was mind-bending, I couldn't have felt more hyped up. And when the response came I could hardly believe it—the simple word took seconds for my mind to absorb: 'No.' Tom looked drawn and confused and there was some stirring in the court room. The judge told the jury that they must go back and try again to reach a unanimous verdict, but if they could not he would direct them on a majority verdict. So once again the jury tramped out of the court room, the judge withdrew and the court broke up again as we returned to our waiting.

Jake arrived as I stood outside the court lighting a cigarette and winding down with the anticlimax.

'The jury have been back and gone out again. They couldn't agree.'

'Really? That's promising.'

'I hope we don't get a hung jury though, after all this.'

'No,' said Jake. 'But a hung jury is better than a hung client, so to speak.'

Joe Delaney stepped out of the court, leaving Mae alone inside with the scattered piles of abandoned depositions. 'All right, Mr Delaney?' asked Jake offering him a cigarette. Joe wasn't a smoker but he was feeling so tense that he took one and Goldberg flicked his gold lighter.

'They had me goin' for a minute in there, I tell yer,' Joe shook his head in a cloud of smoke.

'If the jury can't make up their mind too easily then that's not a bad omen for us,' Jake told him.

'Let's hope so, Mr Goldberg,' Joe puffed on his cigarette. 'All this hangin' about is putting years on me, never mind one of your clients.'

Not a few must have gone through some worries on this very site over the centuries, I was thinking. Throughout this case I had rushed my arse off and boiled my brains out. It had given me a new conviction as a lawyer, though it had taken me far away from the kind of law I had planned to deal with.

Time trickled on slowly and soon 4.30 had come and gone. All other courts had adjourned for the night and the building was less hectic, ready to lock its doors and shut its eyes for the night. But our jury had not yet returned.

Jake's bleep called him to a public telephone on urgent business back at the office.

'Jesus,' he said on his return. 'Hardwick is on in Bristol tomorrow. What a schlep, having to go all the way down there.'

'You should have instructed agents,' I said.

'Agents? What, on a case like that? Don't be silly, I couldn't entrust work like this with a bunch of shmocks! Are you mad?'

'Greta was telling me that you were thinking of giving the bleep the elbow,' I said. 'Why is that?'

'I'm beginning to feel like a space man,' he inhaled on his cigarette. 'You're never alone with a bleep!'

At about six o'clock things began to stir. The jury were back and counsel were sent for again. The empty court filled up quickly and Tom was brought back up from the cells. Then the judge returned to his throne. A few hearts began beating louder as the jury once more filled their seats.

The Clerk of the Court asked the foreman to be upstanding and repeated his question: 'Have you now reached a verdict upon which you are all agreed?'

'Yes.'

'On count one in the indictment do you find the defendant Thomas Gerard Delaney guilty or not guilty?'

'Guilty.'

177

'On count two in the indictment do you—'

Shock waves went through me as my heart took a downward plunge into a pit of disbelief. But before I had time to think there was a scream. It came from Mae Delaney who was now struggling with her husband and the usher who were trying to get her out of the court room. They disappeared through the swing doors and I followed them out. Mae was distraught and hysterical. 'It's lies,' she shrieked, 'It's lies. Can't they see? It's lies, lies, lies ...'

It took at least five minutes to get her to stop shrieking and for the three of us to restrain her. Joe had said nothing for he was also stunned. The outcome of this trial had been a dead certainty. Their son was innocent and he was bound to be cleared. How could this have happened? It wasn't feasible.

By the time I returned to the court the verdict had been heard in its entirety. Guilty on all three counts. And Mr Justice Cassidy was advising Tom of his opinion of the sinister and shady world of drug-and-misery pushers, and of the viciousness of this murder. I was just in time to hear them sentence my brother to life in prison.

Part Three

ECHOES

Chapter Nineteen

Fleet Street was relatively quiet compared with its daytime business and traffic, as I left the hardness of the pavement for the softness of another pub. The barman served me a beer in the midst of twilight lamps and a few other shadows in suits still hanging around the City. I'd already had a couple of drinks and fancied another, in spite of the fact that, having left a conference in Lincoln's Inn a few hours ago, I had some work to take home with me. Gazing around the pub my eyes stopped at a table where I recognised the figure of Kim Harrison, talking to a casually dressed guy in jeans, a blond man in his late thirties.

I crossed over to their table, feeling slightly pissed by now but in the mood for conversation. They both looked up as I cast my shadow over them. 'Nicky!' her face broke into a surprised smile that warmed the cockles of my boozy heart.

'Mind if I join you?'

'Of course not. Sit down. How are you?'

She introduced me to the man—he was her brother Roger, of legal-advice-centre fame, though if I'd had to guess his occupation I would have thought of social worker first, or maybe political lecturer.

'Well—' Kim lifted her glass, 'how did you fare when the big moment came—the decisive examinations?'

'Well, I did enough. Believe it or not I am on the rolls at last. How about you?'

'Yes, I also passed, much to my amazement.'

'You're too modest, Kim,' her brother grinned. 'She got a distinction in equity.'

'Well, congratulations are in order all around,' I said. 'A distinction, huh? There's more to you than fluttering eyelashes, my learned friend.'

181

'Oh,' she laughed, 'you've got a good memory!' Then with mock seriousness: 'I use my distinctions as a final resort! But what are you going to do with your qualifications now?'

'Ah. Who knows! I had all that worked out for years. I was dead sure about what I would do. Now I begin to wonder. I was very single-minded about my future but I've had so much going on that I'm feeling a little unsettled, if not illogical. I haven't made my mind up yet.'

'Are you still in the City?' Kim asked.

'Yes, and my principal there has offered me terms to stay on and help boss the next articled clerk about. I may accept that for the time being. I've also been offered something with Tyler Leon & Co., who have about thirty solicitors—plus a silicon-chip filing system, and all that sort of thing, which I suppose is what I had in mind for myself.'

'Why are you suddenly hesitating then?' she asked.

I couldn't answer that so shrugged it aside and turned the same questions back on her. She was still working for the firm she had been articled to in Chancery Lane, plus she did three evenings a week at various legal advice centres in the East End and North London. This part intrigued me; I asked to hear about it. Roger described his East End work at length and with enthusiasm. 'Obviously it isn't just the affluent who require the assistance of the legal profession. But try persuading the prestigious of the profession to open up a practice in the East End. The prospect does not attract them at all, they stay well within the lucrative boundaries of the City and the West End. This firm Tyler's wouldn't touch legal aid—it's a dirty phrase, it's an eight-letter word to them.'

'Aren't all those tenancy squabbles and trivial matters a bore to deal with?'

'On the contrary. The work is varied and interesting, infuriating and frustrating. One is dealing with all kinds of people; the work varies from tenancy troubles, to black kids getting harassed by the police, to accident claims, and debts, and matrimonial stuff. You see into the lives of ordinary people somehow, in a way that you never could in some carpet-and-glass practice in the West End. These people are inarticulate, some of them don't speak English very well, they're poor, they're unemployed and well below the real poverty level, never mind the official one. Yet their lives are complicated and they need the protection of lawyers as well as the better-off do. Listen, Nick. When I qualified and came down from Cambridge I worked in a swish practice in Marble Arch—Montgomery Tetherstone, Son & Barratt—do you know them?'

'Yes. They're big enough.'

'A similar outfit to Tyler's, employing so many people that I was just a junior figure among a legion of solicitors and partners—there were so many of us that one partner might not know all the faces that worked for him. I spent two years there. Then I just got out and went to Camden Town and Limehouse and haven't regretted it since.'

'I enjoy it as well,' said Kim. 'You meet some real characters. You ought to come along sometime and see for yourself.'

'Perhaps I shall.'

Roger bought a round of drinks while Kim told me about a case that she was handling at the advice centre. My concentration was straying back to Diane and this morning's yelling match, so I missed half of it and didn't click back until the new drink was in front of me.

Roger left at about half-past nine, hoping that he would see me again. I expected Kim to leave as well but when I offered to buy her another drink she accepted. While I was at the counter waiting to be served I wondered what Diane was up to at the moment. She was wrapped up in her work so much these days, and I with mine, that we hardly saw each other, it seemed. Glancing back at Kim my wondering ceased, and the barman served me with a beer and a Bacardi.

'Cheers,' she took the glass from me as I sat down. 'The last time we spoke you were up to your neck in heavy cases with all sorts of clients doing a turn at the Bailey. You still into all that? What an exciting life you lead.'

'Not really. I find it difficult to summon up enthusiasm these days. I have to dig deeper for it, but it's probably just a phase.'

'What's brought all this on, Nick? You've always been constant and full of get-up-and-go. What's the problem? That future that you worked so hard for has arrived. Anybody would have thought that you had failed or something.'

'We did this murder case last year you know. We lost it—it's difficult to explain—but it took something out of me.'

'So? You can't win them all.'

'The client was my brother.'

'Oh Christ ...! I'm sorry.'

'We lost at the trial and a few months ago the appeal was chucked out. Ever since then I've been turning over the pages of the depositions in the case and I'm convinced that Tom is innocent. I'm even convinced that one of the prosecution witnesses was responsible for the murder. We tried to pursue that during the trial but it wasn't taken very seriously.'

'No wonder you're so pissed off about things,' she said. 'D'you want to tell me about it?'

Over the next hour I related to her the events of the past year: Tom, Sandra, Donna, the police, the prosecution, the defence, Galveston and the conviction. To the world at large this was an open-and-shut case but to me it was more, though I felt powerless and useless, especially as the system for which I worked had washed its hands of the matter. Had it been twenty years ago Tom would have been hanged by now. The thought was frightening. So was the thought that he was living and breathing within the confines of prison life for something that he didn't do, and he might remain there for the best years of his life. In some of the national newspapers a few lines had appeared with subtitles like: 'Girl Killer Gets Life', 'Drug Dealer Kills Girlfriend' and 'Life For Drug-Pushing Killer'. 'They're all wrong,' I concluded. 'I've never had such a gut-feeling about something before. Now the family and friends are strenuously trying to get together the funds to finance an appeal to the House of Lords. In their neighbourhood in Liverpool there's a Free Tom Delaney Campaign afoot.'

'What a way for you to become qualified,' she reflected.

'I was positive that there was at least reasonable doubt.'

'It sounded as though the hammer clinched it for the jury,' she said. 'And the alibi witnesses were rather the worse for wear.'

'Anyway, I suppose the whole experience has left me feeling a little adrift to say the least. Tom is sitting up there in Norwich Prison not giving a damn whether the bomb drops at any time, and I am carrying on with other things, but there's nothing left to be done in my brother's favour. One can't help but feel restless.'

'It would be a little defeatist and tragic if this made you throw the towel in,' Kim said. 'You might not be able to do Tom much good but you're skilled enough to assist others that are going to get into the same fix, no matter how you feel. Of course, I've never been in your position—I can only imagine what you feel. But I think a case like this would give me all the more determination to fight back within the system and protect the rights of individuals. Think of the injustices that would take place without people like you.' She mocked herself as she spoke.

'You make the profession sound noble again,' I laughed.

'But it's true, though. Anyway, we'll leave my little lecture at that,' she said, taking her purse from her shoulder bag. 'What are you drinking?'

I felt drunk as we walked down Fleet Street at gone eleven o'clock. The yellow lights, dark shop windows, newspaper buildings, dark passageways leading off, the darkness of St Bride's and the floodlit dome of St Paul's ahead of us seemed to jump at my vision, and everything was beginning to spin round.

'Where do you live?' I asked.

'Clapham. I share a house with some girls there. Do you have far to go?'

'I'm in Kentish Town for the moment. But not for long. If you hear of any flats going think of me because we're in the market for one.'

'I'll keep my eyes and ears open,' she promised as we reached Ludgate Circus. 'Why don't you join me at the advice centre next week? You might enjoy the experience.'

'I'll phone your office on Monday morning and we'll arrange to meet somewhere.'

I stepped towards her wondering whether she would stiffen with resistance or not and kissed her. She was quite receptive to it, and that together with the scent she was wearing managed to register through my alcoholic mist. We wished each other good night and she went off towards Blackfriars as I carried on up Ludgate Hill.

Chapter Twenty

Whenever I needed Diane to come out with me somewhere it always seemed impossible because she was wrapped up in her work. Whenever she wanted me to go somewhere with her it was often at a time when I had to do some last-minute work on a case. Mostly it was my fault—things just kept turning out that way. Sometimes there would be a row, and she would go out alone. She had a lot of new friends and a job that she enjoyed, so things could have been worse.

'But we can't go on like this,' she said one night, drained after a row about God knows what. 'We're growing apart.'

I knew she was right but it still drilled into me a bit to hear her say it. I didn't want us to break up but felt things were changing, as if beyond our control.

'Look, Diane, I have to go before a High Court Master with this in the morning, and it's one of your father's cases. I have to finish going through these papers tonight, so for Christ's sake leave me here to finish it.'

'What are you doing all this for?' she demanded. 'Since Tom's trial you've changed, you're different. You don't seem to be interested in the things we were doing or were going to do. You just lock yourself up with all this! You don't seem to be able to find your own stop-and-think button. Avoidance again, that's all this work is. You don't even have any heart in it.'

That was true to a certain extent. When the court of appeal dismissed Tom's case I had felt as though something in me had been dismissed. His trial had been a peak, teaching me a lot about other clients' cases, though the work that I had done since was naturally at a lower key and I had to dig deeper into myself sometimes to get the necessary done. It was just a restless phase.

'I am the way I am and I can't change that,' I told her, but called myself a liar. I didn't know what I was but I knew it wasn't this. Every time I took a step towards doing whatever I'd always wanted to do I thought of Tom's trial. I could take the steps without difficulty but there was no satisfaction in them.

'You did everything you could, Nicky,' she said. 'Everybody did. But it's over. You have to get on with your own life.'

'I am doing. Or I'm trying to if you'll allow me to get on with this.'

Then she gave up, until the next time. Not that it was always like that but it was becoming more and more so. There were two absorbing jobs competing, two self-willed people trying to live together, teaching us that even living separate lives can be as suffocating as gluing ourselves together.

Once a month I would drive to Norwich Prison to see Tom, now settling into the routine of prison existence. Sometimes he was calm and philosophical, other times screwed up and still unable to believe the situation he was in. He would wake up in the morning thinking that he'd had nightmares and suddenly realise where he was—restless nights of ominous dreams chopped up with ominous reality.

Driving back I would think of something like Joe Delaney's response to the dismissed appeal. 'Is diss British justice then?' he had roared, half in tears of anger. 'Well I don't t'ink much of it if it is! Burrit's not over yet, Mr Faconti, not by a bloody hell of a long rope it ain't. My son is innocent and I won't stop til the bloody weerld knows it. I don't care how bloody long it takes.'

Or I would think of Jake's observations in the Seven Stars over a drink that lunch time. Faconti had argued before the three judges that the trial judge's summing up had been prejudicial. 'But,' as Jake pointed out, 'the transcript of the trial that goes before the appeal court is word for word accurate in clear type. There are no italics emphasising any words that the judge stressed. If the judge said in a sceptical tone: "Members of the jury, do you think that the police would say that?" his intonation is not included in the transcript and therefore the words read differently the scepticism is lost. Neither does the transcript mention that at one stage the judge threw his pen down incredulously at a point made by the defence. Personally, I prefer the American procedure where a judge sums up on points of law and points of law alone, not on points of evidence. It's a small risk, but one that shouldn't exist.'

The appeal was a formality that never stood a chance. And Joe was just another father who could not believe in the guilt of his son. When they appealed to the House of Lords, predictably they obtained the same result. A petition was then sent to the Home Secretary. After a few months a letter came from the Home Office regretfully informing them that after careful consideration they had not found any new evidence or circumstances to question the original court decision. The subject was now closed.

Several months after the Home Office decision I took a trip down to Limehouse Law Centre. It was a damp and dismal collection of rooms over a shop near dockland—not my favourite part of town. When I arrived Kim was already in conference with somebody and the waiting room was full of people, a different-looking crowd from the businessmen I had dined with in the City earlier that day—I smiled to myself as Roger emerged from a room, casually dressed as before. 'Nick, welcome,' he offered his hand. 'Great to see you. Look, we're quite busy this evening as you can see for yourself. What would you like to do—do you want to sit in on a consultation?'

'Sure. I'd love to.'

The first clients were a young couple. The girl had been at a drug party that had been raided by the police several months before. She had had to make a statement to the police which implicated somebody at the party, who was later arrested and charged. She was now worried that she would be called to give evidence against them. She wanted to know what she could do to get out of it. She added that she was now getting anonymous telephone calls and although the police did not think the two events were connected she wasn't so sure. Roger told her that if she was to receive a witness summons and ignore it, legally she would be in the wrong. However, he didn't think the judge would get very heavy about it if she did not attend, especially upon hearing about the anonymous telephone calls—Roger looked to me for a nod of agreement. It seemed that there was quite a bit of evidence against this suspect in any event, and Roger didn't think that she had much to worry about. But in the unlikely event of her being compelled to attend court he promised that he would make sure that somebody from the law centre went

188

to the court with her. The young man was more interested in the telephone caller. 'I'm thinkin a gettin' hold of a startin' pistol or summing,' he said. 'The next time he calls I want to fire it against the phone and do his earholes. Where do I stand as far as the law goes with that?'

'I've never actually heard of anybody being indicted for shooting at somebody on the telephone,' Roger reached out for the bulk of Archbold, and then sat back flickering through the pages for the Fire Arms Act. 'GBH on the eardrums not being in itself an offence. If it were most lawyers would be in prison by now. Now then—starting pistols—according to this it is an offence to possess one for anything other than sporting events. Still! You could always take up racing or something until you've got rid of your unwanted caller.'

As they left he wished them good luck and told them to come straight back if they did receive the witness summons.

I sat there for a couple of hours as Roger dealt with people, relaxed and friendly, his personality and confidence putting them at ease in this dank place which was perhaps not so intimidating to them as the formal area of a solicitor's office.

I found myself becoming immersed in the problems people were bringing in: rent hassles, tenancy disputes, employment disputes. One man was dodging a warrant for his arrest that emanated from the Department of Health and Social Security for the non-payment of maintenance to a wife he had divorced for adultery after she had 'galloped off with this geezer'. He demanded aggressively to know why he should keep her for the rest of his life when she broke the marriage up. 'The law has gone from one absurd extreme to the other by taking overwhelming burdens from the wife and placing it all on the husband, whether he be the guilty party or not,' Roger told him, picking up a biro to take notes with. 'There are no provisions for the middle ground. Now, the first thing we must do is contact the DHSS ...'

By the end of the evening I had gone into the next room, having offered to speed things up a bit by seeing some of the people myself. A young woman with two kids came in, distraught and anxious. Her husband was out of work and couldn't find a job. He had been down to what she called the Jobless Centre so many times and had come back with 'nuffing but the 'ump'. All their money went on food, clothing and rent.

189

They couldn't go out for the evening, so their entertainment was confined to the telly. But because of their financial straits they kept deferring payment of the TV licence and had now been caught out. They had been fined but couldn't get the money to pay it. He had just been arrested and she didn't know what to do. He was due to appear before the magistrates the following morning but there was no way she could get the money together by then. I advised her to tell her husband that he must ask to pay off the fine at a pound a week. The court would almost certainly agree to this. She sat there fiddling nervously with her wedding ring and on second thoughts I conferred with Roger, who agreed to nip down to the court with her in the morning.

Time went by quickly and before I knew it I had seen the last client to the door. Then I sat back on the desk and put my feet up, gazing around at the whitewashed silence of the dreary mildewed room. It was more like a dingy doctor's surgery than anything else, then I suddenly realised that for the first time in months I had been doing something without just going through the motions and pretence of doing something. It wasn't much but to a client it was always something and to me for that moment it was a booster out of the blue. I considered it over a relaxing cigarette, my reverie brought to an end by the opening of the door and Kim looking in. 'Hello. Are you going to join us for a drink?'

'Sure,' I said, stubbing the fag out. 'Why not?'

Chapter Twenty-one

One afternoon in December I was in my office dictating a brief to counsel into the cassette for the audio-typist when the internal phone buzzed loudly. When I answered it Sue told me that there was a Mrs Grafton in the waiting room who wished to see the person who had been in charge of the Delaney case. Mr Goldberg was in court and Mr Markbyss had gone to a conference at Lincoln's Inn, so would I see her?

She showed Mrs Grafton into my office and left us. The woman, who at first glance looked as though she was in her mid to late thirties but after a closer look was maybe in her early forties, was well dressed, slim and olive-skinned. I imagined she was quite good-looking when she was younger, though her looks were on the wane now. I also noticed that she had a slight cast in the left eye.

I invited her to take a seat and she sat across the desk from me. 'Are you the solicitor who dealt with the case of Thomas Delaney?' she asked, and I could detect the vague hint of an accent.

'Our Mr Goldberg was in charge of it but I did assist him. How can I be of help to you, Mrs Grafton?'

'D'you mind if I smoke?' she asked uncomfortably.

'Go ahead,' I said, offering her one from the cigarette box on the desk. She took one and I reached over and lit it for her.

'I got the name of the firm dealing with it from the Old Bailey,' she said, blowing a cloud of smoke away. 'I suppose you must know quite a bit about the background of the lad. Did you happen to know that he was adopted by any chance?

'Yes.'

'He never knew his real parents. Or at least, the last time he saw them he was too young to be able to remember them now,' she said. 'You know, I've been following this case a bit. In fact in some of the regional newspapers there's been a bit of publicity about the campaign led by his adopted parents. There's a lot of people saying he's innocent although the family's having a hard time trying to get anybody who matters to listen.'

'All the known evidence has been heard—at the original trial, the appeal, the House of Lords and the Home Office,' I pointed out. 'Unless new evidence were to come to light at this stage there's nothing more that can be done. What is your interest in the case, Mrs Grafton?'

'Well, I'll tell you,' she nodded, 'and it's not something I'm particularly proud of and it's not something that I openly talk about, of that you can be sure. But you being a lawyer must come up against a lot of not too pleasant things in life, as young as you are. Thomas Delaney was born Thomas Mackin. And I'm his mother. I was Eileen Mackin at the time.'

Looking back on it she must have wondered why I stared at her for so long. Her last sentence had suspended my power of thought so that I must have looked quite blank.

'Well—' she went on disconcertedly—'circumstances that I won't bother you with led me to put him up for adoption when he was just over a year old. He hasn't seen or heard from me since although I've often wondered about him over the years, especially when my circumstances changed. I live a new life now so that the time that I'm talking about seems like the life of a different person. I divorced my first husband—Tommy's father—twenty-one years ago and haven't seen him since, which was the first bit of luck I'd had since I met him. Then ten years later, having moved south, I met my second husband and we started a real family. We've got two girls. My two husbands are as different as chalk and cheese and that's a fact. My second family knows nothing about my past. They don't know of Tommy's existence. It would come as a bit of a shock if they ever found out. But I have thought about Tommy over the years, especially when my mother, who lives in Birkenhead, sent me a newspaper cutting from the local paper about a lad called Tom, born in Dalethorpe and then brought up in Bootle by adopted parents, on trial in London for murder.'

'I think Tom did a fair amount of wondering about you,' I spoke with my heart pounding away like a drum. 'When I met him he was looking around for a family tree to climb.'

'How close was he to finding me?'

'Not very close. He knew your name but that wasn't much good unless he could find your general location.'

'I'm glad he didn't find me,' she said. 'There would have been repercussions on my life as it is now, which has got nothing to do with the past. I've paid for that. I wouldn't want my family to know. You see, I've never discussed the situation with anybody since, except perhaps my mother, who I'm not that close to. I've lived with it quietly and perhaps that's part of me punishment as well. Like leading a double life, type of thing. I suppose Tom wanted to find me to spit in my eye for what I'd done for him. Did he ever express his feelings to you about me?'

'I think he just wanted some sort of explanation,' I told her. 'Naturally he wanted to know where he came from, what his natural family were like, and why he was adopted, given up.'

'He might have become bitter if he'd found out,' she said.

'Well, you can rest easy. He won't be in a position to come looking for you for a long time.'

'That doesn't make me feel any better. I can taste your disapproval, Mr Heyward. How do you think I feel knowing that a child that I gave up is in prison for life?'

'What made you come here, Mrs Grafton?'

'My mother was sure that the boy in the cuttings was Tommy. Born in Dolethorpe twenty four years ago, and now adopted. I now live in Brentwood and for the past couple of years since the trial started it's all been preying on my mind, though I was forced to keep it from my husband. A husband and wife shouldn't have secrets from each other but there was no choice with this one. As often as I could, I came up to London and went into the public gallery at the Old Bailey and I saw my son give evidence in the witness box, and heard the lawyers calling him to his face a murderer. It did something to me, seeing him for the first time in twenty-odd years. All my failures came flying back at me. I wanted to talk to him. But I was an outsider and had nothing to do with him. I was just the stranger who'd given him a bad start in life. I came here because I wanted to speak to somebody who knows him. I want to know how he would react if I just turned up at the prison to visit him. I'd like to try and explain things to him, without hiding the truth, though it's an ugly enough story.

193

He's under enough pressure as it is. Will it do him harm or good? You see, I'm so indecisive about it. I don't know what to do.'

'If you want to talk about it, by all means talk,' I said, settling my heartbeat down, on the verge of telling her a few things myself but holding back for some reason. 'Whatever you say will be in confidence. I know Tom quite well so perhaps I can guide you.'

'I married Tom's father when I was seventeen,' she said. 'Lookin' back it's hard to say why I married him. He seemed nice and he was generous with his money, was a bit flash. He seemed different from the other fellers and was full o' tall stories about his adventures in the merchant navy. I was impressionable enough to go for all that. I came from a big family and at the time we were in a rough part of Liverpool. So I was glad of a chance to get out and make a home of my own somewhere. We got married and moved to Manchester and suddenly life wasn't so flash any more. We lived in rooms, and Neil was more interested in drinkin' than weerkin', and it wound up after a while with me being the one that worked regularly, supporting him. No girl would put up with that sort of thing these days but I did, although it's hard to understand why. I was still impressionable and in those days you never wanted to admit to a bad marriage. Then when I was nearly nineteen I found out I was pregnant and after a while of course I had to stop working. Neil had to go out to work, but even when he could hold a job down for a few months he spent most of the money on booze and that would leave us in dire straits.

'I gave birth to my first son, so there was three mouths to feed but Neil still drank. After one bender he went on he lost his job and we had absolutely nothing and I hated going to the national assistance. I had to get some real money for the sake of the baby. I wasn't too bad lookin' in them days and got chatted up by a lot of men. One day this feller in the park got talking. He offered me some cash to … well, he wanted certain things and said he was willing to pay well for it. He said it was just a few minutes' work. I was desperate enough to do it but I felt sick, and when I was back out in the street I felt empty and the money felt dirty so I just spent it on rubbish to get rid of it, I didn't want to keep it. But with Neil being the way he was and with money being the way it was—that experience put me on the road to easy money. I could earn in an hour what other people sweated their guts out for a

194

week in a factory for. It wasn't easy to do, mind you. You had to act. The worse thing was, you had to pretend you were enjoying it and act as though they were exciting you, in order to get rid of them faster. When Neil found out he got drunk and gave me a hiding. He was pretty loose with his fists when the drink was in charge, and drink was his only boss. But he didn't stop me from doing what I was doing—because the money came in handy. Except for when I was carrying my second child, things carried on ...'

I didn't want to hear much more of this. I wanted her to stop and leave it alone. What was the point of coming out with all this crap now? It was too late now; I had managed to get on in life without hearing this. It was too late for Tom as well. Who wanted apologies or a self-pitying save-her-own-soul confession now that our lives were already shaped, for better or worse, in spite of or because of her? She was my mother but my only registration of that fact was the gut-wrench I felt as I heard about what I'd often wondered at. In this case the end of the mystery seemed worse than the continuation of it.

Her nervousness disappeared as her sordid life streamed out into the office. It was the old, old story of a whore entertaining lawyers and various pinstripe punters, being caught and brought before a magistrate and fined by more lawyers. 'Our David was about eighteen months old when that happened,' she took a pull on her cigarette. 'I was out at work again after being fined by lawyers for selling my body to lawyers. Neil and his sister were supposed to be looking after the boys but his sister apparently didn't come round and so they were on their own with Neil. Our David did something that Neil didn't like and he lashed out at him. The poor little mite fell back against the door and split his head open ...'

The two children were eventually taken into care. She didn't want them to grow up in an institution and so asked for them to be put up for adoption, and she obtained the support of a priest known to her mother. She left her husband and got on a train to London, where she managed to find a room in King's Cross and got a straight job in a City kitchen.

I sat back in the silence that followed these revelations, trying to catch my breath under the weight of my chest. Some minutes ticked by but I couldn't fill them with words. The sensations that

195

were reeling about inside me defied words anyway.

'So ...' she spoke again, 'you see why I haven't rushed up to my son and told him who I am. And you can also see why I don't want my husband to know what I once was.'

Coughing to clear my throat I lifted the receiver and buzzed Sue to tell her that I was going out for half an hour. I led Mrs Grafton out to the Market where Christmas tinsel and coloured lights were on display in shop windows whitened with artificial snow. I was glad of the cold fresh air after being cooped up in the office all day, and I took her into a café in Ship Tavern Passage, where I directed her to a table by the window that looked out at the passing people. I bought two cups of frothy coffee.

She thanked me for the coffee and asked me, as I knew Tom better than she, how I thought that Tom would react to her history. I sighed, because after all that I didn't know. 'Before I speculate on that, Mrs Grafton, I have a little story to tell you,' I said, stirring my coffee. 'Three years ago I was a clerk at this firm and during that time I received a visit from a guy introducing himself to me as Tom Delaney. He had a number of documents with him that he had brought along to give credence to a revelation that he had to make. The documents were birth and adoption certificates and these documents showed that his real parents were also my real parents, and his revelation was that he and I were brothers.'

At first she looked confused: 'You mean—?' Then everything seemed to stop and she looked shocked.

I lit a cigarette to try and soothe my internal pounding. 'Have you wondered about me as well, mother?'

She couldn't believe it, but then neither could I. Yet this was so real that it was our external surroundings that seemed unreal. I wondered what these passing strangers would make of it if they knew what was going down between the two people at the table on the other side of the plate-glass window.

'Oh my God,' she spoke faintly. 'You're David.' The colour had drained from her face and her brain was trying to find words.

'I don't know how my brother will react to this,' I told her. 'He wants to know about you. The question is would it be kinder to leave him in a state of blissful ignorance now that he is suffocating with a life sentence in prison. If his reaction is similar to mine then it would be cruel to tell him.'

196

'I see,' she swallowed hard, suppressing some emotion that was choking her. She put her cigarettes back in her handbag, fumbling and embarrassed, distraught, but trying to keep herself together. 'David, I—'

'My name is Nicholas,' I spoke with more conviction than I had intended. I was trying to keep the thunderstorm in my guts quiet but it was proving difficult.

This flustered her all the more. 'Why didn't you tell me straight away?' she whined. 'Why did you let me go on like that, for God's sake?'

'I wanted to hear the truth at last,' I said. 'After all these years I wanted to know about my beginnings as well. If I'd told you I was more than Tom's solicitor you would have clammed up. I'm sorry.'

'I'm sorry. I'm bloody sorry. I don't know what to say now!'

'I think you've said enough, mother.'

Her hand trembled as she lifted her cup to her lips, and I wondered why I was being so childish. I enjoyed being heavy one moment and regretted it the next, when a wave of animosity was already rushing up the next put-down.

'Of course I've wondered about you as well over the years. If I could only go back in time and change everything I would. But what's the use of talking like that?'

'Give me your address. I'll tell Tom that you turned up and if he wishes to contact you it will be up to him. I shan't tell him any more than that. He can draw his own conclusions.'

'I can't. If my husband found out I'd die.'

'You owe us this much,' I growled irrationally. Then realising that what I was doing was wrong, I pulled back to try and collect together some sort of calmness. 'All right ... forget it. Phone me at my office in about a month's time. By then I will have seen him. If he wishes to meet you we'll arrange a visiting order for you.'

'No!' she said.

'Pardon?'

'Don't bother!' Her eyes were glazed but her face was set, defying the pressure underneath to break down. 'I want to see him but I couldn't go through this again. I don't blame you and I wouldn't blame him either. But I don't want to see another of my children look at me the way you've just done—or speak to me

197

like that, no matter how much I might deserve it. I was a lousy mother, I was negligent and stupid and learnt about life the hard way every time. I was a whore, a slut, as cheap as they come, and I deserve no better than I get when I do find my kids that were snatched away into care. But for what it's worth I've managed to build a new life—and it's a worthwhile life. I can't do anything about the past, only about the future. I'm sorry life had to be this way, but there it is. And I'm sorry I spilled it out to you like this but I didn't know—how could I know who you were?' She picked her handbag up and stood up. 'I have to go now. But before I do there was another question I wanted to ask, if you can bring yourself to answer it. Do you think Tom did kill that girl?'

'No. I don't think he did.'

She looked at me strangely for a few seconds. 'Well,' she said, 'I can see that at least one of you is doing well in life.' And then she hurried out of the café into Ship Tavern Passage, rushing on down the narrow thoroughfare towards the traffic roar of Gracechurch Street.

Chapter Twenty-two

At some time early in the New Year I was working late in the office. It was a murky cold evening, the part of the year that I dislike the most. It was necessary to work late on a case that I would have to go into court with the next morning. Everybody else had gone home, so there was a dead silence around the office, when at about twenty to seven I heard the waiting room door open and footsteps walk across to the reception desk. Wondering who it could be at this time of the evening, I went out to see, and found a small stout man, middle-aged and grey-haired, wearing thick pebble glasses, wrapped up in scarf and donkey jacket.

'Can I help you?'

'This is Marlon Markbyss's, ennit, mate?' he beamed, peeling his woollen gloves off and shaking his hands to get the blood going again. 'Gaw' s'truth. It's enough to freeze the bollocks off a brass monkey art there tonight. There's a fog comin' darn, son. The barstard's gonna be a freezer!'

'Well, you've come to the right place, but at the wrong time. We close up at 5.30.'

'Mr Goldberg's expectin' me, mate.'

'Mr Goldberg isn't here.'

'I'm early, squire. He's expectin' me at seven, but I got 'ere too early and it's too perishin' for hangin' about outside. I'd wait in a boozer but I don't wannhim to fink I'm pissed when I tell him wot I've come to tell him.'

'What's your name?'

'Connors, mate. Sean Connors. Me old man was a Mick,' he laughed. I stepped into Jake's office and checked his diary which confirmed that the man was expected as late as seven o'clock. I went back to the man and told him to make himself at home, then I returned to my room to finish what I was doing.

At five to seven I put my jacket back on and came out into the reception with my attaché case. Connors was still in the waiting room flicking through a copy of *The Times* that had been left there. 'I don't fink much of page three,' he remarked with a laugh.

The waiting room door opened and Mr Goldberg walked in.

'This gentleman is here to see you,' I told him.

'That's right,' he smiled. 'I do hope I haven't kept you waiting too long, Mr Connors.'

'No, Mr Goldberg, no way. I'm at your disposal as far as this goes, believe you me, Mr Goldberg.'

'Good, good. Well, I suggest we have our discussion over a drink in a pub somewhere,' said Jake.

'My sent-iments entirely, Mr Goldberg. No bovver!'

'You've met my colleague Mr Heyward?'

'How d'you do?' Connors offered me his hand, which I shook for him.

'Would you care to join us for a drink, Nicholas?' Jake asked.

'Actually I've had a bit of a heavy day, Jake. And I've got to be at the High Court in the morning pulling Geraint Everard's strings.'

'I think that if you were to have a drink with Mr Connors and myself you would find our discussion quite stimulating,' Jake assured me. 'It concerns a matter that will more than interest you.'

'Really? Okay, just a quick one then.'

'And while I'm checking to see if any messages have been left for me I suggest you have a glimpse at this evening's paper if you haven't seen it already,' Jake slapped a rolled-up copy of the *Evening News* into my hand.

I looked among the headlines to see what he was talking about. The article discussed the idea of video-taping police interrogations to increase the safety factor and cut down court room disputes. Violent crime was on the march and we needed the protection of the police to deal with criminals. A controversy had arisen over a case in which two officers, Detective Chief Superintendent Angus Balfour and Chief Detective Inspector Michael Haskins, were accused of perverting the course of justice in a robbery case in 1981, before Haskins' recent promotion.

Out of the fatigue of a day's hectic work a rocket shot through my soul at the sight of the names that two years ago had damned Tom at the Bailey. I was reading it again and again when Jake returned to us.

'Are we ready then?' he asked.

'Jake,' I said. 'This could be it.'

'Now don't go getting busy at this stage,' he said. 'These are allegations and no more. These officers are innocent until proven guilty, the same as anybody else in the land.'

'Of course. But——'

'Let's go. Before we have Belligerent Bert after us,' Jake said, turning the lights out. 'I'd sooner offend Melford Stevenson than him.'

Connors was right about the weather. A cold foggy atmosphere was drifting into Gracechurch Passage, making the solitary lamp post look like a ghostly beacon in the mist. In Leadenhall Market the mist was drifting up and down the different passages, turning the lights into fluid blurs, and the dustmen clearing up the market refuse looked like ghosts.

We stepped out of the cold into the warmth of a pub in the sheltered archways of the market. It was a pub with a high ceiling and two giant bottles hung above the bar, one green and one orange. My mind was racing around in circles at the thought of the news report as Jake went to the counter leaving Connors and I on hard wooden stools by the frosted glass window.

'It's a good night for a bit of villainy,' Connors said cheerfully, rubbing his hands. 'If that fog gets much ficker the ole bill wun arf av their work cut out tonight. No bovver.' Jake returned to us with the drinks and Mr Connors took his, saying, 'Cheers, Mr Goldberg. Just what the doctor ordered. I don't mind tellin' yer. You know, they reckon hell is hot, but I reckon different. To me hell is freezin' fackin' cold, like ternight. If they told us eternal damnation meant everlasting fog and frost and snow, then I'd make an effort to go straight and be as good as gold. That's a fact!'

'That brandy will keep you warm for the time being,' Jake nodded.

'Too right it will, squire,' laughed the man.

'Now then,' said Jake. 'Let us get down to business. Nicholas, this gentleman, Mr Connors has just completed a sentence at Pentonville Prison. Only a week ago in fact, isn't that right, Mr Connors?'

'Got it in one, Mr Goldberg. I did a slow six months for maulin' nicked gear about. Ole Justice Warren took one look at me form and pulled the trap door switch, so down I went, the barstard. But in the death it seems it mighta done someone a bit of good arter all.'

'In Pentonville Prison you shared a cell with two other blokes,' said Jake. 'Perhaps you'd be kind enough to tell Mr Heyward their names.'

'A geezer called Bradley Morgan, who was in for puttin' hisself about wiv dodgey credit cards and all that lark, and another bloke called Kevin Galveston who was in for assault. He'd given someone a thumpin'—though he didn't look as though he'd say boo to a bloody goose!'

'Galveston' I exclaimed. 'The prosecution's reformed witness back inside!'

'This bloke Galveston,' Connors leaned forward confidentially, 'is full o' wind 'n piss, enn'e! Brad an' me 'ad these pictures up on the wall, of the tits an' bums variety. Well, Galveston don't seem to take to 'em, as if he was above all that sort of thing, like. A young bloke like him—well, compared to me he is. Word gets about the nick pretty quick, like, and the word is that Galveston is in for prangin' the jaw of some ole brass he was wiv. So we starts to fink that he's got a problem about women, see? I mean, I'm clockin' on for sixty, I might as well tell yer the truth, but even I'm interested in a good bit of jack any time I can get me ole robroy near some.'

'You'd charm the birds off the trees, Mr Connors,' said Jake. 'But if we could just stick to the point ...'

'Well, to be honest, Galveston ain't thee most popular wallah in the nick. Nobody is partial to the cunt. A wind-up starts, dunnit! Everybody's tryina get him at it! Extractin' the urine and givin' him the occasional shove, just a bit of good harmless fun. But he takes it all personal, bein' a bit of a humourless slag, like, and gets het up about it which makes the wind-up worse. One night we're banged up in the cell just arter Galveston has had a ruck with some bloke down the landing. He's right steamed up, threatenin' ter top the barstard in question. Brad told him, "Stifle yourself for fack' sake. You ain't got the bottle to piss against the wall." Galveston's who's still got his rag out tells him to shut his clack or he'll do him. We larfed, which made him all the more

202

aeriated. "You ain't got the taste for it, you wally," sez Brad. Anyway, there was a bit of a barney, when all of a sudden Galveston comes out with, "I've dunnit once I can do it twice!"

'A couple of days later, this bloke sidles up to me in the television room and tells me summink about the bloke in our cell. He must've been Galveston's only mate in the prison, except in the death he wasn't such a great mate to have. It seems that Galveston had got talking to him about all the trouble he was having and confided in him that if the other blokes knew that he had killed someone they'd think twice about geeing him up. This bloke, a geezer called Roper, didn't believe him either, but asked him about it and Galveston told him that he'd croaked some bird he was livin' with because she kept havin' a pop at him. He lost his temper with her and belted her one with a hammer he had in his hand, doing a job for her. He was livin' with her down Old Ford way and had a bit of a thing about her, but she was the sort of two an' eight that you never knew who she was kippin' wiv at a given time, like. Though sometimes she made a point of telling him. "Such and such a person was wiv me last night—he was really good," she'd say. "Let's face it," she'd say, "he's got all the equipment to be good with." She wound him up one night and he just blew his top and popped her one. Roper said that Galveston described the bird layin' there, all bruised up and her eyes swollen, and how he couldn't bring her round and realised she was dead. Roper says, "The guy's either got a vivid imagination or he's kosher." I says, "Ain't he afraid of you goin' to the guvnor? It's got to be a load of old Aunt Fanny really, ennit?" And Roper says, "The guy trusts me. He don't bovver me and I don't bovver him, so the geezer trusts me, y'see? But the thing is, he reckons that the filth gave him some intensive interrogation but nicked someone else. There was a trial where they tried to suggest he was implicated, it didn't work and this other guy is doin' time for it. If Galveston is right then this bloke must be doin' life for fuck all except givin' one of the arrestin' pigs a back-hander, for which he should be remembered in the Honours List and not sent down." In the death we started to fink about it and Roper told me the name of the case. When I came out I went to see this DC I know to find out who the brief was and he gave me Mr Goldberg's number arter checkin' up. So then I gets in touch and here I am, no bovver.'

203

'So,' Jake inhaled his cigarette smoke. 'The climate is changing. By a weird twist of fate tonight's press has cast a shadow over a couple of the police officers involved in the case and Mr Connors has come forward. Is Mr Galveston still in the Ville.'

'Only for a few weeks,' said Connors.

'What about Mr Roper?'

'He gets out in July and Brad Morgan in September.'

'Will they corroborate your statement?'

'No bovver. No one likes to see a bloke like Galveston do a few months while someone else is doin' life for summink that's down to a prat like that.'

'So what are you going to do next, Jake?' I asked.

'I'll obtain permission to have a quiet conference with these guys at the prison and see what we have when we have something written on paper. This case doesn't seem to be as open and shut as at first thought. But don't worry, Nicholas. Leave it to me.'

'Thanks, Mr Connors,' I shook hands with him again. 'We appreciate your bringing this to our attention.'

'No bovver, son, the least I could do.'

'Another drink, Mr Connors?'

'I wouldn't say no, Mr Goldberg ...'

I walked across the fog-shrouded orange haze of London Bridge. It was impossible to see the river but I cold hear the waves lapping against the walls, like thoughts sneaking up in the darkness, as I turned over a lot of things in my mind. In the fog it was difficult to see a quick end to Tom's plight but there was something to think about at last, though I remembered Jake saying, 'Once people finally get round to telling the truth they sound like the biggest bloody liars going.'

Chapter Twenty-three

As soon as Jake had in his possession signed statements from Connors, Roper and Morgan he dispatched a bundle of documents to the Home Office with a covering letter highlighting the evidence given at the trial by Galveston, referring to the statements made by the landlord and the patrons of the Four Lanterns, and emphasising that Galveston's present status aroused enough concern about his reliability as a chief witness for the Crown in a murder trial. He also pointed out that certain police officers involved in the case had now been suspended pending an inquiry into their conduct on several other counts. Mr Goldberg urged the Home Secretary to reconsider Tom's appeal as a matter of some urgency. For good measure copies of all this documentation were sent to the Delaney family's MP in Liverpool, in the hope that he might exert any influence that he had on the Home Office.

It was all very uplifting and optimistic no doubt. Joe and Mae were able to transmit their hope down the telephone line but I was more cautious. Mae was all for relaying these events to Tom to give him something to hope for but I had to warn her that things would take a long time still and might peter out into nothing at all.

Soon after we received a letter from the Home Office acknowledging receipt of the documents. But as weeks turned into several months Mae and Joe slipped back into their anxious sense of frustration, though they carried on writing letters and campaigning; they now had the unequivocal support of their local MP, who was himself in communication with the Home Office.

The press, who two years ago had vaguely mentioned that a 'drug dealing killer' had got life, were now picking up on the parents' fight to free their son, and the Delaney family—Mae, Joe, Tom and Kathleen—were getting their pictures in some of the papers. The case was attracting more interest than it had done at the time of the trial, I was thinking as I read the reports and recalled the night Diane and I were blue-arse flying around between the City and Old Ford, the only two people on the outside who knew that Tom was being held in a murder inquiry. Already it seemed like a lifetime ago to me though for Tom the nightmare was just the same.

In any event fate, having lost its way a little, was now receiving a guiding hand from the lawyers at last. We watched the media closely for any reports on the question of Balfour and Haskins as we waited for the slow machinery to deal with the new evidence. It was difficult for Mae to understand these legal time lags, judging by the letters she wrote to Mr Goldberg. Her son was still in prison after all.

My hopes were not as high as Tom's parents'. There was no conclusive new evidence that proved Galveston was guilty of the murder. It was the police question that interested me the most although it was still too soon to build one's hopes on that. I remained distant from the subject and got on with my work in the City and at Limehouse.

At some time in May I was dealing with a client whose husband had recently died and who was on the verge of inheriting his estate, until his secret girlfriend and mother of his secret child suddenly materialised with a large claim on the estate, shocking the hell out of our client, who until then had had no knowledge of the girlfriend's existence. We were interrupted by the internal phone and Jake asked me to step into his office for a moment. So I went across to his untidy room, where I found him sitting behind his desk with the midday post in front of him.

He handed me a letter that he had just received and asked me to read it. It was from the Home Office and read:

Dear Sir,
re: Regina v. Delaney
I write to advise you that I have now re-examined the depositions and transcript of the trial in the above matter and have completed my inquiries into the case. As a result of allegations made by certain persons

206

against another in connection with the death of Donna Maddon the police have now re-opened their file and have made further inquiries into the matter and a report is being prepared by the Director of Public Prosecutions. ...

As a result of these and other events it seems to me that the decision to convict your client at the Central Criminal Court is now open to question. I have therefore referred this case back to the Court of Appeal to be heard as soon as possible.

It hardly seemed possible that after two and a half years the unlikely could happen, that my instinct and bias about this could be backed up by fact, and that all the noise Joe and Mae had made had finally paid off. After all the time and energy spent apparently getting nowhere, at last the establishment was listening again.

New police officers had gone into Galveston's story. His original alibi must have been convincing, but a detective was now pulling the plugs out of it in the light of the various statements that had been taken recently.

The date of the new appeal was set for June. Joe and Mae returned south, wanting to be in court more than ever for this. This time they stayed with my parents in Wichfield and were driven up to the law courts by Alison, who was not used to the heavy traffic of Central London. She saw one-way systems as treacherous devices to send her personally 'all over town just to go around the corner' and was infuriated by the fact that her A–Z did not indicate which streets were one way and which were not.

I woke up that morning with eagles in my guts rather than butterflies. As Diane reached out to turn the alarm off, my first thought was to visualise Tom now travelling towards London in a prison officer's car, perhaps hopeful, perhaps not. Nobody could be more used to disappointments by now.

That same morning I had an application before a Master of the Chancery Division on the other side of the High Court, and it overlapped with the start of the appeal hearing. I had to summon up extra concentration to keep my mind on the matter in hand as I sat in the Master's Chambers.

When I arrived at the Court of Appeal John Faconti was on his feet putting his case before the three judges. He had been advised by his learned friend that another person had in the past twenty-four hours been detained in connection with the death of Donna Maddon and charges were expected to follow shortly. He emphasised the statements of the Four Lantern patrons, of various prisoners at Pentonville, and the findings of an inquiry into the conduct of one of the police officials involved in the case, and he invited the judges to acknowledge that a serious error had been made.

Mr Wetherby was called upon to confirm that a man was now helping the police with their new inquiries; indeed, he had been informed that some sort of statement had been signed but he could as yet say no more than that, and was entirely in their lordships' hands.

Their lordships retired for a brief adjournment, during which time Diane stepped into court with her shoulder bag swinging and came and sat next to Jake and me at the bar. Faconti leaned back with his elbow rakishly hung over the back of his bench, chatting to Scott Hilliard and Jake.

The judges returned after several minutes and Lord Justice Beaumont called for the defendant to be 'brought up'. A few minutes later Tom was brought into the dock by a prison warder who stayed by his side. Tom faced the bench with a blank expression on his face, almost indifferent.

When this case first came before the Central Criminal Court, Beaumont opened his remarks, there was enough evidence to reasonably suppose that the appellant was guilty.

Beaumont went on to explain how and why the jury were justified in coming to a decision which had resulted in Tom's imprisonment. As he rambled on I glanced at Tom who remained expressionless.

... 'We take the view that it would not be in the interest of justice to allow this matter to stand. In our opinion the verdict returned at the Central Criminal Court on 5th October 1981 was wrong and that a miscarriage of justice took place. We therefore rule that the conviction and sentence against Thomas Gerard Delaney be quashed.'

The sense of relief and exhilaration that some of us felt did not reach Tom immediately. He just stared at the judges, not moving, as if movement would wake him up and ruin it all. But there was a stirring from the gallery and a gasp from Mae, who was sitting behind us.

Lord Justice Beaumont addressed his baggy eyes and words to Tom personally. 'Mr Delaney, you have suffered over three years of anxiety and humiliation and imprisonment unjustly. We can give you back your freedom but we cannot give you back the three years spent in custody. Most people convicted in a court of law are undoubtedly guilty but no system can be fool-proof. Go back and pick up the threads of your life, Mr Delaney. We wish you well. You are free to go.'

Tom continued to stare back at them as the three judges and the rest of the court rose to their feet and bowed, and their lordships filed back out, disappearing into the woodwork again. Suddenly there was an outbreak of chatter in the court, a hubbub of noise and people moving about. The dock was opened—Mae and Joe rushed up to their son as he stepped out, not quite grasping the reality of his sudden freedom, looking as though he was expecting the hand of the beefy warder to snatch him back.

His mother was hanging on to him as we approached. He looked overwhelmed and Mae was on the verge of tears as three years' worth of tension came to the surface. Joe glowed with satisfaction and Alison stood by with a told-you-so expression on her chops.

'Well, Tom,' said Faconti, 'this is indeed a red-letter day for you. I am pleased to see it. We have all waited a long time for it, although I have to admit I did not expect it to come about in this way.'

Faconti held his hand out and Tom took it. 'T'anks, Mr Faconti. Thanks for all you've done for us. I can't believe it. I just can't believe thatt I'm free now.'

'It's true enough,' smiled the QC. 'Good luck, Tom.'

Tom shook hands with Hilliard and the hand-shaking went on with the parents before the two barristers walked away with their blue-and-red sacks over their shoulders.

'Nick!' Tom stepped up to me and grabbed my hand. 'I'm free, man, fuck it, I'm free. I can go. I drove down from thatt prison this morning with two screws in sports jackets and shoes like bumper cars and I thought, in about eight hours these blokes will be driving me back to the prison. What the hell, it makes a change to be travelling down the motorway in the wide open weerld.

Now the bastards will be driving back without me!'

'Yes,' I laughed. 'You're free now and that's a fact.'

'Shite,' Tom said, as though it was just beginning to dawn on him.

'It calls for a drink,' Joe's voice boomed. 'Let's go to a boozer. They've been open for an hour!'

There were journalists waiting in the dull corridors outside the court room and they followed us out to the steps in Carey Street, where photographers were waiting. A television camera swung as a microphone was thrust in Tom's face. They asked him how he felt and what his plans were. He didn't know the answers to half their questions but told them he was going to get some compensation for this, they could bet their rocks on that.

Jake hustled Tom, Joe and Mae into Lincoln's Inn where he had left his car, whilst Diane and I climbed into Alison's car parked at a meter in Lincoln's Inn Fields. We escaped from the press following Jake's Rover into the London traffic, eventually arriving outside a pub near Southwark Bridge. A large plate-glass window gave a panoramic view of the silver-grey Thames swirling along and Tom, smoking a cigarette, gazed through the window at the freedom of it all.

Chapter Twenty-four

By the end of that summer I had decided to part company with Marlon Markbyss & Co, as much for a change of scenery as salary. I half-heartedly went for several interviews in larger practices around town but each time I stepped into their waiting rooms and sat there waiting for the interview with the partners I got restless and left after the interview feeling dissatisfied, although I was walking away from precisely what I had been working towards. People change and maybe I'll change back to all that, but it began to seem that I didn't know what I wanted and possibly I hadn't known all along. I sat in a café near St Paul's Church Yard just after an interview in the offices of Messrs Kilo & Sons. I was sipping coffee that tasted as though it had been poured out of a camel's condom, staring at a couple of fat pigeons waddling about on the paving stones. As far as I can remember it was then that I made the decision to work full-time at Limehouse.

Also around that time I wrote to Tom, who had gone back to Liverpool with his parents the weekend after his release. We'd had a night on the booze before he went and I had not seen him since. But I now had something of interest to discuss with him which I felt was too personal for the phone, so I invited him down for a few days.

He showed up looking smart and healthy, dressed in a navy-blue velvet jacket and new black cords, still with his hair well groomed and clean-shaven.

'You don't look like a bloody hippy any more!' I laughed. 'I expected you to revert back to your former self. Did prison life change you that much?'

'I fancied a change, kidder,' he shrugged. 'I don't get off on all thatt feerst impression stuff but you fancied a change youself, I see. You don't look like the stereotype solicitor any more with

211

your jeans and T-shirt. You want to get a hair cut. You look more like a bloody layabout than a lawyer.'

'Come in and park yourself,' I laughed again.

He dumped his holdall on the floor and made himself at home in one of the armchairs. Some things don't change though, and it wasn't long before he was rolling a joint. He looked straight and smooth, 'but life can be a deceptive bastard at times, to put it mildly,' he said, licking the last Rizla down.

'You should know. How's the job situation?'

'If you go into the job centre you'll still see the vacancies boards are vacant, weerse than before. So you see even more kids hangin' about in the cafés, pushing for their turn to get at the silicone-chip space-war machines up against the wall, while the same silicone chip and other things are keepin' 'em out of weerk. It's been a depressing bastard gettin' some weerk together but I got a break last week. A friend of mine fixed it up for me to have this drivin' job at his firm. It's only part time but I'll hang on to it for a while in the absence of anything else.'

'And Sandra? What happened when you found her?'

'Notten much. She's livin' with a guy in Liverpool. I guess she expected me to be doin' time for the rest of me life. I called her all the names under the sun but you can't blame the geerl. We're too different now anyhow. I can't see it ever weerkin' out, so thatt's that. Bollocks to it. I'm too obsessed with freedom and the future to worry a fuck about heavy relationships and poverty an' all them type of tings that I can't do notten about.'

'Well ... maybe things will start to work out for you now,' I said. 'Especially if you get a few quid from the compensation claim.'

'Yeh. Dat'll help when it finally comes,' he passed me the joint.

'Don't hold your breath while you wait.'

'Meanwhile, I've been pretty hyped up about your letter,' he leaned forward. 'It's your turn to sling mysteries at me. What's it about, Nick?'

I told him what it was about. The information that I had switched on his expression of eagerness and anticipation, that old child-like enthusiasm mixed with intensity. The subject was a surprise to him and gave him a lot to think about.

'The rest of it, Tom, will come tomorrow if I can arrange things right, which I'm not sure of,' I finished. 'Tonight, take things easy—just in case tomorrow is unsuccessful.'

Actually we did not take it easy but went out for the night because Tom wanted to enjoy the atmosphere, noise and motion of London again. We did some of the pubs in Portobello Road, Tom warily eyeing the police vans that cruised the streets of Notting Hill as though he was expecting to be pulled in at any time.

He'd always had an air of restlessness about him but now it was intense, you could see it in his face and eyes. 'You know, some nights I wake up in a cold sweat, expectin' to be back in the cell—not knowing where I am for the minute—then hardly able to believe that I'm not in the nick, thatt I'm free. I'll never forget them first few weeks on remand, them walls, metal stairs and landings, the fucken acoustics, echoin' voices and whistlin', doors clanging and keys jangling on me neerves. Even weerse than thatt was the first few weeks in the Scrubs while they were waiting to farm me out to a permanent prison. How I didn't crack up I'll never know—all dem noises were doin' me head up. Then they transferred me to Norwich. Thatt prison out in the country—so quiet you'd lie there in your cell on a summer evenin' and you could hear a pin drop. I tell yer, it's taught me some lessons about time bein' wasted and makin' the most of life. For three years my head was draggin' a corpse around but now I'm alive again and I want to do so much, y'know? And I keep t'inkin' that if it wasn't for people like you—I'd still be in thatt poxy place.'

'I didn't do much. It's Joe and Mae you have to thank. Plus a few old lags from Pentonville who were sharp enough to communicate with Jake. Not to mention the "unexemplary image of the policeman involved in the case", as one judge recently put it—stressing of course that the man was an exception to his profession.'

'Yeh?' Tom looked sceptical.

'Galveston is on remand now. I believe he signed a confessional statement and I think the medical reports are going to come to the conclusion that he's not a hundred percent in the head.'

'He might get a manslaughter then?'

'It's possible.'

'Jeez, it's frightening, it could happen to anyone. It won't happen to me again, though. But how do I know?'

'You'll be pleased to hear that the celebrated Royal

213

Commission have come up with another gem of a report,' I said.
'They recommend that even statements improperly obtained by
the police should be considered admissable in court. How do you
like that for a bag of doughnuts?'

He shook his head incredulously, '*Bastards*,' he hissed ...

'Put it behind you. The only thing left to do is go forward.'

'I intend to,' he laughed, breaking the intense spell of prison
recall, his face relaxing as his eyes turned towards a couple of
girls standing at the bar. 'Providing I can gerra livin', notten is
goin' to hold me back.'

The next morning I took him for a drive down the Eastern
Avenue, pulling off the main roads beyond Gallows Corner into
the narrow country roads outside Brentwood. A warm autumn
sun beamed through the trees and reflected off glass and chrome,
making me feel good at snatching a day away from London and
the office.

I left Tom at a large roadside pub where he could have a drink
while I sorted some business out. I drove along winding lanes and
roads shaded with bushes and trees, wondering what kind of
reception I would receive at my destination. I climbed Weald
Road, where the houses began, and pulled in outside the number
I wanted.

Everything seemed quiet, being on the edge of countryside and
town. The front garden of the terrace house was a small square,
well kept and multi-coloured with flowers. I rang the doorbell
and waited, preparing myself with the right answer if the wrong
face opened the door. After a few minutes the door was opened
and my real mother stood there in a pale yellow sweater and tight
blue jeans. She seemed a bit dismayed to see me—then the
expressive brown eyes looked daggers at me, as if to say what the
hell have you come here for? It suddenly struck me that those
brown eyes were like Tom's. I stood there stupidly thinking Tom
had got her eyes before I jumped back into alertness and asked
her if she was alone. She said she was.

'Have you got half an hour to spare?' I asked, trying to be
casual. She looked hesitant. 'Look ... I have to talk to you. And
there's somebody down the road who also wants to talk with
you. I also think I owe you an apology. Will you come and have a
drink for half an hour or so, so that we can talk?'

'I don't know. I—' still hesitant.

214

'I just thought that we shouldn't leave things the way we did. I don't want to leave them like that, anyhow.'

'All right.' She pulled the front door closed behind her.

I felt awkward as we walked back to the car. I got in and let her in, then did a U-turn and pulled the gearstick comfortably back into fourth as we descended the hill into the winding lanes.

'How did you find me?' she asked.

'You told me you lived in Brentwood. I went through the phone book and found you. I phoned about a week ago but your husband answered.'

'Oh. You were the wrong number.'

'I thought I'd better not phone again in case he wondered what was going on. If he had opened the door just now I would have asked him if Mr Birtwhistle lived there.'

'Thanks. But he's at work.'

'What does he do?' I said, trying not to work overtime to show her my friendly side, though also curious.

'He's an engineer.'

'That's not a bad job.'

'It's better than no job at all.'

There was an atmosphere in the car that the passing breeze at the window could not blow away—not that I had thought it would be easy to break through her defensiveness.

'Well,' she said, 'it made me jump seeing you on the doorstep like that. You're the last person I expected to open the door to.'

'I want to apologise. For the way I responded to you when you came to see me.'

'It was understandable.'

'It was out of order. It was also bloody childish, I know that. And far from sympathetic.'

'I don't want or need sympathy.'

'That's not the point. Understanding, then. Lack of insight. Self-centred and infantile.'

'Like I said. It was understandable. I can see that it must have been a shock when I just turned up.'

My attempts to make peace were doing nothing to dispel her tension but I drove on and clacked on as nonchalantly as possible, trying to put her at her ease.

'Who's waiting for me at this pub?' she asked. 'As if I couldn't guess!'

215

'Tom came down from Liverpool especially for this.'

'What did you tell him?' she asked.

'I told him all about our meeting.'

'Everything?'

'I thought it was best to tell him everything,' I said. 'He wanted to know.'

'And now he wants his turn to have his say, I suppose.'

'Relax. Tom's been through enough in life to be able to handle this. I guess I was just a late starter.'

I took her into the saloon bar of the pub, where Tom sat at a table nursing a pint. I didn't have to point him out to her, she recognised him immediately and Tom had been watching the door for us. They were both nervous and I was hovering in between them as matter-of-factly as possible.

'Hello, Tom,' she spoke uncertainly, but her eyes gleamed at him with something like pleasure at seeing him there in a pub on a country road rather than in the dock of the Old Bailey.

'Jesus,' Tom said. 'I can't believe this. Of all things, I wasn't expectin' this.'

'What are you drinking—mother?' I said, and the last word jarred because it seemed unnatural though I reminded myself that it wasn't.

'Vodka and lime, please.'

'Another drink, Tom?'

'Why not, our kid? I'll risk it for a biscuit!'

I returned to them a few minutes later with the drinks, and Tom was cascading words on the wave of his nervousness again as he had done on the night that I went to meet him at the Spooky Lady. He told her that she looked different from what he had expected and she asked him what it was that he had expected. She laughed when he told her he had imagined her to be older.

'For my part,' she said, 'I wondered if I'd ever see you. I sat in the gallery of the court and wanted ever so much to come down and talk to you and—and be your friend—especially when I could see you being attacked by all those people and lawyers. I don't have to be told that I'd left it a bit late.'

'You don't want to get off on things like thatt,' Tom waved his cigarette as if to dismiss her guilt or to blow it away with the smoke. 'You have to be philosophical aboutt thatt type of thing. It would never have been too late. I've already been on trial mesself,

216

I'm not gonna put you on trial, am I? What's the good of a soul-searching post-mortem now?'

'Me and my husband were watching television a few months ago,' she said. 'The news came on, and there were you, walking out of the court, free again, cleared of that murder. Of course my husband didn't know that we were looking at my son but I felt so pleased. It nearly all came out that night, I can tell you. And now to meet both of you after all these years is a weird thing,' she glanced at me. 'I guess you've both been through a lot.'

'So have you, from what Nick's been telling me,' said Tom. 'I looked for you when I was about nineteen. I went to Warwick Road in Dalethorpe to see if I could find some sort of trace, but after all this time ...'

'No. I pulled away from there over twenty years ago.'

'I even considered at one point gettin' the Salvation Army to look for you,' he laughed. 'But then I found Nick and thought I was makin' progress at last.'

'How did you two find each other?' she asked.

Throughout the next few drinks all three of us relaxed more and more, so that we were gradually able to talk quite naturally. She never totally relaxed but she could smile now and again at some of the stray remarks that Tom made. She wanted to know what kind of lives we had led with our adopted parents. Some of it must have been painful, if not all of it, but she seemed intrigued by the two different lives that she was hearing about—one son who went to university and the other who had drifted through the 'netherworld', as Tom laughingly quoted Matthew Wetherby QC. She asked light-hearted questions about girlfriends, and her mouth dropped open when she heard that Tom had a six-year-old son called Damien. 'You mean I'm a bloody grandmother already? Oh cheers! I feel bloody old again.'

Then Tom turned the questions back at her, wanting to know about her own family in Liverpool—about our father also. She didn't paint an attractive picture of him and she didn't paint an attractive one of herself at that time. 'Nick told you what I was doing at the time?'

'Yes,' nodded Tom. 'He also told me you got busted for it—confirming my suspicions that the two oldest professions in the world have got a lot in common with each other,' he gave me a side glance.

217

'You could put it like that,' I nodded.

'Poor Nick,' she half-laughed, relaxed by the drink and relieved that Tom and I were soft-pedalling. 'When he heard the truth straight out of the blue like that it must have been a hell of a shock. I've made some God almighty mistakes, but, as you said, it was a long time ago and I'd like to forget it. I don't think about it much but sometimes it comes back in spasms of—I don't know— disbelief and horror. It seems inconceivable to me that I let you boys go as I did.'

'Our Damien hasn't had a great start in life either, but I won't do him much good if I spend the rest of my life putting the blame about,' Tom said.

'At least he knows you. But you're right. It's pointless going on about that now. I'm glad of having this chance to talk to you.'

'Perhaps if you talked it out with your husband he might understand,' I suggested. 'All this happened so long ago it can't matter.'

'I've been tempted to tell him a few times over the years but I always chickened out. I value what I have now too much. I don't want to risk spoiling it. Maybe one day I'll take the chance.'

The three hours we spent in the pub were short—there was not enough time to talk or get to know her properly. As the last bell rang Tom said he hoped that this wasn't going to be the last meeting.

'So do I,' I said. 'Although we shan't contact you or come here again. But this is the phone number of my office and that's my home number. Tom's address is on the reverse side of the card.'

'Thanks, Nicholas—Tom.' She looked at the card thoughtfully, then came back to life with a remorseful smile. 'Well! it's chucking-out time, I suppose.'

I downed the last of my drink. 'We'll drop you back home.'

We left her standing at the garden gate and didn't hang around long after she got out of the car. Tom scrambled over into the front seat and we found our way back to the runway to London.

Chapter Twenty-five

Tom and I had a drink at Euston Station on Sunday night, while waiting until it was time for him to board the train to Liverpool. 'I miss London,' he said, 'although I got mesself some trouble here. And a wet Monday morning in New Road, Whitechapel, was hard to beat. But when I can I'll get back down here, because I get a lift off the atmosphere. I'll have to get some money together.'

'Do that,' I said. 'And save your money up instead of buying double rounds. You know London is a bastard expensive place to get into.'

'I'll try and take your advice, big brother,' he scoffed. 'Meanwhile, when do you start at Limehouse then?'

'Next month.'

'When I was talking to Alison on the trombone the other day she reckoned you'd gone daft. She says you'll be losing out on a lot of money by weerkin' this way.'

'I can go in lots of different directions if I wish to. At the moment this is the one that suits me.'

'That's the main thing,' he nodded in agreement. 'It sounds worthwhile to me. You've come a long way from what you seemed to be when I first met you.'

'I don't know about that. It's hard to pinpoint where the change in direction came or why. There were various times when I didn't want to look back at my origins but they came looking for me twice, and in big ways. I'm glad they did now. It took me long enough to absorb it all and come to terms with a few things. But fuck it, it doesn't matter. I'm glad you walked into that office that day, Tom.'

'So am I, kidder. I knew if I could get in touch with the people that I really came from I'd feel more complete than I would have done otherwise.'

219

'Yeh,' I nodded. 'I suppose that's it. In some ways we've had that void filled for us. Enough fat to chew over for a while.'

'We're beginning to know what sort of people we really are after all,' Tom said. 'And thatt can't be bad. I mean, if I never see Eileen again I'm glad that I met her and talked to her at least once. I feel as though I can do other things now without lookin' back too much, whatever happens.'

We walked towards the ticket barrier where we could see the last train of the night waiting at the platform. 'Well, this is it then, for now. I'll see you, our kid,' he punched me gently on the shoulder.

'If we don't get up to Liverpool to see you in the next few months, good luck with the job,' I said.

'Yeh, same to you. Cheers.'

I watched him walk through the barrier and step up into the train. I stayed put for about five minutes, turning things over in my mind. Then I watched as the whistle blew, the bell rang, and the late-night train jolted forward, moving out of the station, taking him back to the town from which we both came.